# THE
# LIZARD QUEEN

## BOOK ONE:

## THIS SHRINKING WORLD

H.L. Cherryholmes

ISBN: 1500727849
ISBN-13: 978-1500727840

# For Ron

with you, everything is possible

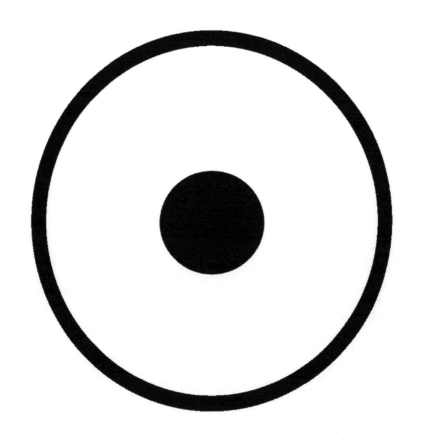

# PART ONE

"**I** saw an orange lizard today."

"Orange? That's an unusual color for a lizard isn't it? I've seen red ones."

Amy Darlidale looked at the wall just above her therapist's head. She'd seen the family photo dozens of times but had never given it much attention. This was the first time she'd noticed the pendant his young daughter wore. Was it a circle within a circle? It was difficult to make out from a distance. "Maybe your red lizard mated with a yellow one and produced my orange lizard."

John chuckled. "Maybe. Where did you see it?"

"That's the interesting thing." Amy stopped bouncing the leg she had crossed over the other. "I saw it in my office." She looked at John. His daughter resembled him. "It ran across my desk."

"You're kidding. How do you suppose a lizard—of any color—made it up to the twenty-seventh floor of your office building?"

"Maybe it crawled through the pipes." Amy glanced out the

window and resumed bouncing her leg.

Pen in hand, John leaned back in his chair. "You seem rather distracted today."

Amy's gaze drifted across John's desk. When he started seeing her alone, he'd moved from the couple's area to the desk. She liked it better this way.

"That damned lizard. I saw it first thing this morning, and I can't get it out of my head." She uncrossed her legs. "I feel a bit silly for saying this, but it stopped and looked at me."

"There's nothing unusual about that. A deer-in-the-headlights response. Animals often momentarily freeze when they think they've been caught."

"Probably." Amy pictured the incident in her mind. She'd been reviewing a quarterly cash flow spreadsheet while leaning back in her chair much the way John was currently doing. She'd detected movement and glanced over the top of the printout. "But that wasn't what it seemed like at the time."

"What did it seem like?"

If she looked at John, she wouldn't be able to say it. She returned her focus to the pendant on the girl's neck in the family portrait. It *was* a circle within a circle. "I swear it was looking at me." She remembered how the small creature had scrambled up a pile of reports centered at the far edge of the desk and stopped there. "We sort of locked eyes for a moment. I had the oddest feeling she had been waiting for me to notice her."

"She?"

Amy looked at the therapist. "What?"

"You said *she* not *it*."

"I did?"

"Yes. Why would you assume it was female?"

"I don't know."

"Was there some sort of marking that gave away its gender?" John leaned forward.

Amy shook her head. "No, there weren't any markings. She was just orange. Bright orange like a ... well, like an orange. Her underside was slightly more yellow."

"Okay, so you and the lizard locked eyes. Then what?"

"Then she blinked a few times and ran off my desk. I shouted for my assistant and we looked in every corner and under every piece of furniture but never did find it."

John wrote something on the pad in front of him. "So what was it about this incident that you can't get out of your head? Not being able to find it?"

That he would assume what bothered her was the lizard's disappearance didn't surprise Amy in the least. John was a marriage counselor, which was why she'd started seeing him in the first place; unfortunately, despite the bi-weekly appointments for nearly a year, she and her husband, Peter, hadn't been able to work out their problems and eventually divorced. Peter got the SUV and the boat; she got condo in Palm Springs and John. They sold the house in Brentwood. One issue that had brought the (then) couple to see a therapist was Amy's inability to let things go. Her husband said it bordered on obsessive. Amy believed she was just determined. As it turned out, John tended to side with her husband on that particular topic and even after the divorce John still thought it was something Amy needed to work on. That's when she started seeing him only once every other month.

"No, it wasn't that I couldn't find the lizard. Although, I will admit that was frustrating. I'm guessing I can't get it out of my head because, for some reason, it made me think of my father."

"Interesting." He made another note on the pad. "What did it remind you of?"

He seemed anxious to hear her answer, which also came as no

surprise; Amy seldom talked about her childhood. Something else that annoyed her ex-husband.

"I don't know …" She crossed and uncrossed her legs again. "I suppose it made me think about when he married my stepmother. A few of months after their wedding I became very ill. My father said that he found me unconscious and rushed me to the hospital. I was in a coma for three days. The doctors never found out what was wrong with me." She paused to clear her throat. Talking about her childhood always made her uncomfortable, mostly because she remembered so little of it. "But to get back to your question, the way that the lizard looked at me was exactly how my father was looking at me when I woke from that coma. I remember opening my eyes and seeing my dad watching me as if he were waiting for me to notice him. That's what the lizard seemed to be doing."

John tapped his pen on the notepad. "I find it interesting that the first thing you said it reminded you of was when your father married your stepmother and not that you were in a coma."

Frowning, Amy asked why he found it interesting.

"Why don't you tell me?" He smiled wryly.

Amy hated that smile; John only used it when he knew how she would respond. "Maybe it's because I found my father marrying Alice more traumatic than being in a coma." She laughed.

"All right." He made another note. "So seeing the orange lizard brought this all back to you. My question then is why do you see it as a distraction?"

As she adjusted her jacket, Amy wished she hadn't brought up the lizard. She'd only done so because she hadn't had anything else to talk about and didn't want to waste a session. "I don't really know. Seeing the lizard just brought out … a feeling, I suppose."

"What feeling?"

"If I knew," she said, mimicking his smile, "*I'd* be the therapist."

He sat back, leaving his pen on his desk. "Do you think this feeling has something to do with you having recently turned forty?"

"You think I'm that shallow?"

"Actually, I don't think you're shallow at all, but milestone birthdays usually bring out thoughts about our past, especially childhood."

She considered his interpretation before rejecting it with a shake of her head. "I don't think it has anything to do with my turning forty. I'm not the type of woman who dreads aging."

"Not dread perhaps, but getting older is a constant reminder of one's mortality. Alice was your father's second wife, yes?"

Amy nodded. "Also his last. They were married for a little over twenty years."

"You've mentioned that your father has passed away, but what about your stepmother? Is she still alive?"

"Oh yes. Alive and kicking and living in Ojai."

"Are you still in contact with her?"

"Holidays, mostly."

"Even though Ojai is only an hour and a half from here?"

Amy looked at the family photo again. "Surely I'm not your only client with stepmother issues. Why do you ask?"

"Curiosity."

"You think this may have something to do with her."

John shrugged.

A glance at her watch informed Amy that the session was up. Close enough, anyhow. "I don't think so." She stood. "I think it has something to do with that damned lizard."

◉    ◉    ◉

Although Henry had offered to come over, Amy felt tired and wanted to make it an early evening. Henry hadn't sounded disappointed when she said wasn't up for company, which was good. They'd only been seeing each other for three months and Amy wasn't sure how serious she wanted the relationship to become. Not that she didn't enjoy Henry's company; he was kind, generous in bed, a good kisser, had a great sense of humor, was as tall as she (five-foot-eleven), and—even more importantly—as an EVP for a finance company he understood her job's complexities. That had been something Peter had never seemed to comprehend. She had already made COO when she'd first met Peter, but he never quite understood what that meant and therefore was unable to really grasp her career ambitions. He'd known that she was driven, just as she'd known that he was not. They'd laughed and embraced the axiom that opposites really do attract. By the end, though, they'd learned that opposites repelled, as they almost always do once the novelty wears off. Amy's laid-back husband refused to understand her interest in such a demanding, time-consuming job, and when she became CEO their problems quickly amplified. Peter asked for a divorce. They were seeing John then and he had tried to talk them both into working out their differences, but Peter didn't think it would do any good. And, to be honest, Amy didn't want to spend more evenings arguing about why their relationship wasn't working.

Henry, however, understood how little time she had to devote to her personal life. He also embraced making the most of their time together rather than whine about its brevity. He didn't mind that she sometimes had to take calls when they went away for the weekend or that she checked her email whenever and wherever possible. Sitting in a coffee shop, each busy with their smartphones, still meant they were spending time together. Amy appreciated this, even if she never said so.

After ending her call with Henry, Amy curled up on the sofa with a salad she'd bought on the way home to watch a little television before bed. She eyed her briefcase, leaning against the hall credenza where she'd dropped it, and briefly considered reading one or two divisional earnings reports stuffed inside before turning on the TV, but decided they could wait until the morning. She would read them over coffee. Her assistant reminded her again and again that she didn't have to read the entire report; each one came with an executive summary, but Amy never listened. While she trusted all the people who reported to her, she couldn't bring herself to withdraw completely. She refused to call it micromanaging, preferring to think of it as being thorough.

Amy pressed a button on the remote and waited for the television to come on. When they'd split, Peter had insisted he get the huge widescreen television they'd bought their last Christmas together and Amy hadn't argued about it. She kept the smaller set they'd had in the bedroom even though it was ancient, technologically speaking. The tube blinked on and off, as if the screen were winking at her, and when the somewhat skewed picture finally came on the color was wrong. On the screen was a commercial she'd seen a hundred times, the one with the talking gecko. Usually the lizard was green. Currently it was orange. Amy thumbed the settings button on the remote until she was able to correct the background color, which had previously been blue. The talking gecko, however, remained stubbornly orange.

"I wonder what John would make of this," she mumbled.

She turned the television off and stared at the blank screen, muttering to herself that it was just an odd coincidence that the television had picked tonight to go on the fritz and screw with the color. She set the salad on the coffee table and reached for her cell phone. Resisting the urge to check her email, she scrolled through her contacts list until she came to her stepmother's name. The hour was late, but Alice had always been a night owl, even in her seventy-seventh year. Forgoing her earpiece, Amy pressed the call button and held the cell to her ear.

"Hello?" Alice Darlidale's voice had become gravelly in her golden years, but it hadn't lost all of its British lilt despite her having been an American citizen for over forty years.

"Hi, Alice." Already Amy regretted making the impetuous call. She wasn't even sure why she'd done so.

"Amy, dear," her stepmother said. "What a surprise. When I heard your voice, I actually glanced at the calendar to see if I'd missed a holiday."

"No, not a holiday."

"Well, it certainly wouldn't have been the first time I've forgotten what day it is. Those *senior moments* happen more and more these days, I'm afraid. What brings you to ring me, dear?"

Amy couldn't think of an answer. Certainly, she couldn't inquire whether her stepmother had seen an orange lizard lately. Nor did she want to ask Alice about the days leading up to or following her childhood coma, which was what seeing the lizard had brought to mind. Yet here she was on the phone, and she had to say something.

"Does that friend of yours still own a winery in Napa Valley? A colleague of mine is taking a road trip over the weekend and I thought she might enjoy a stopover."

"Oh, no, dear. That winery closed years ago. I'm surprised you don't recall, being as it happened shortly after Christopher passed on."

She did recall, actually. The winery was where her father had the first pangs of what would become a fatal heart attack. "I guess it's my turn for a senior moment." Amy managed a chuckle. "I'm sure my colleague can find somewhere to visit on her own."

"Of course she can, dear."

For the next few minutes, Amy asked the obligatory questions concerning Alice's health and general welfare before saying goodbye. Alice seldom asked Amy any questions because Amy seldom had anything to say. Stories about her job were of no interest to her stepmother and, unfortunately, those were about the only stories she had to tell. Mentioning Henry was pointless (she wasn't sure how long he would be around) and enough time had passed that even her divorce was no longer fodder for conversation. Probably just as well. Alice had never been a very good listener.

Once she hung up, Amy used the remote to turn the television on again. The color had returned to normal, so she skipped around the channels until she found something that interested her. She ate the remaining salad before retiring for the night.

Something woke her.

Lying on her side, Amy opened her eyes and looked at the blue numbers on her bedside clock. Three thirty-three a.m. When she rolled over onto her back, her heart stopped. At the foot of her bed was the silhouette of someone at least seven foot tall. The figure raised its arms and the silhouette went from rectangular to hourglass.

Amy lunged for the light and switched it on.

She was alone in the room.

Had she dreamt it? If so, it was the first time she'd recalled a dream since her childhood. That seemed so unlikely that she decided it had been an illusion. Her eyes had played a trick on her while trying to compensate for the darkness. Whatever it had been she was awake now and couldn't possibly fall back to sleep, so she got out of bed and slipped on her robe. In the kitchen she flipped on the light switch and poured herself a glass of water from the pitcher in the refrigerator. Feeling a bit unsteady, she sat at the small dining table and looked out through the sliding glass doors that opened onto a balcony. Shortly after the divorce she'd rented an apartment in a newly renovated building so that she would be closer to work, cutting her commute from forty-five minutes to ten. Downtown Los Angeles had been in the throes of a revival for a few years and she'd thought it a good time to take advantage of it. What she loved most about her new place was, due to the emptiness of downtown at night, she didn't have to draw the blinds (it also helped that she was on the thirty-third floor) and she always kept the sliding glass doors uncovered so that she could see the Hollywood sign in the distance. The view was especially lovely at night, framed by the tall downtown buildings—particularly the Library Tower, an office building with seventy-two floors across from the main public library. Of all the tall downtown buildings she liked the Library Tower the most because of its distinctive crown-like top.

Since she was up she figured that she might as well be productive. She went through the living room to the front hall and removed her laptop from her briefcase. Back at her small dining table, she turned the computer on, accessed her email, and started her workday a bit earlier than usual.

◉   ◉   ◉

"Wendy, where did this come from?" Amy called out to her assistant. When the young woman came into her office Amy had one hand tapping away on her keyboard and the other waving a gold bracelet in the air.

"What is it?" Wendy stepped farther into the room to get a better look at what Amy held. "Oh, *that*. When I unlocked your office this morning I saw it on the floor next to the couch." She pointed to the sofa at the front of the office where Amy would sit when she had visitors. "I thought it had probably fallen off when we were looking for the lizard yesterday."

Amy stopped typing. "Isn't it yours?"

"No," Wendy said. "I assumed it was yours. I don't own any expensive jewelry."

Amy placed the bracelet in the palm of her hand and looked at it closely. The bracelet was relatively heavy, about an inch thick, and gold-colored. The only distinctive elements were the three peaks on one side, the center peak higher than those on either side. "You think this is expensive?"

"Looks like solid gold to me."

Puzzled, Amy tilted her hand so that she could see the inside of the bracelet where there should have been a stamp to indicate the carat, but saw that it was smooth. "I don't know about that, but it doesn't belong to me."

"Really? Then who could it belong to? We didn't have anyone in here yesterday."

Amy spun the bracelet around one finger. "Maybe it belongs to the cleaning crew."

"I don't think so. I'm telling you that is real gold. Even if someone on the cleaning crew could afford it, she wouldn't wear it to work."

Amy shook her head. "I'm betting that it's fake or at most, gold plated." She stopped spinning it and dangled the bracelet from her finger. Something about it seemed familiar. "Doesn't Wonder Woman wear a bracelet like this?"

"It's not wide enough to be Wonder Woman's bracelet." Wendy held out her hand. "Here, I can tell if it's real or not." When Amy gave it to her, Wendy slipped the bracelet on. "If my wrist doesn't turn green by the end of the day, it's real. I have a knack for exposing fake jewelry." She pushed the bracelet up her thin wrist. "Just ask my boyfriend."

A few minutes after six that evening, Wendy returned to Amy's office with her purse slung over her shoulder, her coat over her forearm, and her car keys in hand. She set the keys on Amy's desk and pulled off the bracelet that she'd worn all day.

"Told ya." She held up her arm and twisted it so that Amy could see that she hadn't any marks on her wrist. "It's real."

Until Wendy handed her the bracelet, Amy had no idea what her assistant was talking about.

"Oh, right." She looked at the inside of the bracelet and saw that, like Wendy's wrist, it too was free of discoloration. She set it next to her keyboard.

"I thought that Monday morning I'd send out an email about finding it," Wendy said.

"Good idea; although I still think it could belong to the cleaning crew."

Wendy picked up her car keys. "You need me for anything before I go?"

"No, I think we're good." Amy returned her attention to the computer screen. "Have a nice weekend."

"You too." Wendy turned to leave but stopped in the doorway. "You're not planning on staying late tonight, are you?" When her boss didn't respond, Wendy stepped back into the office. "Amy, it's Friday night. You can't—"

Amy held up her hands without taking her eyes off the computer. "No, I'm not going to stay late. Henry's son is in a play and we're going out to dinner afterwards."

"Oh, you're going to meet his son?"

While Amy made it a point not to discuss her personal life with coworkers, she'd had to make a few concessions when it came to her assistant. She'd read somewhere that people in their twenties believed that the word *assistant* meant more than secretary, and Wendy was no exception. Whether or not Amy agreed, she knew that sometimes it was important to play along. "No. I think it's too early in our relationship for that."

"Really? How long have you guys been dating?"

But it didn't mean she had to play along *all* the time. She cocked an eyebrow.

Wendy bit her lips in an obvious attempt to keep from smiling. "Sorry. Not my business. Well, have a good night. See you Monday."

"See you Monday."

An hour later, when she'd finished the shareholder presentation she'd been working on for nearly a week, Amy leaned back in her chair and looked at the bracelet next to her keyboard. Was it possible that the bracelet was solid gold and not plating as she'd first suspected? Wendy had thought it looked expensive, but Amy thought it was too plain, too ordinary. If it had some sort of design etched into it she could have been convinced that it was genuine, but it was as smooth as it was shiny. She picked it up and slipped it over her left wrist. While it wasn't as loose on her wrist as it had been on Wendy's, the bracelet easily slid up to her watch, which *was* gold-plated. The coloring of the two looked the same, but that didn't necessarily mean they were made of the same substance. There had to be a better way to determine whether or not the bracelet was real gold other than waiting for her assistant's wrist to turn green. Surely a jeweler had a process that could test it for authenticity.

As she glanced at the clock on her computer screen, she was surprised to find that it was almost nine. The curtain would be coming down on Henry's son's debut performance at some middle school theater. That Henry had two children was slightly troublesome for Amy, if there were to be any permanence to their relationship. She had never aspired to be a mother and certainly not a stepmother. She'd had one herself and that was as close to the role as she wanted to get. Of course Henry's children were older than she had been when her father had brought Alice around seven years after her mother had passed away. That alone would separate their experience from hers; also, they wouldn't have to move because they didn't live with their father. When Christopher Darlidale married Alice Frye, Amy had been uprooted from the only home she'd ever known and plopped down in the middle of what might as well have been a foreign country. She'd grown up in Indio, a relatively small

Southern Californian town renown for its date crops and immigrant population, and wasn't prepared for the affluent life ensconced in Northern California where her father's new wife lived.

That they'd move in with Alice was a foregone conclusion. Besides having a more luxurious home, Alice also had connections and found Christopher a job that paid much more than the one he'd had in Indio. They'd met at a hotel where Christopher was attending a convention. Alice was in the bar waiting for a friend, who never showed. What happened that night, Amy didn't want to know. But after that weekend the two talked on the phone every night and met up every chance they could. A little over eight months later, Christopher ended their long-distance relationship by proposing. At the time, Amy hadn't been terribly thrilled with the idea of having a stepmother. But even at the age of ten she could see how happy Alice made her father. That was what mattered most.

Her cell phone rattled on the desk when it buzzed to announce she had a text message. She was grateful for the interruption. Surprisingly, or perhaps not, the text message was from Henry. He wrote that he hoped she'd understand but his son wanted him to join the rest of the family for a late dinner. Amy returned the text telling him that of course she understood and to have fun; nevertheless, she was annoyed. He shouldn't have told her that he would meet her after the play to begin with. If he had, she wouldn't be working late in her office on a Friday night thinking about her father. She turned off the computer monitor and gathered what she would work on over the weekend.

The trip was a spontaneous decision. She told herself that it was because she'd been thinking about her childhood in the desert earlier and it had nothing to do with not wanting to be readily available when Henry called. Instead of going home, Amy jumped onto the freeway. The hour was late enough that the traffic on the I-10 wouldn't be too congested and there was no better time to head out to her condo in Palm Springs. She listened to music and let the drive, one she'd taken so often that she could do it with her eyes closed, soothe away her irritation. It worked well enough that, two hours later when she left the Interstate for Highway 111 near where the huge electricity-producing windmills churned, she'd already decided that when Henry called in the morning she would invite him to join her. She'd even blow off work and relax—for a while, at least; she wouldn't guarantee that she could relax for the *whole* weekend.

Amy sped down the highway, slowing only when she reached the sign welcoming her to town. Moonlight glinted off the bracelet that she'd forgotten she still had on.

◉   ◉   ◉

Saturday morning she woke early. She began her day sitting out in the courtyard next to the small plunge pool sipping coffee and skimming through months-old magazines. When her coffee mug was empty and the magazines had lost her interest, she decided to take a walk while it was still cool. In the bedroom she exchanged her robe, nightgown, and slippers for a tank top, capri pants, and running shoes. As she bent to tie the shoes, the gold bracelet bumped into the heel of her hand. The previous night, when she'd readied for bed, she'd discovered that removing the bracelet wasn't as easy as putting it on. She'd taken off her watch but when it came to pulling the bracelet up over her hand she found that it stuck at the thickest part, no matter how much she squeezed her palm together. Too tired to struggle with taking the bracelet off, she'd removed all her other jewelry and had gone to bed. The bracelet still wouldn't come off when she gave it another yank and she thought it best to wait until she showered so she could use soap as a lubricant. She grabbed her driver's license, sunglasses, and her keys on her way out and, as she stepped over the threshold, the sunglasses slipped from her hand

and bounced off the outdoor tile. When she picked them up, she saw that the bottom of the left lens now had a small crack. Rooting around the condo or the glove compartment of her car for another pair wasn't worth the trouble, so she put them on anyway. After locking both the condo door and the courtyard gate, Amy left the complex for her morning stroll.

Just west of the airport she saw something small scurry across the sidewalk into a field and could have sworn it was orange in color. She would have thought that her eyes were playing tricks on her again but when she reached the spot where the something small had scurried across and looked into the field, there it was—an orange lizard. The tiny creature had stopped and was looking back, as if waiting for her.

"You *cannot* be the same lizard," she said to the motionless creature.

If being orange weren't peculiar enough, the lizard turned and slowly, as if trying to impress with its skills, rose up onto its back legs. Amy could have sworn it was smiling at her before it scuttled into the dry brush. Without thinking about what she was doing or why she was doing it, she gave chase but quickly concluded that she would never catch the lizard (and what would she do with it if she did?). During her short energy burst, however, she'd somehow mixed up her directions. The sidewalk she'd been strolling on wasn't in the direction she thought it would be. As she turned in search of it, a wave of dizziness crashed over her and the sun suddenly seemed as if it had doubled in size. Its brightness bleached the field and its heat pressed down like a flatiron. Amy didn't understand what was happening when her knees started to give way.

As she felt herself falling, she wondered how long it would be before someone found her.

# PART TWO

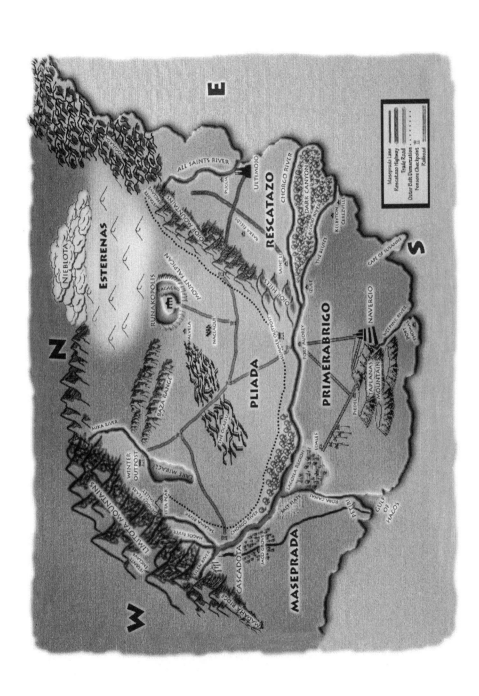

**H**er eyes stung and she felt grit under her eyelids. Rolling onto her side, Amy fumbled for the bottom of her tank top to gently dab at her eyes. Her lashes seemed crusted over, as if she'd slept for a very, very long time. With some gentle rubbing and a little spit, she was able to clean her lashes and open her eyes. She pushed herself to her knees and paused to get her bearings. She recalled going out for a walk and crossing into a field when she'd suddenly become dizzy and fallen. While the dizziness was gone, it had been replaced by a nearly overwhelming thirst, leaving her to wonder how long she'd been lying unconscious in the heat. As she sat back on her haunches, she noticed that, from head to toe, a thin layer of red dust coated her and bits of rock had somehow also found their way into her hair and down her shirt. After futilely trying to wipe off the red dust, she brought her head up. Her pulse began to race. Sand surrounded her, miles and miles of white sand.

Her first clue that something was amiss should have been when she brushed at the red dust. That alone indicated she was no longer in the same field where she had fallen. Not seeing the adjacent street or the housing cluster next to the field was certainly another clue. The biggest piece of evidence, however, was the missing San Jacinto Mountains. Utterly confused, Amy pulled herself to her feet. There had been times when she'd woken up from a deep sleep and for just an instant had no idea where she was, but that hardly compared to how she presently felt. Nothing about the situation made sense. Had she somehow blacked out after falling? Was it possible she could have, in an amnesia-like state, returned to the condo, gotten into her car, and driven farther out into the desert? Surely she couldn't have walked. Maybe in some addled stupor she'd tried to find a spot where she once hiked with her father. She had no memory of any of that, though. She had no memory beyond feeling dizzy.

She tried to comprehend how she had gotten herself into such a predicament. Maybe someone found her and then … No, that seemed even less likely than going for a drive. The sand beneath her had no footprints, no markings at all except those she'd made while rolling over, sitting up, and standing. She couldn't have appeared in the middle of nowhere, yet nowhere was exactly where she seemed to be. With no landmarks to guide her Amy was unsure in which direction to head but she desperately needed water and shelter. She knew that the San Jacintos were west of Palm Springs and, if the dark bumps on the horizon were those mountains, then the sun should be heading in that direction. She also knew that waiting for the sun to move was akin to waiting for water to boil, so she slowly turned in a circle to scan the horizon for something other than the dark bumps. She saw nothing until, just shy of the 180° mark, she found herself looking at what appeared to be low-lying clouds that, like the mountain bumps, tapered off at each end. The cloud formation gave her some hope, though, because it could mean rain. Amy set off in that direction.

The sun seemed to be leeching every bit of liquid from her body so that even her breath felt void of moisture. She could feel her lips cracking. Each dune she staggered across appeared to lead to a hundred more beyond it and after hours of walking, the cloudbank seemed no closer than it had been when she started. The sun seemed to move so slowly she feared it would never set and she would be baked alive. Still she trudged on, robotically lifting one leg, then lifting the other. Over and over her body moved in that manner until it could no longer repeat the process and once again, she fell. The sand was hot, but it was soft and she managed to roll onto her side, facing away from her enemy, the sun. As Amy lay there, barely conscious, she thought she saw something moving across the dunes. She was too weak to lift her head but managed to lift her left hand and sunlight glinted off the gold bracelet she couldn't remove. She tried to wave but her arm felt too heavy and she let it drop. Amy closed her eyes.

◉　◉　◉

"Wake up, now. You must eat."

She was prone, that much she was aware of. And she could smell something odd—like rotting flowers, cloying and dusty. Her eyelids fluttered until they opened slightly. Through blurred vision, she saw a bald boy sitting beside her prone body holding a bowl and a spoon. He seemed to have a black mask around his eyes. She wanted to go back to sleep, but the boy (or was he a young man?) held the spoon to her mouth and automatically she parted her lips to slurp up his offering. What he gave her was watery and cool—wonderfully cool. When he offered her another spoonful, she was able to lift her head a bit and with every swallow thereafter, she felt strength returning to her limbs. Once the bowl was empty, the young man set it on a small table next to where Amy lay so that he could gently pull her forward to place pillows at her back.

While he adjusted the pillows, his face was close enough to hers that Amy saw he didn't have a mask around his eyes. If it were an actual

28

mask it would have stretched from one eye to the other across the bridge of his nose. Instead, each eye was surrounded in black and feathered out downward along his cheeks as if smudged. The slightly oval markings seemed to be painted on or possibly tattooed, but the rest of his skin was smooth and unblemished, although it seemed to have a blue-gray hue. He had a large forehead and a small chin. A long, brown garment covered his body.

"Where am I?" Amy tried to say as he laid her against the pillows. What came out, however, was more a whispered croak than a question.

The young man understood her, though. "You are in our camp," he said. He seemed to take delight in her speaking to him. "We found you lying out on the sand and brought you here."

Despite, or possibly because of, her muddled state, Amy had the inescapable feeling that he was looking at her as though she were the prize found at the bottom of a cereal box. Her eyes darted across her surroundings. She was inside a canvas tent. The sloped roof was highest in the center where a pole stood, surrounded by open flaps. The bed, the chair the young man sat in, and the small table were the tent's only furnishings. Amy wondered what sort of camp she'd been brought to. On the table, next to the empty bowl, a thin tendril of smoke rose from a brass tray.

"We are Carados," the young man continued. "I am a seguidost under Apósto Baruti. For hundreds of years we've been waiting for the prophecy to be fulfilled." His brown eyes moved from her face to her bare shoulder and then down her left arm.

A light, rough sheet covered her body and to avoid his intense gaze, Amy put her arm below it. When her hand pressed against her hip she felt only bare flesh. Realizing she was naked, the bud of concern in her stomach quickly blossomed into fear. She'd read about women being kidnapped by little-known cults. The strange-looking young man must have seen the alarm in her eyes because he told her not to worry. He gently placed a hand on her sheet-covered arm.

"You are safe with us."

Amy recoiled from his touch. She wanted to tell him to get away from her but a ruffling noise took her attention and she turned toward the sound. The tent flap opened and a young woman, alabaster-white, came in. She stood at the opening holding a pile of clothes in her hands atop which sat Amy's running shoes. The young woman didn't seem quite as young as the young man sitting beside the bed but she was just as bald and she too wore a brown, floor-length garment. She came to the center of the tent and looked at Amy with obvious concern, but she addressed the young man.

"Jandro, what have you done to frighten her?"

The young man, Jandro apparently, shook his head vehemently. His forehead wrinkled as his eyebrows shot up—except he didn't have any eyebrows. "I did nothing, Licha," he said. "I only told her she was safe with us."

The young woman snorted. "Ha, not many quimeras would feel safe waking up with a stranger hovering over her like that." She sat her bundle at the foot of the bed and squatted next to it so that her face was level with Amy's. "But Jandro is right. You *are* safe with us."

She had an accent that sounded slightly Mexican. Most of Amy's friends prior to moving to Northern California had that accent. None of them, however, looked like this woman named Licha. When she had entered the tent carrying the clothing, Amy had assumed Licha was an albino due to her extremely white skin. But seeing her up close, Amy wasn't as sure. Licha's eyes were dark blue, which surely wouldn't be the case if she had actual pigmentation deficiency. And the underside of her nose from the tip down to the midline groove above the upper lip was pink, although it could have been painted or tattooed on like the young man's black mask.

"I think you'd be more comfortable if you had on your clothing,"

Licha smiled warmly at Amy before standing and looking at Jandro expectantly. "Well?"

He seemed confused by her question.

"You should leave, Jandro."

"Oh. Sorry."

Standing, he was the same height as Licha—neither could have been more than five-foot-four—and in two broad steps Jandro was out of the tent. He closed the flap behind him. Licha set the running shoes on the ground. She gave Amy her panties first and waited patiently for her to put them on under the sheet. When that was done, Licha gave her the pants and the tank top. Amy put on her pants. She hadn't worn a bra just to go out for a quick morning walk so she turned away when she sat up to put on her top. Licha looked at the running shoes almost reverently.

"I've never seen footwear like that. But if not for them, we may never have convinced the apósto that you are truly *Lacáruna*."

"Who?" Amy whispered. Licha didn't seem to have heard her.

"He said that the Cocúlta on your wrist could be fake," Licha continued, "like those sold in the cities."

Amy slowly swung her feet to the ground, which was covered with what appeared to be several woven carpets. She looked at the bracelet on her arm. It was the only piece of jewelry she had on, but only because she hadn't been able to take it off the night … How long had it actually been? Had that really happened just the night before?

"Even if others think it false we must keep the Cocúlta covered. I brought you this to wear." Licha picked up the last article of clothing and unfolded it to reveal the same brown floor-length robe that Jandro and she wore.

The garment served to confirm Amy's suspicion that she had been found by some strange cult. She looked at the simple, brown robe and it occurred to her that she may not have blacked out after falling in the field in Palm Springs, as she'd come to believe while stumbling over the sand dunes. She considered the possibility that she'd been drugged, and waking up alone in an unknown area of the Coachella Valley hadn't been an accident. She very well could have been kidnapped. With that in mind, she ignored the robe Licha held out for her and slipped on her running shoes. She bent as if to tie the laces and then with every ounce of the strength she had recovered, abruptly shoved herself off the bed. Her momentum was more than she had anticipated and it sent her reeling into the alabaster-white woman, knocking Licha over and nearly pulling Amy down on top of her before she caught her balance and fled through the tent flap. The heat was the first thing she ran into. The second was a man well over six feet tall.

"Ho-ho there, friend." The huge man wrapped his arms around her.

She struggled as best she could but the burst of energy she'd mustered had run its course and Amy quickly fell limp. Feeling sweat drip down her neck, she lolled her head in defeat. The arms that held her tightly were covered in thick auburn hair. The tall, burly man swept one hand under her knees and picked her up, cradling her with ease. When she looked up at his face, she saw that it too was covered in hair. In fact, she thought he had to be the hairiest man she'd ever seen. The auburn hair on his head started midway up on his forehead leaving only an inch or so of skin between it and his thick uni-brow. His beard started above his cheekbones, nearly eye level, and ended somewhere under the collar of his blue robe. The man carried Amy back into the tent. He had to squat to make it through the flap and even while standing next to the center pole had to duck to avoid scraping the top of the tent. Licha had pulled herself up off the ground where Amy had knocked her.

"Oh thank *La Reina*." Licha helped the man gently lay Amy on the bed. "She's still frightened." When Jandro stuck his head through the tent flap, she added, "I blame this on you. Go get her some water."

Jandro ducked out the flap.

"No one is to blame," the large hairy man said. "Anyone delivered here in such a manner would be terrified. Even the Primeróte were frightened when they arrived."

Licha nodded solemnly.

Instead of sitting on the chair as Jandro had done, the big man practically folded himself in half in order to sit cross-legged on the ground beside the bed. He was still so large that Amy had to look up to see his face. His green eyes seemed kind and his baritone voice was oddly comforting, rumbling in her chest when he spoke.

Though most of her strength had been sapped by her escape attempt, Amy's voice was stronger, though hoarse, than it had been since waking. "What do you mean *delivered*?"

Before anyone answered her question Jandro returned with a ceramic jug, which he handed to Licha after pulling the tent flap closed. Licha removed the cup-like top and filled it with water from the jug. She held the cup to Amy's lips, careful to keep Amy from taking in too much at one time. Once the cup was empty, Licha used it to cap the jug and then gestured to Jandro that he should sit. He sat on the ground beside the hairy man and she sat on the opposite side. The chair remained empty.

The auburn-haired man looked at Amy for a moment, as if gauging his words before speaking them. "I am Baruti Tigrezo, an apósto of the Carados," he said. He gestured to the youngsters on either side of him. "This is Jandro Mapanode and Licha Conenode. They found you. You were delivered here to usher in the *New Morphósis*." He seemed to expect Amy to respond. When she didn't, he continued. "Three millennia ago it was prophesized that *Lacáruna* would be delivered to us to make the world right again." He smiled almost bashfully. "I wasn't certain it was true. Even when Licha pointed out the symbols on your unusual shoes, I continued to have doubts. But after spending these past hours in escalétre I've concluded it doesn't matter that your arrival isn't exactly how we'd thought it would be."

"Or *when* we thought it would be," Jandro piped in.

Licha hushed him.

The large man nodded. "Yes, that as well doesn't matter." He laid his very large hand on Amy's forearm just above the bracelet on her wrist. "You are *Lacáruna*."

The words the man named Baruti used weren't at all familiar, but there was no doubt in Amy's mind that they had some sort of religious significance. Her suspicion that she'd been kidnapped by a cult was all but confirmed. Trying her best to remain calm, she asked the question she'd wanted to since first waking in unfamiliar territory, hoping the answer would give her a clue as to how to escape. "Where am I?"

Baruti took his hand off her arm and placed it in his expansive lap. "You are in Pliada, in a region known as Esterenas, south of Nieblota."

None of the locations he mentioned were part of the Coachella Valley. They sounded Spanish, though, and she wondered if she had been brought to Mexico. That could also explain Licha's accent.

With some effort, Baruti hoisted himself to his feet, towering over the bed where Amy lay. "I know that this is all very confusing to you. Believe it or not it is confusing to us as well. Soon, however, apóstos from other factions will gather here for communal escalétre so that we will better be able to answer your questions." He nodded at Licha who quickly stood.

"Make her comfortable so she can get some rest." When Jandro stood as well, the bigger, hairier man said to him, "And *you* stay out of here."

Jandro looked a bit disappointed but nodded in agreement. He said nothing as he followed the huge man out through the flap, but he turned briefly to offer Amy a smile. Then he was gone. As much as she wanted to pepper Licha with more questions, Amy's body had other plans and, in moments, she was asleep.

Amy fell out of bed. When she hit the ground her eyes opened. The cot she'd been laying on was still at her back. She hadn't fallen; the cot had been pushed over. Crawling on her hands and knees, Licha scrambled around the cot to Amy's side.

"Shhh." She held a finger to her lips.

Despite that, Amy started to speak. Licha used her other hand to cover Amy's mouth and shook her head. When the tent flap opened, light coming from somewhere outside appeared and Licha ducked down. Amy saw the fear in the young woman's dark blue eyes. She held her breath until the light disappeared. Slowly, Licha rose and peered over the edge of the cot. Once certain the coast was clear, she handed Amy something.

"Put this on. Quickly. I'll get your shoes." Moonlight filtered down from the open flaps at the top of the tent and reflected off Licha's white skin like sea foam on a summer's eve.

Amy sat up and unfolded what Licha had given her—the brown robe she'd been told to put on earlier. Fully awake now, it occurred to her that Licha might be trying to help her escape. Amy pulled the robe over her head, spinning it until her arms found the appropriate holes. She stood when Licha did and let the robe fall to her feet. Licha took her hand.

"Now, stay very, very close to me," Licha whispered. "And don't make a sound." With Amy's running shoes tucked under one arm, the young bald woman parted the tent flap no more than an inch. She looked outside cautiously before going through it and tugged Amy along behind her.

The air was many degrees cooler than it had been during her feeble attempt to flee, but even at night it was warm enough to draw sweat from Amy's upper lip. The warm sand felt good on her feet. Several other tents, many bigger than the one she'd been kept in, stood nearby. Most were dark, but a few glowed with an inner light and she could see shapes moving about within. Licha pulled her along between the tents, always careful to peek around corners to make sure they weren't seen. Twice they had to press themselves against a tent to stay out of sight. They crouched behind a barrel at the last tent as several people wearing dark robes passed by. Amy could hear voices coming from within the tent next to her. The canvases didn't quite meet at the corner and through the gap she could see inside. Two men were talking. One had the hood of his dark robe up and the other, also wearing a blue robe, had his back to her. She could make out only bits and pieces of their conversation, but what she heard made little sense. They were arguing about something—the tone of their voices made that clear. Two words were repeated by both of them: *den* and *dough*. Were they talking about ransom? The man with the hood held up a knife. When he did so the other man turned and Amy could see his face. Apósto Baruti, the hairy man who had stopped her earlier attempt at escape, backed away from the hooded man. Licha yanked Amy's arm and pulled her away before she could see what happened next. She followed the white-skinned young woman around the tent into the darkness behind it.

In the light of the full moon, Amy searched for some clue as to where she was and whom she was dealing with. If Licha proved unsuccessful in helping her to escape, understanding her captors could save her life. The robes they wore and the fact that they lived in tents suggested they were a religious cult. Even so, she'd never heard of a cult demanding ransom, which was what she thought the hairy man and the hooded man had been arguing about. So if they weren't a religious cult, then who were they? She didn't have much information to go on nor did she see anything familiar. The camp seemed to have no vehicles or buildings. Amy spotted someone working a hand lever to pump water into a bucket up ahead. The lever was attached to a spigot of a large metal cylinder five feet in diameter, sitting atop what looked like wide skis. As they neared, she saw that it was the young bald man named Jandro at the pump. Because of his painted on or tattooed mask, in the semi-darkness the whites of his eyes seemed to float alongside his nose.

"I feel bad for taking this much," he whispered. "What about the others?"

"That's not for us to worry about," Licha said. "We need to go."

When he finished filling the bucket with water, Jandro picked up another bucket already filled. "I harnessed one of the avestrandés to the trinéot. She wasn't happy about being separated from her mate."

"She'll be reunited soon enough." Licha handed Amy her running shoes. She picked up cloth bag next to the pump. "What were you able to get?"

"Mostly cheese. But there are a few turnips and leeks in there and one loaf of bread. I hope it will be enough."

"It will have to be." Licha nodded toward a large tent several yards out from the pump. The tent was the only one in the area. "Hurry."

Jandro led the way, carrying the two buckets. Following Licha, Amy clutched her shoes against her chest. She had no intention to try to make a break for it on her own; there didn't seem to be anywhere to go. As far as she could tell, nothing but white sand surrounded the camp and there were no lights indicating anything off in the distance. She'd already tried to make her way through those dunes alone and had no desire for a second trip.

Nearing the large tent, Amy smelled a musty, animal scent and heard rustling. Jandro had mentioned a harness, so she assumed he was taking them to where the horses were kept. Then she heard a shrill squawk that sounded like a parakeet screaming through a trumpet. They rounded the tent and Amy gasped when she saw what had made the noise. It certainly wasn't a parakeet. Standing before a small covered wagon was a creature that had to be ten feet tall and looked like a bird from a nightmare that only a frightened, over-imaginative child or someone completely insane could produce. The beast's head was oval-shaped, made up mostly of a frighteningly sharp-looking beak. From the top of the creature's head dark feathers fell like a mane down a long, thick neck. Its body seemed nearly round due to the huge breastbone that puffed out like that of a cocky, barrel-chested man. The creature's wings were small and flipper like, but the legs on it were huge and thickly muscled and its webbed feet had to be three feet wide, ending in sharp talons. The feathers on top, from its head down its back to its stubby tail, were much darker than the feathers underneath. The beast's eyes were saucer big and one look from it brought a startled, and somewhat prolonged, squeak out of Amy. Licha dropped the bag with the food in it and reached up, clamping her hand over the taller woman's mouth. Her attempt to silence Amy came too late, and the beast screeched in return.

Jandro quickly, but carefully, set the buckets of water on the sand and hurried to the creature to calm it. He used both hands to rub its feathered breast, cooing at it as a mother would a baby. Although agitated, the beast stopped rocking back and forth on its monstrous feet and lowered its head until its beak rested on the young man's shoulder. If it opened its mouth it could easily have bitten off Jandro's head. He didn't seem worried, though, as he wrapped an arm around the beast's neck and stroked it like a pet.

Stunned, Amy remained frozen in place until Licha shoved her past the gigantic bird to the back of the covered wagon sitting atop wide skis like the water cylinder

"Get in," Licha said. "I'm sure someone heard the avestrandé bellow and will come to check on it. We don't have much time."

Amy couldn't decide which disturbed her more, the beast or the way Jandro reacted to it. "What is that thing?"

Licha pushed at her. "Get in."

Amy climbed through the arched opening on her hands and knees. The wagon, or trinéot as Jandro had called it, was about six feet wide and twelve feet long. Compartments ran along one side of the interior and opposite that was what appeared to be rolled carpets and bedding. With a shoe in each hand, Amy crawled up to the front and looked out an opening to see Jandro pouring the buckets of water into something attached to the side of the trinéot. Once emptied, he tossed the buckets into the dark tent, which caused a commotion inside and more screeching and squawking.

Licha climbed in and crawled to the front next to Amy. As Jandro stepped up onto the driver's box, she told him to hurry.

Jandro took the reins in hand. "What about Apósto Baruti?"

"He will join us near Nieblota, where we made camp a year ago." When he still didn't get the wagon moving Licha asked him why he was waiting.

"The nightwinds. If we don't wait we could be followed."

"They'll come up soon enough," Licha said. "Now go!"

With a flick of his wrists Jandro snapped the reins. The beast took off at a surprising speed. Unprepared, Amy fell back against the rolled bedding and hit her head on the side of the wooden trinéot. Seeing the stars brought on by the jolt left her to wonder whether she was hallucinating all of this. Being drugged was the only explanation for the enormous beast pulling the wagon-sled over the sand. She'd been to many zoos in her life, had watched dozens and dozens documentaries and television shows about the creatures of the world, but never had she seen anything like it. For the first and probably only time in her life, Amy wished she'd dropped the acid that had been offered to her more than once while in college. Maybe then she'd be better able to tell if she'd been doped. She'd tried marijuana on occasion and had been drunk more times than she cared to admit but in all those instances she had known, had felt, that the substances altered her consciousness. This was entirely different. Other than being disoriented because of the strange situation, she felt normal, leaving her to wonder whether there were psychotropic drugs that could cause hallucinations without the feeling of being under the influence.

"Are you hungry?" Licha's face was in darkness.

Amy pushed herself up off the bedrolls she fallen against. "What?"

"I asked if you are hungry. We don't have much, but you must keep up your strength." She opened a compartment on the opposite side of where Amy sat and took something from it. A moment later, there was a flash, as she turned on a small lantern that glowed with a greenish light. Licha placed the lantern on the floor. "That should be all right, but we shouldn't leave it on for long. We don't want to be spotted."

The bag Licha had carried in was at her side and she rummaged through it before pulling out a small round cheese. From a drawer below the compartment where she'd retrieved the lantern, she removed a knife. Although the knife was only about three or four inches long, it was sharp enough that it easily cut through the red rind. She sliced the cheese in quarters and handed one to Amy.

Amy brought the cheese to her nose. Despite its orange hue, the cheese had a pungent Roquefort smell. She pulled back the rind and appeared to be studying the cheese in her hand but was actually looking at the knife Licha had laid on the floor next to the quartered cheese. When the bald woman leaned forward to ask Jandro if he were hungry, Amy lunged and grabbed the knife. Faster than she thought possible, she clutched the neck of Licha's robe, yanked her to the floor, and held the knife to the woman's bone-white throat. Wide eyed, Licha opened her mouth but when Amy pressed on the knife, she closed it. Amy straddled her, not an easy task due to the robe she'd put on before leaving the tent.

"Who are you and where are you taking me?" Her voice was just loud enough for Licha to hear. She held up the piece of cheese that Licha had given her. "What are you drugging me with?"

Licha seemed confused. "Dragging?"

Although Amy found it odd that Licha wasn't fighting back in the least, she refused to allow the woman's apparent submission fool her into letting down her guard. "No, *drugging*. That's how you got me here, isn't it? You must have …" She struggled to make sense of it. "You must have broken into my condo and put something in my water. Or the coffee." Water and coffee was all that she had consumed before going out on her walk.

Licha insisted that they weren't the reason she was there.

"Then who is?"

Licha's dark blue eyes filled with tears. "The prophecy says—"

Amy pressed on the knife slightly. "Stop. I don't want to hear anymore of your religious nonsense. I only want to know what you have done to me." She could feel Licha wanting to shake her head.

"We're trying to help you." She sounded so earnest.

"You're trying to help me to escape? Is that it?"

"Yes." Licha nodded as best she could. "Yes!"

The adrenaline pumping through her blood wouldn't last much longer. Already, Amy could feel her strength ebbing. "Then why have you given me something that would cause me to hallucinate?"

"Hallucinate?" Licha stammered over the word as though she'd never heard it before.

"See things."

The bald woman's eyes grew even larger, but apparently not from fear. "What are you seeing?"

Her reaction surprised Amy. "How about that Frankenstein ostrich out there pulling us over the sand?"

Licha seemed confused as to what Amy was referring to. "You mean the avestrandé? Everyone sees that."

Amy rose up so that she could look through the front arch.

Jandro had his back to them. When she realized that she'd pulled the knife away from Licha's neck she turned back, expecting the woman to try to throw her off. Licha remained passive. The tears that had gathered in her eyes had run down the sides of her white face and Amy felt a pang of guilt for causing them. She kept the knife close to Licha's neck without pressing on it. "If you're trying to help me escape then tell me how you plan to get me home."

The young woman's lower lip trembled. "I ... I don't know. Apósto Baruti didn't say."

"This was his idea? This escape?"

"Yes, but I don't know why beyond that he said you were in danger. After some other apóstos arrived he came to Jandro and me and told us that we had to take you away from camp because your life was threatened. He said he didn't have time to explain but told us where to go and not to tell anyone. He also said that if he wasn't be able to join us, we were to go on without him."

"Go on where?" Without realizing it, Amy had taken the knife from Licha's neck and was holding it flat against her own breast.

"To Winter Outpost. To find the Trotéjo."

The wagon lurched sideways for a moment and she fell off Licha. Still, the bald woman remained prone, even when Amy backed away. Amy looked out through the front of the wagon again and saw that the trinéot was headed straight for what looked like an enormous sandstorm, a giant wall of white sand as big as a mountain.

"What is *that*?"

Licha sat up. "Nieblota. That is Nieblota. We will be safe there."

The knife fell from Amy's hand.

"It will cover us, smother us, why—"

"Shhh. It will be all right. We're not going into it."

"But—"

Licha picked up the knife and returned it to the drawer she'd taken it from. The young woman gently placed another slice of the orange cheese into Amy's hand and urged her to eat. When Amy only stared, Licha found the cheese slice that Amy had dropped earlier. Holding it up for Amy to see, she peeled back the remaining waxy red rind and popped the wedge into her mouth. After much chewing, she swallowed, opened her mouth, and stretched out her light pink tongue to prove that the cheese was gone.

"There is nothing in the food or water to make you see things. I vow to *La Reina* that what I say is true. We are only here to protect you, never to harm."

Slowly, and with great care, Amy removed the rind from the cheese and bit into it to quiet her stomach. When she had swallowed the last bite, she took from Licha a bladder canteen filled with surprisingly cool water. The exhaustion that followed the adrenaline burst fell over her like a soft blanket and she leaned back into the bedrolls. When she closed her eyes, Licha turned off the green glow of the lantern.

◉   ◉   ◉

When Amy woke, the sun was out and she was soaked in her own sweat. She heard an odd buzzing and listened for a while. Eventually, she decided it sounded like the static noise of an old-fashioned television not receiving a signal. Surprisingly, the buzzing wasn't bothersome and was more akin to white noise, background noise. If she hadn't been so hot, it might have lulled her back to sleep. She found the bladder canteen and gulped as much water as her stomach would allow. Licha must have opened one of the bedrolls for her to lie upon because she was stretched out on the covered trinéot floor. She was alone.

Amy sat up and looked out through the arched openings, front and back. She could see nothing but sand through the back but through the front opening she saw something that took her brain a moment to comprehend. The sled-wagon had stopped near the wall of clouds she seen the night before. Up close it looked less like a bank of clouds and more like an enormous crazy quilt made of rain pockets that moved in various directions: vertical, horizontal, and circular. Again, she was reminded of the snow on a signal-less television screen. The cloudbank was fascinating in its improbability, but like the avestrandé there was no denying its existence.

The giant bird-like thing wasn't harnessed to the trinéot and the driver's bench was empty. Though she was alone under the arched canvas, it seemed unlikely that she'd been abandoned. She searched the interior until she found her shoes, which had been placed neatly in a cubbyhole beside the shelf of compartments. Because it had been dark when she had boarded, she hadn't noticed that the wagon part of the trinéot looked to be made entirely of a reddish burl wood, although what tree the burl came from she couldn't say. The patterns within the wood—swirls, arches, waving lines, and dark irregular spots—were nearly as visually fascinating as the crazy quilt cloudbank, but she would have to admire it another time. Of more importance was finding the bald two who had spirited her away into an even stranger place than that from which she'd escaped.

After tying her shoelaces, Amy pulled off the robe that Licha had given her to wear. Under it, her tank top was stuck to her skin and her capri pants were damp with sweat. She used the robe to wipe the moisture from her face and then tossed it onto the open bedroll before climbing out the back of the trinéot. She shaded her eyes with her hand and wished she had her sunglasses. She remembered putting them on before going for her walk but she didn't think she'd had them when trudging over the dunes. She really couldn't remember much about what happened before she woke in the tent with Jandro at her side.

Squinting as she looked across the endless expanse of undulated sand that looked like a frozen sea covered with snow, she turned and viewed the opposite direction. As much as it had shocked her when she'd seen it the night before, the giant mountain-like sandstorm took her breath away. Licha had called it Nieblota; Amy would have called an haboob, but that couldn't be right. Haboobs, the enormous sandstorms that swept across deserts, moved and this ... this Nieblota seemed rooted in place. It loomed over the trinéot and in the daylight looked more like a wall of clouds whiter than the sand it seemed to sit upon. The cloud-mountain spanned the horizon in both directions, although Amy knew that it didn't fill it entirely because she'd seen it from afar when she'd stumbled across the dunes before being found by these strange people. Nieblota had seemed like a mountain then too, yet clearly it wasn't a geological formation, more like a weather front. Something was keeping the cloud anchored in place. She would have guessed wind, but the air was still.

She found it difficult to take her eyes off the anomaly to look for her captors—or liberators, she'd yet to decide which. When she did look away, she found Licha and Jandro on the starboard side of the trinéot. They sat facing her in the shade of a tarp unfurled from the top of the wagon-sled and attached to wooden poles stuck in the sand on the opposite end. They'd spread out a carpet and were perched atop colorful pillows, cross-legged. Ramrod straight, they sat with their hands on their knees and their faces upturned. Their eyes were closed and they seemed to be meditating. She stepped under the tarp into the shade, prepared to quietly sit and wait for them to notice her but when she moved onto the carpet covering the hot sand, she saw over their bald heads the bird monstrosity behind them. The creature was lying with its long, powerful legs underneath its feathered body and its head and lengthy neck stretched out over the ground. In the daylight it was even more frightening and, once again, Amy was startled by it.

Licha and Jandro both opened their eyes when she gasped. Jandro wobbled a bit until he fell over.

"What is it?" Licha hopped up from her cushion. "Are you all right?"

Amy nodded. She pointed at the avestrandé. "I wasn't expecting it to be there."

After righting himself, Jandro sat on the pillow and leaned back to gently stroke the head of the beast. "She is exhausted from running all night." He smoothed down its dark feathers, which popped back in place as his hand passed over them. "She will sleep most of the day, I'm sure."

Amy recalled how, the night before, Jandro had comforted the fierce-looking creature, whose beak she was sure could bite her in half. She found it difficult reconcile the fact that she was looking at a beast that didn't exist. And then there was that cloud wall …

"I think I need to sit down."

Licha immediately offered her pillow and helped Amy to sit on it. She knelt on the carpet before her. "Are you hungry or thirsty?"

Amy shook her head. "I drank some water when I woke up."

Jandro leaned forward so that he was sitting upright on the pillow again. "You took off your robe. You should wear it to keep the sun from your skin."

"The robe was too hot."

"That's because you had those on underneath." He indicated the clothing Amy wore. "You should do as we do and you will stay cool." With that, he lifted up his robe and proved that he was naked underneath.

"Jandro!" Licha slapped his hand so that he would drop the robe. He looked at her as if he couldn't understand why she was upset.

Amy sat stunned, not from being flashed; penises had long ago lost their ability to shock. What she found surprising were the black stripes circling Jandro's thick thighs. She was sure that they had to have been tattooed on because paint would have smeared under the robe. His legs and … other parts … were several shades lighter than the skin on his bald head, which, in the bright sunlight, continued to look a pale blue-gray. The rings on his legs reminded her of a kachina doll. Maybe, like the tattooed mask around his eyes, the rings had something to do the cult she found herself in.

Licha looked apologetically at Amy. "You *would* be cooler."

"I'll think about it," Amy said, although she had no intention on doing so.

The bald woman jumped to her feet and scurried around to the back of the trinéot. Jandro shrugged when Amy looked at him for explanation. He pulled his robe over his knees. The shoes he wore looked like moccasins. Licha, who Amy noted wore the same kind of shoes, returned with something in her hand, which she held out for Amy to see. Licha had the driver's license that Amy had taken with her when she'd gone out for her morning walk. She also had Amy's house keys.

"These were in your pocket. I took them out before I washed your clothing. If I'd found them earlier I wouldn't have needed your shoes to convince Apósto Baruti who you were." She held up the driver's license. "I saw your image on that along with the writing of *La Reina*."

She held out both, but when Amy only took the driver's license, Licha put the keys in her pocket.

Jandro leaned in to see the license. "Can you read it?"

"Of course I can."

"What is it?"

"My driver's license. Can't you read it?"

"Lie sense?" Clearly, Licha thought it was two words.

"Is that what it says?" Jandro drew a finger along the card.

"No, that's my name," Amy said. "Amy Mildred Darlidale."

Licha and Jandro looked at one another, their eyes growing wide.

"Mil ..." Licha cut Jandro off with a look.

"Mildred was Meemaw's ... was my grandmother's name. Everyone just called her Millie." The bald two responded to this by gasping. "What?"

Jandro shouted and pointed out into the desert. "Look!"

Both women turned their heads. Far in the distance, something glinted.

"What is it?" Amy asked.

"I hope it's Apósto Baruti," Jandro said.

"Of course it is." Licha poked him. "No one else knows we are out here."

"Unless someone found out that the apósto sent *Lacáruna* into hiding."

"Hold on." Amy held up her hand. "What do you mean *into hiding*? I thought you were helping me to escape."

"We are." Jandro exchanged looks with Licha. "We just don't know who you're escaping from yet."

Licha stood at the edge of the carpet. "I think I know who. I just don't know why he would want ..."

"Want what? Out with it."

Licha looked at her. "Want to harm you."

"Harm me?"

Amy looked out at the dunes, where something sparkled between the white sand and the blue sky. Apprehension prickled the back of her neck. "Maybe we should arm ourselves."

"Seguidosts don't carry weapons," Jandro said.

"You have knives don't you?" Amy smiled guiltily when Licha put a hand to her neck where Amy had threatened her with a knife the night before.

"There's no reason for weapons." Licha dropped her hand to her side. "If that isn't the apósto whoever it is wouldn't be signaling us."

Jandro's eyes grew wide with worry. "What if they want us to think it's the apósto?"

"Stop it." Licha gave him a little shove. "How would anyone but the apósto find us?"

"How about following our tracks?" Amy looked at the wagon. Although it was on sled, the trinéot had to leave deep impressions as it moved across the sand.

"The nightwinds would have erased our crossing hours ago." Licha turned around to face Jandro. "That has to be the apósto."

"Apósto means what?" Amy asked. "Is he the leader of your … whatever this is?"

"Apósto Baruti is the head of our faction, yes." She motioned for Jandro. "We should prepare for him."

The two began unloading the trinéot in silence. What Amy had assumed to be bedrolls were actually more cushions to sit upon. They placed the cushions in a semi-circle facing away from the avestrandé. In front of the semi-circle they placed a taller cushion with an elaborate print of conjoined triangles, every third triangle taller than those beside it. The lines of triangles alternated blue and yellow.

Jandro filled a large wooden goblet with water and Licha sliced up a cheese wheel—keeping a firm hold of the knife, Amy noted—and removed a thick loaf of bread that resembled a baguette. When she saw Amy eyeing the bread, she pulled off a piece to give to her. Amy accepted it and took a bite. The bread was chewy, the way she liked baguettes, but it had a nutty flavor and was yellow, not white, inside.

Licha arranged the food on a wooden tray and Jandro added the goblet of water. She asked him where the small cushion that went under the tray was, but Jandro didn't know so she placed the tray next to the tall cushion. With some trepidation, Amy watched the spark on the horizon near. The oppressive heat was only slightly more bearable under the canopy than it had been out in the sun but still her clothing stuck to her like a second skin. Her cushion companions, however, looked as dry as the sand. Maybe it had something to do with being bald; all the body heat escaped right out the top of their heads. As she watched them, Amy noticed several things: Licha's eyelashes were as white as her skin, as were her sparse eyebrows and slight the stubble on her head, and her thin lips were as pink as the underside of her nose. Jandro had not even a trace of stubble on his head or his face. All he had were the odd markings around his eyes.

He caught her looking at him.

"Sorry. I was just … um … admiring your tattoo."

"My what?"

She twirled a finger in front of his face. "Tattoo. The black around your eyes."

"What is tattoo?" He seemed confused and glanced at Licha again, as if he expected her to say something.

Amy frowned. Not knowing what a tattoo was seemed as unlikely as not knowing about driver's licenses. This was a strange cult indeed. "Markings like what you have there."

Jandro touched his cheekbones where the black markings sloped across. "Many Mapanodes have these."

"Mapanodes?"

"My family."

"Mapanodes," she repeated.

"Yes." Jandro slid his robe up to his thighs, careful not to reveal anything more. "But not many Mapanodes have these rings."

That had never occurred to her. "You mean those are birth marks?"

"If that means I was born with them, then yes." The short young man returned to preparing for the apósto's arrival.

Amy walked to the edge of the carpet and looked out at the wide expanse of sand toward the spark, which was now accompanied by a dark blot, headed their way. Soon the blot took on a more substantial form. Whoever it was, was riding a bird-creature smaller than the one that pulled the trinéot. Assuming the rider was the large, hairy man who had introduced himself as Apósto Baruti, Amy felt sorry for the beast, no matter how scary it may be, that carted his bulk over the hot sand.

Licha and Jandro stopped what they were doing, stood beside her, and watched the bird-creature lope across the white sand. As it drew closer, Amy saw there were other differences between it and the one sleeping beyond its size. The creature's head was less oval-shaped and its small beak looked considerably less dangerous. The feathers covering it were amber except for those on its head that spilled down its neck, which were brown.

"Where on earth did you find these birds?"

No one answered.

When creature and rider came to a stop a few yards from the trinéot, the rider dismounted and stuck the reflective tip of the staff he carried into the sand. On the beast's back was a saddle that had no stirrups and its reins dangled from the straps around its head rather than a bit in its mouth. The rider wore a blue robe, but it was hooded and hid his face. Only the man's size and his hairy hands exposed him as the man who had carried Amy into the tent. Although the apósto was tall, the creature's head was at least a foot and a half above his. Behind Amy, the creature, called an avestrandé, snorted and raised its head. She hadn't realized it was awake until it squawked. She stepped closer to Jandro to be out of the creature's direct line of vision.

Jandro smiled at her. "She smells her mate."

"Oh." That didn't make her feel any better. "So, that's the male of the breed." In nature, males were often smaller than females. She'd watched a television program dedicated to the subject.

"No. That is a radamia. They are related closely but not the same."

"But you said it was her mate."

Jandro looked at her as if she said the silliest things. "It is." He left her and hurried out into the sand where he greeted the rider with a bow before pulling the staff out of the sand and taking the radamia's reins. As he led it around to the opposite side of the trinéot, Amy saw that its widely spaced talons were also webbed. No wonder the creatures could run across sand.

Apósto Baruti stepped into the canopy shade, flipped back the robe's hood, and smiled broadly at Amy. "I am relieved to see that you are safe."

"I'm not so sure I am. How about you tell me what's going on here."

The apósto took the tray of food and water and sat on the tall cushion. He drank the water from the goblet in one gulp. Jandro appeared from behind with a bladder canteen and refilled the cup. Amy looked at the avestrandé and expected its smaller mate to be with it, but the radamia was not. Bending slightly to look under the trinéot she saw the creature's legs on the other side where Jandro must have left it.

As the apósto drank more water, he kept his eyes on Amy, always smiling. Instead of making her uncomfortable, his gaze was comforting and reminded her of how her father would look at her when she was a child.

Apósto Baruti set the cup on the tray at his feet. "You must be more confused than ever."

"You could say that." Amy crossed her arms. "Why don't you help clear it up by telling me why we sneaked off in the middle of the night?"

The apósto took a deep breath and let it out slowly. "I think I need to start before that."

*Now we're getting somewhere,* Amy thought. She nodded and, when he gestured toward a cushion, she sat.

The big man smiled. "Tell me what you remember from before."

"Before what?" Amy asked.

"Before"—he raised his hands over his head—"all of this."

She assumed he meant since she'd gone out for her morning walk. "I felt dizzy and fell in a field not far from my home. When I woke, I was no longer in the same field." Muttering, she added, "I'm not even sure I'm on the same planet."

Apósto Baruti nodded somberly. "In the Extiguos—"

"Extiguos?"

"Writings as old as this world. In the Extiguos it is revealed that the Primeróte were aware that they had been taken from their homes and delivered unto a new place as well."

"Who or what are the Primeróte?"

"The first six who started the world. This was before the *Morphósis*, of course. This was at the beginning."

She couldn't believe he was going to start his explanation as to why she had been brought into his cult by telling her about its folklore. "If they came from someplace else, then how could they have *started* the world?"

Again the apósto raised his hands. "*This* world. Or, more precisely, this world as it was before the *Morphósis*. There are many worlds."

"Um … I was only joking when I said I wasn't sure I was on the same planet."

"Planet?"

How could he not understand that? "World. Not in the same world."

Apósto Baruti laughed. "You're not."

Amy looked over her shoulder at the Nieblota. She looked down at the avestrandé that had gone back to sleep. She looked back at the apósto. "You're telling me that I've been taken from another world and brought here."

"That is my understanding of what occurred in the Extiguos. Since the *Morphósis* the appearances have stopped—until you; although, you didn't quite arrive how we Carados had expected you to." He looked at Jandro and Licha, who sat on the cushions like Amy's bookends with their hands on their knees palms up. "Only a few speak of their home worlds in the Extiguos. Mostly it is the Primeróte who give accounts of their lives before their arrival."

Jandro turned his palms down and when he did, Apósto Baruti called on him. "Yes, Jandro?"

"Is it not also written that *La Reina* and her attendants also speak of their home worlds?"

"That is true." When Jandro turned his palms up again, the apósto continued. "It is written that the Winged-One, an angel, brought the Primeróte to this world. Did you see him?"

"An angel?" Amy scoffed. "Can't say that I've ever seen an angel."

The apósto nodded as if he'd expected that would be her answer.

"I did see an orange lizard, though."

The two at her sides gasped and the apósto's mouth dropped open. She'd meant it as a snide comment regarding their folklore, but they obviously didn't take it that way.

"You saw her?" Jandro's eyes were wide. "What did she look like?"

"Like a lizard." Amy stretched out her forefinger and thumb. "About that long and oddly orange in color."

Jandro looked at Licha and Apósto Baruti. "That doesn't sound like—"

The apósto stopped him. "*La Reina* never left us." He glanced at the cloud-mountain. "She sent an emissary to bring *Lacáruna* to us."

"I don't know what that means," Amy said. "Or what an orange lizard has to do with it."

"It means that you have been brought here by *La Reina* to fulfill the prophecy."

Amy could feel the sweat running between her breasts. She

couldn't understand how the other three could remain dry while she was all but dripping. "What is this prophecy you keep speaking of?"

"*The Promise of a New Morphósis.*"

That sounded vaguely Christian. "And what happens then?"

Apósto Baruti smiled broadly. "The world will expand again."

"Expand where?"

If he heard the question, the apósto declined to answer. "After three millennia the world has begun to contract. But when the prophecy is fulfilled, the world will expand again. Do you understand, *Lacáruna?*"

"Don't call me that."

Apósto Baruti seemed surprised by her reaction. "Very well. How would you like to be addressed?"

"By my name, Amy."

"Amy," the large man repeated. He noticed that Licha had turned her palms over. "What is it, Licha?"

The bald woman glanced at Amy before speaking. "She has several names. But one is forbidden."

Amy looked at Licha and recalled how Jandro and she had reacted when she'd said her full name. "You mean my middle name? Mildred?"

Licha shook her head. "Not that form, but the other."

Because she had the notion that they would try to stop her from saying it at all, Amy said the name quickly. "Millie?"

The apósto jerked back as if struck. "That is her name as well, but it is forbidden to say. We only call her *La Reina.*"

"The queen, yes. I know what la reina means."

Licha nodded. "She knows because she is *Lacáruna.*"

"I know because I understand Spanish."

The apósto's hairy brow furrowed. "What is Spanish?"

Amy grunted. "A language."

"*La Reina*'s language?" Jandro looked at the apósto and back at

Amy. "Is that how you pronounce her writing?"

"I don't know what you mean."

Jandro picked up her driver's license from where she had left it next to a cushion. "The symbols on this."

"No, that's English."

"That's the language of *La Reina*," the apósto said.

Amy pointed to her name on the card. "I don't know who *she* is but that's *my* name right there."

Apósto Baruti looked at the license closely. "I cannot read this. No one in this world can read the language of *La Reina*." He reached into his robe pocket, pulled out a piece of beige parchment, and handed it to Amy. "Can you read that?"

Amy took the piece of paper from him. She was surprised to see it covered with what she thought looked like Chinese characters made from dots. Maybe it was the heat but she found it difficult to focus on the symbols; they seemed to fluctuate. "These are words?"

"Yes. As it was with most everything, our written language changed with the *Morphósis*."

She returned the paper to the apósto who put it, along with her license, into his pocket. "Tell me why it is forbidden to say that name."

The apósto clasped his hands between his robe-covered knees and stared at them in thought. "It happened not long after the *Morphósis*. Not everyone believed that the world had changed, because many did not remember it as it had been. This is why *Dendos* brought the Extiguos with him and created the Carados to help him spread the word. Some were so opposed to the very idea that the world had expanded they tried to stop the Carados going so far as to eradicate entire factions. To keep this from continuing it was decreed that the Carados could only spread the word in Pliada and, to keep others from believing what *Dendos* had come out of Nieblota to say, *La Reina's* true name and even her face became forbidden."

Amy shook her head. "All I got from that is Carados is the name of your religion. I haven't a clue as to what all the rest of it means."

The apósto looked at Jandro and Licha. "I brought a few provisions. Take them and prepare the trinéot for the journey. We will leave when the moon rises."

The bald duo nodded and left the canopy. The apósto watched them and when they disappeared into the trinéot, he turned to Amy.

"Yes, Carados is the name of our religion. We are nomadic, following the tradition of *Dendos*."

*Den doughs,* Amy thought. She'd overheard him say that to the hooded man in the tent. "What are den doughs?"

"Not what—who. *Dendos* is he who spread the truth after the *Morphósis*. He lived for five hundred years, reminding quimerté what *La Reina* had done for them."

Apparently she'd misunderstood what she'd overheard and surmised it was two words.

The large man reached a hairy hand into his robe's collar and pulled out a medallion that hung around his neck. Leaning forward, he held it out for Amy.

She had to rise from her cushion to see the patina medallion, which was nearly as big as her palm. The raised image on it was difficult to discern, but to Amy it looked like two heads back to back. "Are those men wearing masks?"

The apósto shook his head. "I don't know this word—*men*. Is it more of *La Reina*'s language, this Spanish?"

She almost rolled her eyes. "It's not Spanish. Men. Like you. Male."

Understanding came into the apósto's eyes. "Ah, you mean quimero."

"Now *that* sounds Spanish."

"But it's our language."

"Never mind that. Forget I ever mentioned Spanish. What does whatever you just said mean?"

Apósto Baruti used the hand not holding the medallion to touch his chest. "Jandro and I are quimeros, male. You and Licha are quimeras, female. Together we are quimerté." He thought for a moment. "There's no other name for that."

"People? Group?"

"Yes. Group." He looked down at the medallion. "*Dendos* was a quimero. He—"

"He?" Amy pointed at the two heads on the medallion. "That looks like two ... quimeros."

The apósto grinned. "*Dendos* is two who are one."

She looked closely at the medallion. She knew of a Roman, or maybe Greek, god that had two faces, but couldn't recall the name. "Why are they wearing masks?"

"They are not wearing masks. Those are the faces." He pointed to the face on the right side. "That is *La Rata* and the other is *El Hámster*."

Shuffling backward, Amy returned to her cushion. She didn't need a translation for those words. "A rat and a hamster? *That's* who you follow?"

Apósto Baruti dropped the medallion and it dangled against his blue robe. "*Dendos* is *Dendos*."

Worshiping rodents wasn't all that different than what ancient civilizations deified, she supposed. "So why were you telling me about Dendos?"

"Only to explain that we follow his tradition of spreading the truth, a truth that not many believe in anymore. Yet, we still try to do what we can. The Carados are many, but we are few."

Two who are one, many but few ... She wished she could take notes; religions were always so convoluted.

"And this has to do with me how?"

The apósto slipped the medallion beneath the robe's collar. "The prophecy was supposed to have been fulfilled three hundred years ago. Some became disillusioned when that didn't happen and left the Carados. Most continued to spread the word, however, and continued to trust in what had been passed down. At least that's what I'd always believed." He sighed and his shoulders slumped. "When I sent out word that the first part of the prophecy—your arrival—had finally come to pass, I assumed there would be rejoicing throughout our factions."

"I take it others didn't feel the same."

"Correct. I didn't know that, within us, there are those who believe the arrival of *Lacáruna* at any time other than the time of the prophecy is *La Arañota*'s work."

Already as confused as she thought she could stand, Amy didn't ask who or what this *La Arañota* was. She assumed it to be something generally not good and certainly not good for her.

"That is why I sent Licha and Jandro to take you from the camp. I understand now that we must keep you hidden until we learn what must be done with you."

Amy didn't like the sound of that either.

"We will go to Winter Outpost and contact a Trotéjo comrade who can help us."

She strained to comprehend what the apósto was telling—or trying to tell—her, but she felt somewhat dizzy, not unlike how she'd felt when she'd fallen after chasing the orange lizard into the field. All of this would have been so much easier to accept and understand if she had gone through a hidden door at the back of a wardrobe. Then she would know that she hadn't truly lost her mind. She wasn't aware that he'd moved until she felt the apósto's arm slip around her shoulders.

"The heat is affecting you."

He called out for Jandro to bring water before he noticed the bladder canteen on the carpet next to his cushion. He swept it up and flipped the cap off with his thumb. When he brought the spout to her lips, he bid her to drink from it. The water, although warm, soothed her throat. She felt herself being lowered to the ground and shortly thereafter a wet cloth slid across her forehead. Amy wanted to say that she was fine, that she only needed a moment to gather her thoughts—to digest her sudden understanding that her reality had been replaced with another. She said nothing, though, and closed her eyes as Licha gently stroked her face with the wet cloth.

When she opened her eyes, she noted that the canopy shadow stretched over the sand away from the trinéot. Lying on her left side, Amy felt a slight breeze against the back of her neck. She rolled over and saw Jandro sitting on a cushion. He fanned her with a cloth stretched between two poles while he looked out toward the cloud mountain, not noticing that she'd woken. Feeling more relaxed and rested than she had in months, maybe even years, Amy wiggled up to her elbows. Seeing her toes peeking out from the bottom of a brown robe was a bit disconcerting. She snagged a finger under the robe's collar and looked down it to see that she was indeed naked underneath. She wasn't sure whether or not to complain; she was certainly cooler than she had been. When she looked up she saw that Jandro was watching her.

"I didn't do it," he said, quickly. "Apósto Baruti insisted that Licha put that on you. He was afraid you were overheated."

Amy sat up.

"There is water and a bowl of broth on the tray next to you. You should drink both. The broth is very nutritious and the water … Well, you know what water does." He grinned boyishly and ducked his head. His skin had a stronger bluish tint in the waning sunlight.

She drank from the canteen first, taking deep swallows that seemed to spread out from her chest, filling her. Once satiated, she picked up the wooden bowl with both hands and sipped the milky substance within. The flavor was unlike any she'd ever tasted, both sweet and salty and the tiniest bit bitter. She finished it in only a few gulps.

As he continued to fan her, Jandro looked back out into the distance.

"Where are Licha and the apósto?" Amy asked.

"Out there." He nodded in the direction he was looking.

Amy's gaze slid over the sloping dunes toward the cloud-mountain, which to her continued to look like a white, static sandstorm. It moved as if it were slowly crawling over the sand but never came any closer. The oddity they called Nieblota seemed almost alive. She didn't see anyone in the distance. "What are they doing?"

"They're in escalétre."

"I don't know what that means."

Jandro thought for a moment. "It's when the Carados clear their minds so they can better hear *La Reina*." He grinned again. "I'm not sure I understand what it means, either."

Amy had to laugh. She assumed this endearing, oddly-marked …quimero … was talking about some sort of mediation, or perhaps prayer.

"That's what Licha and I were doing when you woke up before the apósto arrived." Jandro looked at the cloud-mountain. "Now he and Licha are doing it out there. Apósto Baruti hopes being so close to Nieblota will give him the answers he seeks."

"How close are we?" She estimated they were under a mile from it—that is if it were indeed remaining in one place and not advancing like it should be doing.

"Several wheels. Any closer and we wouldn't be able to hear one another."

"Wheels? How far is a wheel?"

"Over a thousand threestrides."

"And how far is a threestride?"

"A bit more three feet. And there are twelve knuckles to a foot. Smaller than that is just a half-knuckle and so on."

Now they were getting somewhere. Amy looked at the cloud-mountain again and guessed Jandro meant that it was several miles away, much farther than she'd thought.

"What is it? Why doesn't it move?"

"But it does move." He hadn't taken his eyes off it. His expression was of unmistakable awe. "You can see that even from this far off."

"I mean why hasn't it advanced on us? It looks as if it should be coming towards us but yet it's no closer than it was when I saw it earlier."

"It stays in place to hide *La Reina*'s mountain where her castle sits. She created it when she expanded this world. I've heard it said that Nieblota is part of Mid-Realm that has broken through."

"And that is?"

He didn't seem to hear her, so mesmerized by the odd phenomenon.

"I don't know if it is true, but I do know Nieblota is where *La Reina* lives now, watching us." Finally, he broke away and looked at Amy. "And waiting for you."

That sounded a tad ominous, although she doubted that was Jandro's intention. "Has anyone tried to go in there to find her?

"Many, but none have returned."

Amy turned back to Jandro. "You don't have to keep fanning me."

"Are you sure?"

He looked so relieved that Amy had to smile. "I'm sure."

Jandro twirled one of the poles so that the cloth between them wrapped around it and placed the fan next to Amy's running shoes. Everything but his cushion and the bedroll where she had lain was gone. Even the avestrandé was gone. Amy looked under the trinéot and saw four giant bird legs on the opposite side. The mates were together again.

She watched Jandro as he gazed at the cloud mountain. His expression was one of longing. "When the cloud scatters, she will be revealed and the world will expand again."

Amy stood and tugged on her robe until it felt more comfortable at the shoulders. "Is that part of the prophecy the apósto spoke of?"

"Yes. But that is really all I know. I've only been a seguidost for a little more than year. When I was sent to Pliada, I came across the Carados first and even though I knew that they were outcasts, I chose to follow them and learn their ways."

"Pliada." Amy looked out at the dunes. "Is that where we are?"

"Yes," Jandro said. "Well, this is Esterenas—" He stopped and jabbed a finger toward Nieblota. "I see them!"

Amy saw two figures in the distance, one considerably larger than the other.

"I hope they heard an answer," Jandro said.

Amy wasn't sure she understood the question. She chuckled when she saw Jandro hopping from foot to foot excitedly as he watched the others approach.

"You don't have to stay with me, Jandro. I'm not going anywhere."

A quick grin spread over Jandro's face and he trotted out into the sand to greet the others. He was short, but solidly built and his youthful exuberance made running across the sand look easy. Amy picked up the bladder canteen and drank from it as she sat on the remaining cushion. Despite what Licha had earlier said about tracks disappearing, she could see Jandro's footprints easily enough. But she knew little about this type of desert, the sandy kind. The only time she'd ever seen sand like this was when her father took her to see the white sands of southern New Mexico right before he'd married Alice. That had been the last trip the two of them ever took alone. Amy stood when the three came up under the canopy and addressed Apósto Baruti.

"I need to know my part in this."

The apósto smiled. "Of course you do."

She was actually caught off guard by his answer. She'd simply wanted, now that she felt more herself than she had since first waking up in the sand, to seize control of her situation.

"You want to know your part. I want to know it as well."

That caught her off guard too. "I thought you *already* knew."

He shook his head. "No. I told you that I only know of the prophecy, not how it is to be fulfilled. That is why I had called for a gathering." The second time he shook his head it was with sadness. "I made a horrible mistake, it seems."

Amy pointed at Nieblota. "Is that what you learned out there?"

The apósto looked across the sand. "Yes, it is."

Jandro, who had been rolling up the bedding Amy had slept on, stopped and looked up at him. "Then she talked to you? *La Reina?*"

Apósto Baruti smiled down at him. "No, Jandro. That, of course, would have been a blessing beyond all, but during escalétre I am better able to hear my *own* thoughts. That is how she guides us, through ourselves."

She could see that Jandro didn't quite understand. Neither did she. "And what did your thoughts tell you?"

"That the only truth you can follow is your own and right now my truth tells me that in calling together my brethren, I inadvertently fed the forces that don't want the *New Morphósis* to come to pass." He moved off the carpet, gently nudging Amy along with him, so that Jandro and Licha could roll it up. "In the excitement of you finding us—"

"Actually, I think it was you who found me."

"Don't be so certain of that." The apósto grinned. "Either way, I had forgotten to take into consideration three hundred years of doubt."

"Doubt about what?"

"Doubt there ever was a prophecy. Those were the very words out of the first apósto to arrive. I was not acquainted with him. He was from one of the mountain factions and was in direct disagreement with everything I had to say. I was baffled by his conviction. He kept demanding to see you, and it's only because you were sleeping that I wouldn't allow it. Thank *La Reina*. He said other apóstos would soon arrive and they would expose you as an imposter. That's when I told Licha and Jandro to bring you here."

Licha stopped what she had been doing. "But she's not an imposter. They wouldn't have exposed anything."

"That's exactly what I told him. We argued heatedly and he demanded to see *Lacáruna* herself and drew a knife. I knew I was right to send you away."

Amy was certain that's the exact moment she'd peered into the tent when Licha was taking her to the trinéot and saw the two apóstos. "Jandro said you don't carry weapons."

"We don't." He looked away, back in the direction in which he'd come. His expression was troubled.

Jandro finished rolling up the carpet. "What do we do now?"

"Be more cautious in who we talk to about the prophecy." The apósto gestured at the rolled carpet. "Now get that put away so we can have a meal before the sun goes down. We have to cover as much distance from the camp as we can tonight, and let's hope we can get to Winter Outpost quickly."

The first night they traveled twenty wheels across the sand. When they moved away from the phenomenon called Nieblota, angling slightly to the south, Amy was surprised by how accustomed she'd become to the white noise now that the sound was gone. All that could be heard was the trinéot creaking as it slid over the dunes and the occasional squawk of the radamia, which was tethered to the back, when it called out to its larger mate. As the evening wore on, however, she heard something else coming from the dunes and looked out the back of the trinéot. In the light of the full moon almost directly overhead it looked as if the sand were swirling. Licha explained that was exactly what it was doing.

"Those are the nightwinds," she said. "It happens all across Esterenas. When the Carados first came into being there were many who did not want *Dendos'* truth spread and they came after us to stop it. *Dendos* asked *La Reina* to create the nightwinds so that our footprints would disappear and we'd be harder to find."

Dendos. La Reina. Lacáruna. Amy had a lot to contemplate and a lot of time to do so, as the trinéot slipped across the sand. She got past that a religious order would put so much credence in a revelation they didn't seem to fully understand because the more she thought about it the less it surprised her. Religions were replete with vague ideas. This, in turn, spawned myriad interpretations, which led to disagreements and separation, which led to war and destruction, and up would pop another religion built upon the same ambiguous notions as its predecessors.

*That* was the real circle of life.

The Carados didn't seem to have many rituals to go along with their religion, as far as she could tell. So far, other than when they were in escalétre, their meditative state, or talking about La Reina and Dendos, they hadn't exhibited any actions suggesting a religious order. Of course, they hadn't done any proselytizing around her so perhaps that's where their creed was most evident.

The second evening, when they woke from their daylight slumber, Apósto Baruti announced it was time for learning. Jandro and Licha seemed eager to hear what their elder had to say, but it was clear to Amy that the lessons were for her benefit. Over the next two nights he spoke and the others listened as they traveled over the dunes. The first of the apósto's lectures had to do with geography. Amy learned that Pliada was the largest of four nations but the least inhabited. Even so, it was the strongest nation. Though a neutral country, Pliada was the home of the

Fensoré, a military established to keep the peace between the other three nations. The Fensoré also controlled trade.

"Legend has it that the Fensoré were the protectors of *La Reina* before the *Morphósis*." Apósto Baruti sat backwards on the driver's bench toward the interior while Jandro, sitting beside him, took the reins. "It is said the Fensoré guarded *La Reina*'s castle on her mountaintop but during the time of the *Morphósis*, when the world expanded, they were sent to what is now called Pliada and *Dendos* soon followed."

"Jandro mentioned that the Carados are considered outcasts."

"We are. Pliada is the only nation that does not persecute us. We are allowed to mingle freely, and spread the word among the populace, although most of us tend to keep to the outskirts."

"Not a very good way to convert the masses. I would think you would want to be in the cities."

"Our intention is not to convert as much as it is to convince. The more quimerté who believe in *Dendos'* words, the sooner the world will expand. Some Carados believe it was because we hadn't convinced enough to have faith in *Dendos* that *Lacáruna* didn't appear three hundred years ago."

"So you've convinced enough now?"

"I don't—"

"Then why am I here?"

He clearly had no answer to either of those questions and continued on with what he had been saying. "Our presence is felt in the cities, but it is in the Outer Belt, which borders the other nations, where we spend the majority of word-spreading. The quimerté there, for the most part, believe as we do that *La Reina* expanded the world. They have stories passed down among them from elders who remember."

"Do they believe she'll do it again?"

"Some."

Amy tried to find a more comfortable position. Sitting cross-legged for too long made her hips ache. "Does anyone in this Outer Belt ever join the Carados?"

"A few. But mostly it's those crossing through the Outer Belt who chose to join us. That is where we find curious quimerté like Jandro, here."

Jandro briefly turned his head and grinned. "I was lucky enough to come across the Carados first when I was sent to Pliada; otherwise, I would have become Fensoré."

"What does he mean he was *sent* to Pliada?"

"Every family is required to send their firstborn to Pliada on their fifteenth birthday."

Amy was shocked. Her eyes were wide, as she looked at the back of Jandro's head and spoke loudly enough for him to hear. "You mean you're conscripted?"

Jandro looked over his shoulder. "Is that Spanish?"

"No. Forget about Spanish. It means you had no choice but to join the military."

"Oh, I had a choice. As you can see, I didn't become a fensoré."

"But you had no choice in being sent here."

Apósto Baruti nodded. "All firstborn must come to Pliada to join the Fensoré. From the highest to the lowest. The only alternative is to become a seguidost."

Amy asked Licha if she had been sent to Pliada as well.

"No. I was born here as part of the Carados. My mother is a seguidost and will soon become an apósto."

The requirement that every family send their firstborn into the desert was incomprehensible to Amy, yet these three accepted it with nonchalance.

The apósto must have seen her bewilderment. "Joining the Fensoré is seen as an honor. Each family is sending a representative who will uphold the law between the nations. And, because the Fensoré control trade, it is in every family's best interest to have one of their own among them."

"But Jandro didn't become a fensoré. Would his family still consider it an honor?"

"They won't ever find out," Jandro called out.

"So you never go back? Can they visit you?"

"They can, but they won't." He didn't say that as loudly as the other, but Amy heard it nevertheless.

Apósto Baruti patted him on the shoulder. "With few exceptions, firstborns aren't allowed to leave Pliada."

"And families think this is an honor?" Amy couldn't mask her incredulity.

The apósto seemed disappointed with her reaction. "This is how it's done."

He turned and faced forward on the bench.

Amy looked at Licha, who smiled and nodded in agreement with the apósto.

"It's how it's done."


On the sixth night, Amy sat with Jandro at the front of the trinéot while he flicked the reins. Having become more accustomed to the huge beasts, she was amazed by their resiliency—especially the avestrandé. Jandro explained that both it and the radamia were breeds called sandrunners. The name was apt considering that from dusk till dawn they trotted without pause across the dunes, the smaller one tied behind the trinéot and the larger tugging the trinéot along until it felt the reins gradually pulling to halt it just before dawn, after the nightwinds had stopped. The instant both trinéot and beast stopped (which happened slowly because the wagon-sled had no actual brakes), the avestrandé would collapse to the ground. Jandro, in charge of the beast's care, would gently remove its harness and bring it water. He would tilt the creature's head back so that its ferocious beak opened and he would pour the water slowly into the exhausted and apparently slumbering avestrandé's mouth. Once past her aversion to being near the giant bird-thing, Amy would stand behind Jandro and watch the creature's thick, pointed red tongue bob as it instinctively swallowed the water. The trinéot was always stopped on the dune's downward slope so that it could be pushed alongside the sleeping beast and the canopy unfurled over it. Jandro would then lead the radamia, who wasn't quite as tired and didn't fall to the ground immediately upon stopping, under the canopy where it would sleep with its neck lying across the avestrandé's body. At dusk, when Jandro would re-harness the avestrandé and tether the radamia to the back, he would feed both with what looked to Amy like enormous birdfeed pellets.

As she sat next to Jandro on the driver's bench, mesmerized by the swirling nightwinds, Amy wondered how long it would take before someone back in L.A. realized she was missing. She had no family that would suffer because of her disappearance (save her stepmother Alice, who Amy doubted would grieve for long) and in that, she was fortunate. Her friends, colleagues, and coworkers would be left with a puzzle and would probably always wonder what happened to her. Unless she returned ...

She knew Jandro wouldn't have the answer to the question she wanted to ask and excused herself. She climbed off the driver's bench to sit in the back of the wagon. Licha and the apósto were sitting on cushions in escalétre. Though it was undoubtedly rude to do so, Amy tapped Apósto Baruti on the shoulder. He opened his eyes.

"You say the prophecy foretold my coming here. Does it say anything about me leaving?"

The apósto seemed surprised by the question. He crawled off the cushion and sat with his back flush with the sideboard. He brought his knees up to his chest. His exposed ankles were as hairy as his hands.

"Maybe when this world expands again you return to your world."

"But you're only speculating, aren't you?"

Apósto Baruti nodded. "The prophecy says that *Lacáruna* will arrive and usher in the *New Morphósis*. I've never heard anything regarding what she does after that."

"You've never heard? I thought it was something you've read."

He shook his head. "The prophecy has been passed through the Carados orally, but it's said the Trotéjo have it in writing."

Amy found it a bit disconcerting that the three she had no choice but to travel with knew so little of the prophecy of which she was allegedly a part. She wanted answers but all they seemed capable of was generating more questions. "So nothing you've told me has been written down. I thought you said something about ancient texts."

"Yes, the Extiguos. Those were written down in the language of *La Reina*. This Spanish you speak of."

"It's not all …" She shook her head. "I told you to forget I mentioned Spanish. But if it's written in La Reina's language, then you haven't read them either."

"No, but there are translations."

"Let's talk about those then. You said before that there were others like me, who were taken from their worlds. What happened to them? The … I forget what you called them … the first to arrive. The ones who came from other worlds like me."

"The Primeróte, the first six. What about them?"

"Is there anything in the Extiguos translations about the first six returning to where they'd come from?"

"Not to my knowledge."

Amy carefully climbed over the still-meditating Licha so that she could sit next to the apósto. "But you've read them, right? So you should know if they returned."

"Yes, I've read them—a very long time ago. And, although I have no recollection of anyone returning to the world of the origin, the Carados believe that not everything within the Extiguos was translated."

That seemed odd. "Really? Why? Who did the translation?"

"*Dendos* himself. He brought the Extiguos with him out of Nieblota after the *Morphósis*. Only he could read them, but he translated the Extiguos so that the truth could be spread."

"What happened to the originals?"

"There are nine Extiguos and they were given to the Fensoré who split them up and gave three to each of the other nations."

"Why didn't the Fensoré keep them?"

"Because if they had, there would be no peace. The Fensoré gave up the Extiguos in exchange for controlling the trade between the other three nations. This kept Pliada a neutral nation and because none of the other three had complete control over the Extiguos, they couldn't claim *La Reina* favored them. No nation was above another."

"So despite that her name and face were forbidden, nations still wanted to claim her for themselves."

"This happened long, long ago. Perhaps long before she became known only as *La Reina*."

Amy rubbed her face with both hands. "This doesn't help me. I just need to know how to get back."

"When we reach Winter Outpost and find the Trotéjo I'm sure we will learn more."

"How much longer until we get there?" As Amy asked the question, she felt the trinéot slow.

The apósto looked out through the front of the trinéot. "Four or five days once we're out of Esterenas. "

The trinéot came to a stop, which surprised Amy because they had only been traveling for a short while and dawn was still hours away. She saw Jandro climb down from the bench and heard him talking to the avestrandé. "What's going on?"

"It seems we're out of sand."

From what she could see out the back of the trinéot there was plenty of sand. The apósto, however, was looking out the front. Rather than ask what he meant, Amy crawled back over Licha and climbed onto the driver's bench. She hadn't thought that the apósto's words would be literal until she gazed out at the horizon. Only a few threestrides beyond where Jandro stood, the nightwinds swirling around his shins while he detached the avestrandé's harness from the trinéot's wooden tongue, the white sand they'd been traversing for days simply ended. The delineation was so well defined it looked as if someone had actually drawn a line in the sand and swept it away on the other side. The nightwinds seemed to stop at that line as well, although it was difficult to be certain. The moonlight reflected off the white sand, but the dark ground beyond the dunes seemed to swallow it.

Amy looked back at the apósto. "So what do we do now?"

"We dismantle the trinéot." He smiled broadly.

First they ate some broth, spiced with something that looked like a potato but tasted like a radish crossed with a carrot. Jandro was happiest about the addition, having complained about the broth for the last two days. Licha told him not to get used to it because there weren't many of the turnips left and they would have to make separate meals of the two. Even Amy was a little put off by the thought of having nothing to eat but the milky broth until they reached their destination. Fortunately, according to Apósto Baruti, they wouldn't have to wait that long because apple and pear trees grew along Mika River, which they would follow to Winter Outpost. The river was only a day or so away.

The notion of jumping into a river sounded like heaven to Amy. She felt grimy and was certain she stank, although she couldn't possibly reek as much as the apósto. The hairy quimero smelled like a moldy carpet and she did her best to remain upwind from him when she accompanied him out of the white sand and onto firmer ground.

Still marveling over the distinction between one area and the other, Amy said, "I can't believe the sand just stops." She straddled the two regions, a running shoe on either side. The nightwinds didn't quite come to the edge.

"More proof that this world is shrinking." Apósto Baruti nodded toward the west where the peaks of a long mountain range stood tallest. "Some say the sand used to reach all the way to Mika River."

Amy looked at the expanse they were about to cover, which was filled with low shrubbery and a few scraggly mesquite-like trees. "I guess the trinéot can't be pulled across that. How are we going to get to the outpost?"

"You'll see." The apósto laughed.

When they returned to the trinéot, Licha was unloading it and carrying what she'd gathered out into the dark desert. Jandro was removing the trinéot's canvas cover. Amy offered her assistance but after everything except the rolled carpet had been taken from the interior, there was nothing more she could do because she had no idea what needed to be done. It frustrated her that she could only watch and she felt antsy. Right now, more than ever, she really missed her smartphone. Although even if she did have it with her, she couldn't use it. It wasn't as if she could connect to Wi-Fi and surf the Internet. She didn't even have games on her phone. Maybe it would just feel good to press buttons and swipe glass. She sat where the nightwinds didn't go, near the avestrandé and radamia (the beasts were already asleep despite the fact that they hadn't been running for very long), as the others dismantled the wagon-sled almost entirely. The cover was removed, along with the arched wooden bows that held it up, and the sideboards. From underneath the bed, Jandro unstrapped two large, spoked wooden wheels and two long poles that Amy hadn't known were there. While Licha packed their belongings in tight bundles, Jandro and the apósto set about constructing what looked to Amy like a large rickshaw using the sideboards and the poles and wheels. The canvas top and two wooden bows were used to cover what Licha told her was called a srudas. The canopies were folded and, along with almost everything else from within the trinéot, were packed into the srudas. Jandro filled several canteens, as well as a large ceramic jug, with water from the container attached to the trinéot and removed the feed trough from the back. All of this went into the srudas, which didn't leave much room for anything else.

"I take it we're walking from here on." Amy stood and dusted herself off.

"You could ride the radamia, if you'd like," the apósto said.

She wasn't sure he was joking. "Not on your life."

Apósto Baruti tightened a rope covering one of the many bundles. "I didn't think so. You, Licha, and I will walk alongside the srudas and, acting as our scout, Jandro will ride the radamia ahead of us."

"What is he scouting for?"

"Many things." He looked up. "Now we will rest and at dawn the next leg of the journey begins."

"You mean we have to walk in the sunlight?" Amy recalled how difficult that had been the last time she'd attempted to walk through a desert.

"I'm afraid so. As bright as the *Eye of Dendos* is, it won't light our way as it did across Esterenas. We'll need sunlight."

Licha handed Amy a piece of cloth. "Here."

"What is it?" Amy turned the cloth over.

"A hood. That is if you want to continue to wear the robe. I can get your other clothing if that's what you would prefer."

Amy shook her head. They'd been telling her the truth when they claimed that wearing the robe would keep her cooler than her clothing. "I'll keep it on."

Licha took the hood from Amy's hands and stood behind her. As she attached the hood with tiny hooks to the back of the collar, the robe became a cowl. When Licha finished, Amy pulled the hood up over her head. The way that the brim stuck out left her face in shadows and reminded her of the kind of bonnet pioneer women wore while crossing the prairies, which she found more pleasing than thinking she looked like a medieval monk.

"You'll need to keep your head covered at all times, especially when we get to Winter Outpost."

Amy pushed the hood back. "Why?"

"Because seguidosts shave their heads. Only apóstos grow out their hair."

Licha offered another option. "I could cut off your hair so that you won't have to keep the hood on."

"No, no." Amy quickly pulled the hood over her hair. "I prefer the hood."

Apósto Baruti again looked up at the sky. "Then let us rest. We have a few hours until dawn and best make use of them."

A carpet was spread on the hard packed ground and they lay on it side by side. As Amy breathed through her mouth to avoid the apósto's smell, she reminded herself to always make certain she was upwind.

◉　◉　◉

The sun hadn't yet crested the horizon when the apósto roused Amy from her slumber. Jandro and Licha were already up. While Jandro was busy doing something to the radamia's feet, Licha harnessed the avestrandé to the srudas. Through unusually groggy eyes, Amy saw something in the fire that the apósto attended and, as her mind cleared, she realized that it was her capri pants.

"What are you doing?" She ran to the fire but it was too late. The pants were almost gone.

"You won't be needing them." Using the staff with the glass piece at the top (which was now covered so it wouldn't glint in the sun) that had signaled his arrival back at Nieblota the apósto poked at the fire. "Space will be limited to only the essentials and everything else will be left behind. I don't want anyone to find what you wore when you came to this world."

Amy looked at her feet. "You're not getting my shoes."

"Of course not. Those are necessary but please don't let anyone see them unless I ask you to."

She helped him roll up the carpet they'd slept upon and return it to the bed of the trinéot where it, along with all that was deemed nonessential, would be left behind.

"Aren't you afraid someone will come along and steal all of this?"

"Not many quimerté come this way except the Carados, and we would never steal another faction's transportation."

"How would they know it's another faction?"

"Each faction has a different pattern that separates it from the others." He tapped one of the cushions covered in fabric with the lines of triangles being left behind.

Amy looked at the white dunes in the east. The rising sun created shadows, giving the sand the depth it lacked when the sun was directly overhead. She looked back at the cushion. "What if someone who is looking for *us* comes across that? Won't they know who it belongs to?"

Her question gave the apósto pause. He called out to Jandro, who was saddling the radamia, and told him to bring a shovel. Fortunately for the bald quimero, the apósto only wanted the items they were leaving behind that would identify their faction, and not the entire trinéot, buried under the sand. The wagon, broken down as it was, offered no clues as to which faction it belonged. Jandro threw sand over it so it would appear to have been there a while.

The apósto explained that Esterenas was a large expanse and they were hundreds of wheels from their camp. "It is doubtful that our trail would be picked up here."

Amy turned around. "Unless they come from that way." She pointed toward the mountain range in the west. "The nightwinds may have covered our tracks in the sand, but it won't do anything about that." She pointed at the ruts in the ground put there by the srudas when it was moved only a few feet.

Jandro, with the shovel over one shoulder, trudged through the sand toward them. For the first time Amy actually saw him sweat. His bald head was dotted with perspiration. "Do the others know we are going to Winter Outpost?" he asked.

The apósto shook his head. "I told no one where I was going. Of course, everyone expects that I would seek out Trotéjo but there were closer places I could have chosen." He clapped Jandro on the back and put an arm around Amy's shoulders. "Enough of this worrying. Let's get going."

Amy tried not to breathe until she moved a few feet away from the huge quimero. Jandro didn't smell too good, either.


Perhaps because the ground they trekked across wasn't as reflective as the sand, Amy wasn't as hot as she had been in Esterenas. The hood that Licha had attached to her robe helped considerably, but it was odd to have to turn her entire head to see her companions. The hood kept her focused on where she was walking, however, which was a good thing. The ground was uneven and full of holes and exposed roots. As Jandro rode on the radamia a wheel ahead of them, Amy asked again what it was he was supposed to keep an eye out for and Apósto Baruti said he was making sure they wouldn't stumble across any surprises.

"What sort of surprises?" She and the apósto walked side by side to the right of the srudas. Licha walked next to the avestrandé, holding its reins like a leash.

"There are many."

Amy would have turned to look at him but it would have been pointless; he too was wearing a hood and she wouldn't have been able to see his face. "Why do you keep doing that? Both times I've asked that question you've avoided actually answering it."

"I have?" the apósto said, with exaggerated innocence.

"Yes, you have. "

He chuckled. "Maybe so. For the most part, Jandro is making sure we are headed in the correct direction."

"And?" Amy knew there had to be more.

"Flocks of pomalvados."

"Flocks? You mean birds?"

"First you must define what is birds."

"Birds," Amy said. "You know, with feathers and wings. Kind of like that thing over there." She pointed to the avestrandé, making sure the apósto could see what she was doing.

"Yes, they are similar to the avestrandé and radamia in that they have feathers and beaks."

"Then they are birds."

"Very well."

"So why is he looking for them?" She stopped and scanned the nearly cloudless blue sky. "If it's a whole flock I would think he could see them from back here."

The apósto stopped as well. "Why would you think that?"

"They fly, don't they? And if there are a lot of them, they would be visible even from far off."

"Oh, no, no, pomalvados don't fly. None of our … birds … fly, although when small, polluelo will flap their wings and glide to the ground if thrown in the air."

"Really? None of them fly?" She found that surprising and a little sad. Birds represented freedom, and she'd always hated seeing one caged.

"It's true."

They started walking again.

"So why is Jandro looking for them? For food?"

"No, the Carados abstain from eating flesh. Our faction doesn't even eat fish, although some of the others do."

That was also a little sad. Amy would have loved to have had something other than a vegetable to sink her teeth into. "Then why would Jandro keep an eye out for them?"

"In order to avoid them. They are vicious creatures, especially a flock of them."

Amy pictured a flock of angry quail and chuckled.

"Two or three of them could bring down an avestrandé within minutes."

That didn't sound much like a quail. "Just how big are they?"

"Bigger than either of our ... birds."

The quail in her mind grew horse-size and took on a decidedly unfriendly look.

"But don't worry." The apósto pulled at his hood so that she could see his face. "It is highly unlikely that he will come across even one, much less an entire flock. This time of year they tend to stay in the Límitotas."

"The what?"

Apósto Baruti pointed toward the mountain range that had been on the western horizon since leaving Nieblota. "The Límitota Mountains, the tallest mountains in this world. Pomalvados nest there and in Baza Range."

Amy almost asked what else Jandro was keeping an eye out for, but after some consideration decided that maybe it was better not to know. She found out later, however, while she'd built a fire. Finally, when Licha realized they'd inadvertently left the flint rock behind, Amy found a way to make herself useful. Having been taught by her father, she knew how to use a pointed stick and friction to start a fire. Jandro had returned and was watching her.

"I just hope this doesn't attract any digging spiders," he said, when the sticks and dried roots caught flame.

"Spiders?" Amy's voice rose an octave. "There are spiders around here?"

Few things terrified her, but spiders were, and always had been, at the top of the list. The tiniest spider made her skin crawl and she couldn't even see a photograph of a tarantula without wanting to flee.

Jandro looked at her questioningly. "Of course there are spiders."

Amy hiked up her robe to her knees and tiptoed over to the srudas. She sat on a clear spot made when Jandro took down the feed trough and pulled her knees up to her chest.

"Do digging spiders bite?" She tucked the hem of her robe under her running shoes.

"Yes." Jandro added more sticks to the fire.

"Is it fatal?"

"Can be. But don't worry; they seldom go after prey that is too large to drag back to their dens."

Licha, who stood over him as he stoked the fire, smacked him on the top of his head with an open palm. "Jandro, you are frightening her. Stop it." With a pot under her arm, she turned to Amy. "The holes I've seen are empty, which means the spiders have probably moved on long ago because there is nothing out here for them to eat."

"Except us." Jandro giggled, and Licha smacked him on the head again.

The apósto laughed. Though he'd thrown back his hood when the sun went down, in the darkness his eyes were hidden by his thick, unruly hair. When the firelight caught them, they were a mere twinkle above his beard. "Don't fret. Many quimerté have an aversion to all spiders because of *La Arañota*."

Although she really wanted to be done with all the spider talk, she had to ask. "You mentioned that name before."

"*La Arañota?*"

"Yes, what is it?'"

"Licha, why don't you tell Amy. Let's see if you've been paying attention to your mother's and my teachings."

The young quimera set down the pot she carried. "*La Arañota* is the opposite of *La Reina*. She is all that is bad and *La Reina* is all that is good. There was a momentous battle between the two and *La Reina* killed *La Arañota*. But, worried *La Arañota*'s influence on the world would continue, *La Reina* knew the only way to take the world out of her grasp was to bring about the *Morphósis*."

"So when good overcame evil the world expanded," said Amy.

"*La Reina* created a larger, better world, and she sent *Dendos* to spread her truth."

The apósto took over when Licha paused. "But *La Arañota* was never forgotten and many believe that, in the past three hundred years, since the passing of the time of the prophecy, she has found a way into this world. That is why the world is shrinking."

Amy turned to him. "Is that what you believe?"

The apósto spread out his bedroll and stretched out on it. "I believe that it no longer matters because *Lacáruna* is here among us." He smiled broadly before laying his head on his arm. "The world will soon expand again." The large quimero closed his eyes and, without the firelight reflecting in them, he was but a shadow.

The next three days were a repeat of the first day out of Esterenas: Licha, Apósto Baruti, and Amy walked alongside the avestrandé across the desert floor while Jandro rode the radamia ahead of them. They spoke very little, except when they stopped so that Licha could prove to Amy that the spider holes that pocked the ground in certain areas were empty.

Slowly, the landscape climbed in elevation, but there was no respite from the heat and virtually no change in the scenery. Amy had little faith that young Jandro truly knew that they were headed in the right direction because she couldn't discern any rock formations, unusual plant clusters, or even a fissure in the dry ground that would guide him. There didn't seem to be anything that would distinguish one place from another. Her walking companions, however, didn't seem worried.

On the third day a dust plume on the horizon caught Amy's attention. She wondered if it could be someone coming towards them and considered her options. If it were a stranger and if he or she came close enough, she could ask for help. She could say religious fanatics had kidnapped her. She considered it but only for a brief moment; no need to jump out of the frying pan into the fire. Like her meemaw often said: better to stay with the devil you knew. The dark spot at the bottom of the plume took on shape and she soon saw that it was Jandro speeding toward his fellow travelers. Amy's first thought was that he'd seen a flock of the vicious quails (she couldn't recall what the apósto had called them), but when he was close enough to see the wide smile on his face, she relaxed. The young quimero shouted that he had spotted the Mika River that would lead to Winter Outpost. Upon hearing the news, they picked up the pace. Half a wheel from the river its tree- and bush-lined banks came into view. As they maneuvered around huge trees that looked like enormous cottonwoods into a clearing a few threestrides from the river, Amy convinced herself that she could actually smell the fresh water. The others must have wanted to submerge themselves as badly as she because without stopping to remove the avestrandé's harness or the radamia's saddle, the seguidosts and the apósto ran to the riverbank, pulled off their robes, and kicked off their shoes. They were naked before Amy could untie one shoe.

She knew she should probably avert her eyes, but their brazen race to the water seemed to indicate they didn't care if she looked. A quick glimpse of Jandro before he dove into the river didn't reveal anything to Amy that she hadn't already observed when he'd pulled up his robe to show her the markings on his thighs. She was able to catch that not only was he bald, but he looked to be completely hairless. In stark contrast was Apósto Baruti who, as he waded into the water, was so covered with hair that it looked as if he still wore clothing. Oddly, though, it was his chest and stomach that were the least hairy, and his groin looked completely hairless. Licha, whose pert breasts had the pinkest nipples Amy had ever seen, also seemed to have no pubic hair. Amy thought that maybe it was a religious requirement.

The three in the river seemed to be waiting for Amy to join them, and she regretted having stopped to ogle. Feeling very much on display, she started to pull off her robe but remembered she was naked underneath. Not wanting to appear prudish she took off the garment but held it in front of her until she reached the river. She tossed it on the bank and quickly dove in. The apósto warned her not to go in too deeply because of the swift current, but Amy was a good swimmer and she swam to the opposite bank. The middle of the river, where the current was strongest, was icy and she swam through it quickly. Crouching in the shallows on the opposite bank, she looked upstream at the mountains to the northwest. Although she couldn't tell from a distance, she assumed there had to be snow on them otherwise the river wouldn't be so cold. The mountains to the southwest were the highest and were most definitely capped with white. Amy wondered whether that was the location of the winter outpost. The vegetation that grew along the riverbanks was thick and brightly colored, a wonderful departure from the drab desert they'd traveled across. All shades of green, yellow, and red spread out through the brush as if splashed there by a careless painter.

Across the river Licha and Jandro climbed out of the water. The young quimera removed the harness from the avestrandé and Jandro removed the radamia's saddle. Once he was done, he led both beasts to the water so they could drink from it and then into the shade under one of the tallest trees. Licha dug through supplies in the srudas until she found whatever she had been looking for, which she then took to the river's edge and tossed to Apósto Baruti. He was waist deep in the water and began to wash himself. Licha's find had apparently been some sort of soap that he lathered over his hairy shoulders. Amy swam back across the river, but not too close to the apósto because she was sure that he hadn't possibly had time to wash away his stench.

"I didn't know there was soap," she called out.

The apósto held up a small white block. "Pulabaza has many uses."

Pulabaza—another word that sounded Spanish in origin, but which Amy had never heard of. Although she wouldn't say she was fluent in the language, she'd taken classes in high school and college and had been around it her entire life. She knew enough to understand most of what was being said when it was spoken to her. If not for the words that actually *were* Spanish, she would have chalked it up to similar pronunciation alone. Even Licha, the only one among them who had what sounded like a slight Mexican accent, only said certain words as if they were Spanish. Yet, the majority of those words weren't the actual language.

"What is pulabaza?"

Amy swam to the apósto's side when he offered her the pulabaza. It was covered with hairs. She held it under the water, rubbed it in her hands until it was hair free, and then brought it to her nose. The pulabaza had no smell. She held it up to her eyes. The block was smooth and milky white, like Licha's skin.

"What other uses does it have?"

"It's what we make the broth from."

"You're telling me we can bathe with something we can also eat?"

"You find that strange?" He caught the pulabaza Amy tossed

back to him.

Jandro returned to the river carrying two pieces of the milky brick. He gave one to Amy and as dubious as it seemed to clean her body with what was essentially a bouillon cube, she began to wash herself. Jandro and the apósto did the same, although Jandro did so standing in ankle-deep water. He said it was because he wanted to be sure to wash everywhere, but Amy had a feeling he was showing off. His short, stocky body was nicely muscled and well proportioned and if it weren't for his markings and the odd blue-gray tint to his skin he would have looked no different from any young man in his early … But was he a young man or still a boy?

"Jandro, how old are you?" She could see by his expression that the question came as a surprise. More surprising to Amy was that he hesitated before answering her.

"I'm seventeen."

"Seventeen *years*?" She hoped they didn't measure time the same way they measured distance, in moons or cycles or what have you.

Jandro turned around and walked out of the river. "Of course years. What else would they be?"

Something about that didn't seem right, but she couldn't put her finger on why she felt that way. Jandro definitely acted like a teenager at times, even if his body looked more mature. Then again, what did she know about how a seventeen year old male with no body hair, blue-gray skin, and black rings around thighs and black ovals around eyes was supposed to look.

She finished bathing and afterwards, joined Licha, who had returned to the river, washing out the robes with what was left of the pulabaza bricks. Amy wanted to dress in her capris and tank top but they had been burned. She wasn't, however, content to walk around naked like the others and wrapped herself in part of her bedroll before helping Licha. While it was understandable that the apósto was still naked (he had a lot of hair to dry off), Licha and Jandro had no excuse—unless, of course, they had nothing else to wear except their robes, with or without the hood. She brought it up with Licha.

"We didn't have time to pack our belongings. Why? Does it bother you that we are bare?"

"Well ... no. I mean ... I'm certainly ... "

"Is it that you have hair where we do not?" Licha's gaze flicked towards Amy's covered crotch.

"No, it's not ... It's just that ..." She didn't know what to say and felt foolish.

"You find it distracting."

Amy glanced at Apósto Baruti sunning himself on a large rock outcrop. "Yes, I suppose I do."

Licha found Amy's unease amusing, but once the robes and hoods were washed and hung on bushes to dry, she gave both the apósto and Jandro canvas strips to wrap around their waists. Licha draped herself in part of a bedroll like Amy.

For their meal, the apósto made a surprisingly tasty concoction of what looked and tasted like apples and blueberries (both of which grew by the river) along with the turnips that tasted like a radish but were the color of carrots. By nightfall the robes had dried and everyone was dressed as they sat around the fire Amy had made.

Finished with her stew, Amy looked up at the dark sky. Living in Los Angeles for so long, she'd become accustomed to not seeing any stars but she wasn't surrounded by bright lights here and thought there should be at least a few stars visible somewhere—possibly near the horizon where it was darkest—but couldn't find any. She considered again that maybe the full moon was too bright to see them. She tried to recall if the moon had been full when she'd driven into Palm Springs, but couldn't. As she thought about her vacation home, it occurred to her that she hadn't really thought much about the life she'd been taken from. Her desire to return to her world was driven more by the fact that she was in danger in this one than longing to be home. She did, however, long for something familiar, something that would make her feel less out of her element. The full moon was about all she had to make her feel connected to what she had left behind. Every night since leaving the Carados camp she'd found comfort in looking up at it and admiring how it dominated the darkness.

Every night.

She'd looked at the *full* moon *every* night.

While she didn't know exactly how long a full moon should last, she was certain that it didn't stay full for well over a week. She looked at Apósto Baruti. "How long does a full moon cycle last in this world?"

He seemed confused by her question. "What do you mean *full*?"

"Round, like that." Amy pointed up. "All of it visible to the naked eye."

Jandro gathered the empty bowls to clean. "That's how it always looks. Is it not that way where you come from?"

"Not always. Sometimes, depending on its cycle, it is half or a quarter full."

Jandro stopped and looked at her with his mouth agape. "Your moon shrinks?"

"No, no. It has to do with the shadow of the planet. The moon never changes size, but the shadow will make only part of it visible." They looked at her as if she were speaking another language, Spanish probably.

Licha seemed as in awe of the possibility as Jandro. "Does that happen to your sun as well?"

Amy shook her head. "The sun actually ... See depending on the time of the year the sun ..." She could see that her words were falling on deaf ears. "Forget it."

The apósto must have sensed her frustration and tried to put her at ease. "There is a very old Carados proverb that comes from *Dendos* himself: *La Reina* lights our way through the darkness. That is why the moon is so much larger than the sun."

"Is that why I can't see stars, because the moon is so big and bright?"

Again the apósto didn't seem to understand.

"Stars. Other tiny points of light in the night sky."

"There are no other lights in the night sky. The moon is all we need. Often we refer to it as the *Eye of Dendos* because we believe he watches over us. This is why we face upwards when in escalétre."

"You do that during the day, though."

He smiled and nodded. "Yes, and also at night. The proverb has many meanings."

Amy lay back on her bedroll and mumbled to herself. "Of course it does." She rolled over so she wouldn't have to look at the sky. Now even the moon was unfamiliar to her.

When Licha asked the apósto what he planned to do when they reached the Winter Outpost Amy flipped over so that she faced the others.

Apósto Baruti paused in his effort to dig something out from between his teeth with a makeshift toothpick. "I will seek out a Trotéjo comrade."

Jandro stopped what he was doing and looked at the apósto excitedly. "Do you think they know what she's supposed to do to make the world expand again?"

"Of course they do."

Amy sat up. "Tell me again who it is we're looking for."

"The Trotéjo," the apósto said. "A clandestine order that came into being immediately following the *Morphósis*. It is said that *Dendos* trained them himself, with the instruction that they were to remain in hiding."

"Why?"

"Because *Dendos* knew that the Carados would be persecuted for spreading his truth. The Trotéjo were instructed to remain in secret until they learned of *Lacáruna's* arrival and assist at the time of the prophecy."

"But you said that time has passed."

"Yes, but their covenant of assisting *Lacáruna* has not."

"How do you know they still exist?" Amy picked up a stray twig and tossed it into the fire. "It's been—what did you say—three thousand years since the first Morphósis? And in all that time Lacáruna never popped in. What makes you believe they are still around?"

"Because I've seen them."

"Did you speak with them?"

"No, I didn't need to until now. I know that when *Lacáruna* came the Trotéjo will help to bring about the *New Morphósis.*"

"So we're just gonna march into this outpost and start asking around about this clandestine order?"

"Absolutely not. *La Reina* will guide me to whomever it is I need to find." He must have seen by Amy's expression that this wasn't a good enough explanation. "There are also signs to look for. Trust me."

She turned away and looked out into the darkness, wondering if maybe she'd been too trusting already.

As they moved down river, Licha pointed out smoke rising from a chimney in the distance. Although he left his off, Apósto Baruti told the others to quickly don their hoods. He climbed onto the radamia (who didn't seem too happy to have him on its back again) and took the lead of their party. They moved off the field and onto a wide rutted path, which left the srudas lopsided because the ruts were too far apart for it to roll in but too narrow for it to roll between. While Jandro guided the avestrandé, Amy and Licha walked along the tilted side of the srudas ready to steady it if it began to tilt a little too far.

As he approached the building with the smoking chimney,

Apósto Baruti called out. "Ho-ho there, friend!"

Forgetting that she was supposed to keep her head down, Amy looked up and saw someone standing at the side of the wooden structure wearing a full, gray skirt. The skirt itself wasn't enough to indicate the quimerté's sex, but the bare breasts above it were. She held in each of her hands tufts of some feathery type of green plant, at least that's what it looked like from a distance. The way the quimera danced about and flailed her arms, it looked as if she were leading a cheer and working up an invisible crowd. Her movements were accompanied by words but Amy only caught two of them, both of which definitely sounded Spanish: *maldad* and *tierra*. She wasn't certain what the first word meant but the second she knew meant land. When the quimera heard the apósto call out, she stopped what she was doing and dropped the tufts.

The quimera was wide and thick and seemed unconcerned that she was topless. Her skin was reddish-brown and her black hair was pulled into a bun at the back of her rather large head. Like two partially filled water balloons, her breasts hung down to her waist and swayed as she walked to the road. Her face was as long as it was wide and her jowls bobbled when she spoke. She was certainly the strangest looking female Amy had ever seen.

"Might be a friend. Might not be." The quimera stood with her hands on her hips and faced the apósto.

Apósto Baruti looked at the sky. "We could use the rain."

The quimera threw a thumb over her shoulder. "That wasn't for rain. You Carados should have spent more time learning evocasado from him and less time spreading word of expanding the world."

"We do as *Dendos* asked of us, señora."

*Another* actual *Spanish word*, Amy thought.

"What do you want?" The quimera seemed a bit testy.

"We want nothing more than to be told we are on the road leading to Winter Outpost."

Scowling, the quimera nodded. "You are and you might as well keep on going because there's nothing here for you."

"We each are on the paths he cleared for us, señora." The apósto seemed to be as unfazed by her rudeness as he was her bare breasts. "May *La Reina* bestow comfort and prosperity on your house."

"She's not listening either." The quimera turned and stomped back to the wood building.

Apósto Baruti flicked the reins and the radamia moved forward. Without prompting, the avestrandé followed. Amy waited until they were well away from the house before speaking.

"She didn't seem too happy to see us."

"That happens all the time," Licha said.

Inwardly, Amy groaned. Now it was clear to her that she was traveling with the sort of religious followers that would knock on doors with pamphlets in hand and wear a smile even when the door never opened. She couldn't wait to take off the brown robe.

A bit later, to break the silence more than out of real curiosity, Amy asked Apósto Baruti what the quimera had been doing when they'd approached.

"An evocasado ritual. Seemed to me she was asking for rain, but apparently I was wrong."

"She was sending wickedness from the land," Jandro said quietly.

Amy looked at him. He must have heard what she had only he'd understood more of it. Yet, he—nor any of them—claimed to know Spanish as a language. She returned her attention to the apósto. "Is evocasado another religion?"

Jandro looked as if he were about to say something more but, for a change, kept it to himself.

Apósto Baruti shook his head. "It is an ancient custom followed by many tribes. That was the first time I've seen it performed outside of the Outer Belt."

"What did she mean about the Carados spending more time learning it and less time expanding?"

The apósto found that highly amusing. "The Carados don't expand. That is *La Reina*'s doing."

Licha turned and walked backwards so that she could talk to Amy. "Many in the Outer Belt believe that *Dendos* came to them first and taught them things we Carados don't know. Some, especially those who've left their tribes, hold that close to heart. We are the true followers, though, because we alone spread his word."

Amy had heard that sort of thing before. Every religion wanted to take credit for something or someone, which usually meant snatching it away from someone or something else. "I take it no one found it unusual that she was topless."

Jandro broke his unusual silence. "Some quimerté in Pliada come from clans that run around naked all year 'round."

"Clans?"

"He means the Isolationist Tribes," Licha explained. "They refer to themselves as clans, but most everyone else refer to them as tribes."

"Do those tribes have to send their firstborn into Pliada too?"

"No. As long as they remain in the Outer Belt they aren't considered part of any nation so it's not required."

As the rutted road slowly curved, color began to appear in the empty brown fields on either side. Bushes, trees, tall grasses, and eventually wild flowers emerged. Subtly, the landscape announced that they were out of the desert. The air was slightly cooler, but not enough to keep the sweat from running down the back of Amy's neck. She'd twisted her long brown hair into a knot and the sweat seemed to pool there before continuing on. Regardless of the heat, Apósto Baruti insisted that she and the two seguidosts keep their hoods up.

The following day they came across other travelers. The apósto saw them coming and bid Amy and the others to move off the road to make room for a team of six avestrandés harnessed to a large flatbed wagon carrying something very big covered with a tarp. Driving the wagon were two quimerté but the hood hindered Amy's ability to clearly see their faces without being obvious. The apósto also insisted they keep their heads down. As the wagon rumbled toward them, she was able to see that the drivers were each dressed in beige tunics with a wide strap crossing from shoulder to waist, left to right, and black trousers that were tucked into knee-high boots. One of them carried what looked like a long-barreled rifle.

"Fensoré," the apósto said. "Whatever was under the tarp must warrant protecting. Usually they carry only swords."

They moved back onto the road. Amy took one last look at the tarp covered wagon heading in the opposite direction and then kept her head down and her eyes on the road.

A short time later they encountered more travelers, some on foot and some riding either a wagon or a radamia. Most of the quimerté they passed were dressed as the flatbed drivers had been, although the tunics varied in color. Jandro whispered that, like the Carados robes, the tunic colors indicated rank, although he was unclear on the hierarchy of the colors. From what Amy could tell, the soldiers, or fensorés as the others called them, seemed to be of both sexes. Some looked to be nearly as hairy as the apósto while others as hairless as Jandro. A couple had been as white as Licha, but most were varying shades of brown. One radamia rider was actually slate gray and another practically orange. The colors were so odd Amy found it difficult not to believe that their skin had been painted or dyed. One traveler had markings like Jandro (who pulled his hood down even further when the traveler passed) but most of the markings on the passing quimerté were stripes or spots. Most shocking, however, were two quimeros driving a wagon. As the wagon neared, Amy saw that they had horns on their heads. *Actual horns.* She was so surprised by what she saw that she completely forgot about keeping her head down and with her mouth agape, stared right into the eyes of the one with tan-colored skin, white markings on his face, and two horns protruding from his forehead. His horns were about five knuckles long, bone-colored, and forked at the top. When he saw her gawking with obvious astonishment the horned quimero angrily shouted something she couldn't make out. She quickly looked away and, following Jandro's example, pulled her hood down.

The road they'd followed since before the encountering the topless quimera merged with another much wider road. The three Carados and one imposter soon joined yet another road that Amy guessed passed through a smaller mountain range to the east, but she didn't take more than a cursory glance in that direction. After encountering the horned quimeros she understood the necessity of keeping her reactions in check. Apósto Baruti wanted her to blend in and she doubted that gasping every time she saw a strange-looking being would work to her advantage. Only the apósto spoke, although even he didn't say much. Mostly he greeted those he passed or who passed him, but received few responses. Amy had to wonder how he was going to find a Trotéjo when no one seemed willing to speak to him.

Five wheels past the juncture in the road, Winter Outpost appeared on the horizon. Risking a quick glance, Amy saw smoke rising from its many chimneys long before she saw the enormous wall that surrounded it. When she was first told about the outpost, she had expected it to be a camp with many tents or possibly a few cabins. She never pictured it as a fortress surrounded by a towering wall that had to be wheels long. The wall seemed to be constructed with enormous trees trunks more two hundred feet high. Despite spending much of her early years in Northern California where sequoia trees grew, she couldn't fathom the size of the forest from which these trees must have come. As awe inspiring as the outpost itself was, it didn't compare the excitement of knowing that within it was her ticket home. Someone within would answer the question of what her part in this prophecy entailed. Then all she had to do would be to find the solution, get the job done, and go on her way. As she thought about it she decided that, basically, this was just a consulting job, and she'd always been good at that sort of thing.

The traffic on the road doubled then tripled in number as they met with more crossroads, creating a bottleneck at the bridge over Mika River. Crossing the bridge took a very long time because, as Carados, they were constantly being pushed aside while fensorés and civilians alike bullied their way past. Although Amy was impressed by the apósto's ability to take it all in stride, she was ready to grab somebody's sword and slash her way through the crowd. Once they finally made it across the bridge the road turned west again as it headed toward the gargantuan wall. Amy could feel it in her thighs as the road sloped steadily upward. She'd always considered herself in good shape, but walking for several days had taken its toll on her. Nevertheless, the mere notion of finding resolution to the mystery she'd fallen into dangled overhead like a carrot and propelled her forward. When they reached the crest upon which the outpost stood, she had to stop for a breather. Jandro stopped with her and while she caught her breath pointed out a large lake to the south that was barely visible through a copse of exceedingly tall pine trees.

"That's Lake Miracle. "It's said that *La Reina* created it to keep two warring groups apart before the *Morphósis*."

"I thought the Fensoré were supposed to keep the peace."

Jandro shrugged. "It happened before there were fensorés."

The jostling of passing quimerté propelled the two forward and they caught up with Licha and the srudas, but the apósto was nowhere in sight. Licha explained that he went on ahead to secure their passage through the gate.

At the western end of the towering wall, the road turned sharply north. Directly ahead was the entrance to the outpost. The gate Licha spoke of looked to be a hole or gap in the wall as wide as the road. Traffic slowed as it approached the gap but there was no shoving to get around the three hooded seguidosts and their avestrandé-pulled srudas. Screeching and squawking from the beasts of burden came from all directions. Most of it seemed to emanate from huge bird-creatures Amy had never seen before. They were the size and coloring of an avestrandé but much less fierce-looking. Their beaks were rounded and their talons smaller. Jandro told her that they were the offspring of avestrandés and radamias, called avestrotés.

"They are easier to tame than avestrandés, but they are stubborn and willful. They prefer being in a team than being alone and are mostly used to haul wagons. They can make a lot of noise."

Amy also noticed that none of the beasts, including the avestroté, had webbed feet. Jandro said that was because they were not sandrunners like the beasts that were accompanying them.

Several threestrides in front of the gate stood a tall watchtower and on it, fensorés with ridiculously long-barreled rifles slung over their shoulders scanned the crowd below. Jandro said the weapon was called an esacado. At either side of the tower were more esacado-toting fensorés, some of whom were directing the traffic. Jandro spotted the apósto on the opposite side from them standing with the radamia aside an equally hairy fensoré waving traffic through the gate behind him. Getting to the apósto meant darting through openings when they became available, something the avestrandé wasn't too happy about. As soon as it started to pick up speed, it would be held back or stopped entirely and it began to squawk in protest as loudly as the avestrotés. When they finally made it to the apósto's side, Jandro took the radamia's reins from him.

"These are my pupils," the apósto was saying to the hairy fensoré who seemed not to be paying any attention. "We are here not to spread the truth but for educational purposes." When the fensoré didn't respond, the apósto nodded and turned to his so-called pupils. "I'm afraid our lesson about the esteemed Fensoré will have to be conducted outside the outpost." With his staff, the glass tip of which was no longer covered, he gestured toward the opening. "Many quimerté from all nations come through this outpost operated by the Fensoré—peace-keepers of this world and protectors of the Carados. Becoming a fensoré is a true and honorable tradition held only by those with the noblest of hearts, trustworthy, and honest above all—"

His effusive speech either made the hairy fensoré feel guilty about ignoring the apósto or he was simply tired of hearing the quimero's voice. Whichever, it had the desired effect.

"All right, all right. Go now before I change my mind and make you wait a few days."

"Thank you, señor." Apósto Baruti bowed and gestured for the others to quickly follow. The four hurried past the fensoré joining the other quimerté making their way through the gate. The apósto guided them out of the traffic once they entered the outpost so that he could look about. Amy raised her head enough to see her surroundings. Looking through the hood, however, was like looking through a periscope; she could only see it one segment at a time and had to turn her head slowly to view the bustling scene. Large flatbed wagons filed down an interior dirt road that ran parallel to the enormous wall. The smaller carts and srudas flowed along with the foot traffic down one of five cobblestone streets that fanned outward from the gate. The buildings were reminiscent of an American city in the mid-1800s. The structures nearest the terminus of the road leading into the outpost were multi-leveled and triangular in shape and each seemed to be the cornerstone of the streets on either side. Signs with the Chinese-like symbols she had a difficult time focusing on hung over most doors. Despite her narrow view, Amy felt a sense of relief. Though filled with strange beings and beasts, the outpost was a city and cities were something familiar. Cities, Amy knew.

Jandro seemed entranced by the spectacle and several times his hood bumped Amy's shoulder while he craned his neck from right to left and back again. Fortunately, no one gave them the slightest notice. With few exceptions, everyone seemed to know exactly where they were headed. Unfortunately, Apósto Baruti was one of those exceptions. His seeming confusion worried Amy and she moved closer to him so that she could be heard above the din.

"I thought you'd been here before."

"I have, but it's been a few years and things have changed considerably." With his staff, he pointed to the second street from the right. "There used to be a wrangler shop right there owned by a friend. I had planned to question him about securing a stable for us."

"A stable?" There went her sense of relief, right out the barn door. "We have to stay in a stable?"

"Of course. No one will take us in and we have no coin to rent a room. Usually there is an empty stall in a stable where we will sleep alongside the pájastias."

"Pájastia?"

"Feathered creatures." Apósto Baruti nodded toward the radamia just behind Jandro. "What you call birds."

She didn't care what they were called and, more importantly, she didn't want to spend the night in a stable stall with the giant beasts. "Can't we just set up camp somewhere? A place this size has to have a park or empty lot."

The apósto shook his head. "The Winter Outpost has been here for centuries and believe it when I say every available spot on the ground has been put to use." He scanned the five streets one more time before moving. "Come along. We need to get away from this commotion."

Amy was in complete agreement. Jandro and Licha kept held the reins tightly, as they led the pájastias down the street. The avestrandé seemed to take the excitement in stride but the radamia was jittery, jerking its head back as if trying to loosen Jandro's grip on it. Only a few threestrides down the street, they had to stop to do something about it.

The apósto suggested using a blinder but Jandro hadn't taken one when they'd left the camp.

"I didn't think we'd need it."

Grumbling, the apósto told the young quimero to hold his staff and went to the back of the srudas. He rummaged through it until he came across the strip of canvas that had been the skirt Jandro had worn at the river while he'd waited for his robe to dry. Once the radamia was blindfolded it immediately calmed.

"There." The apósto took back his staff.

When she saw a quimera pointing their way, Amy quickly lowered her head but not before noting that the quimera was speaking with two fensorés. The apósto must have seen them as well because he quietly told the others to keep moving forward. The srudas didn't get farther than a single turn of the wheels before one of the fensorés shouted for them to halt. The apósto told everyone to do whatever they were told. Amy's heart began to thump rapidly, as she nervously kept her head down on the fensorés' approach. Apósto Baruti greeted them jovially.

"Ho-ho there, friend."

"Are these the seguidosts that just passed through the gate?" one fensoré asked the other, who turned out to be the hairy sentry who had allowed them into the outpost.

"They are."

The apósto continued to smile. "Is there something we may do for you, señor?"

The fensoré who seemed to be in charge wore a brown tunic rather than the guards' beige. He thumped the apósto in the chest with a short thick baton. "Yes, there is. You may answer my questions." His skin was almost the same color as the sentry's tunic and his dark eyes were widely spaced. He told the sentry to return his post and addressed the apósto. "Where have you come from?"

"From Esterenas. We are here on a learning excursion." He

gestured at the others standing behind him. "I have brought these young—"

The fensoré thumped the apósto's chest again, effectively knocking the words out of his mouth. "And before Esterenas?"

The apósto rubbed his chest where the baton had struck him, but he didn't step back or complain. "We camped near the southern border."

The fensoré blew a whistle he'd taken from his trouser pocket and, almost instantly, the sound of feet stomping across the cobblestone filled the street. Amy turned her head just enough to see six fensorés in beige tunics running in formation behind a fensoré in blue. They stopped before the fensoré in charge.

The fensoré commanded them to look through the srudas to find out where the Carados were from and returned his attention to the apósto. "If you came from Esterenas, then you must have heard of the slaughter."

Amy's stomach tightened.

"Slaughter?" the apósto asked.

"An entire Carados camp burned to the ground and all the seguidosts and apóstos, more than one hundred, were killed."

Without having to look above the trembling hands at his sides, Amy could tell how much the apósto was staggered by the news. He'd dropped his staff to the ground.

"Who would do such a thing?" The apósto's voice quivered.

"We don't know," the fensoré said. "But we've heard that it was another Carados faction."

One of the fensorés rifling through the srudas shouted out as he removed the only cushion that they hadn't left behind. "Captain, they're part of the same faction as the one slaughtered."

"Take them into custody." The captain kicked away the apósto's staff.

The apósto began to sob. "But why? Why arrest us when it was our brethren who were killed?"

As if he'd given his permission, Licha and Jandro began to sob as well, but the fensoré took no pity on any of them.

"Because you are now suspects. Let's go."

He blew the whistle again and Amy felt a fensoré grab her arm. She couldn't see above the waist of anyone nearby, but she could hear others approaching. Tilting her head slightly, she caught a quick glimpse of a female fensoré taking the radamia's reins from Jandro. When the young quimero started to protest, the fensoré struck him with her baton and he doubled over. Licha put up no resistance while the avestrandé was taken from her. As the four were led down the street deeper into the city, the pájastias were taken away in the opposite direction.

While the others grieved for their fallen brethren Amy found herself numb. Maybe it was shock because, although she knew she should have been frightened, she wasn't. The sound of the fensorés' boots beating the cobblestone drowned out most of the shouting that seemed to be coming from the sidewalks. Whether the shouting had something to do with them or if it was simply the clamor of a crowded city, she couldn't tell. Dark sewer water dribbled down a gutter on one side of the street and the farther they were taken into the depths of the outpost, the stronger the stench. Amy had to breathe through her mouth to keep from gagging. Without being able to look up and see where they were going, she lost all sense of direction as they turned corners again and again. All she knew was that the grime on the street lessened and so did the smell. Eventually, the unpleasant odor disappeared entirely.

The fensoré let go of her arm and shoved her forward to a set of steps. Ahead of her, Licha was already climbing them. A quick glance upward revealed that they were entering a large, white stone, unadorned building. They passed through an arch, crossed a wide courtyard, and were marched under another arch down a long hallway lit with bare bulbs. Brought to a halt, Amy heard the distinct clank of metal on metal as a door was opened. Forced inside, she nearly knocked Licha off her feet. Her hood pushed back and, since she no longer had a reason not to, Amy looked up.

They'd been shoved in a cell consisting of three stone walls and half a wall made of iron, above which vertical iron bars were placed no more than two knuckles apart. The iron door beside the bars opened into the hall. The only light in the windowless room came from a single bare bulb in the center of the fifteen-foot high ceiling. The cell was only slightly larger than the trinéot had been. Amy's three companions were to her left with the apósto farthest from her. The hoods had also been pushed back from Licha's and Jandro's heads. Their cheeks were wet from tears. A fensoré wearing a blue tunic stood before them. Flanking him were two quimeros in beige tunics. Amy hadn't noticed when the other fensoré who had taken them through the outpost had left. The one in the blue tunic stared at her with what looked like mild surprise.

"I didn't realize that seguidosts could keep their hair."

The apósto cleared his voice, which still sounded shaky. "She is still a novice and has yet to commit herself to the Carados."

"You allow novices to wear the robe?"

"Only because we were coming from Esterenas, señor."

"Sergeant," the quimero corrected.

"My apologies, Sergeant."

"Now answer the question. Why do you allow a novice to wear the robe?"

"I worried she would become overheated."

The sergeant in the blue tunic took a step closer. His face was only a foot or so from Amy's. He had a tuft of brown hair at his forehead and some circling the back of his head above tiny ears. His eyebrows were thick. If his mouth and nose had been painted bright red, Amy thought he would have looked like a clown without the white face paint.

"You look rather old to be a novice. Where are you from?"

The apósto started to speak but the fensoré held up a hand to stop him. "I didn't ask you." He kept his hand up as he waited for Amy to speak.

Worried that if she waited too long he would know she was lying, she said the first thing that came to mind. "I was born in Pliada."

"Were you now? You sound like you hail from Maseprada. What made you decide to throw your life away to join the Carados at such an advanced age?"

She couldn't help but take umbrage; after all, forty was hardly an advanced age. Then again, she didn't know how long quimerté lived. Maybe they had a life expectancy of fifty. If so, she was an old woman.

"La Reina called to me."

The sergeant stared at her for a while longer, apparently waiting for Amy to flinch. When she didn't, he lowered his hand. "It's good to see that they take in the crazy ones."

When the other two fensorés laughed, Amy silently let out her breath.

The sergeant ordered his underlings out of the cell and he followed behind. Using his body weight, he swung the iron door shut. He then moved in front of the bars so that he could be seen. "You will remain in custody until we have determined whether you were involved in the slaughter."

"But, señor"—the apósto quickly corrected himself—"But, Sergeant, how can you determine anything, if our entire faction was killed?"

"Because a quimero from another faction was spared and reported what happened to the nearest patrol."

Apósto Baruti nodded vigorously. "So he would know who committed the atrocity. He would have seen."

The sergeant studied the apósto for a moment. "You would think so. But the Carados are sniveling cowards. The visitor hid and did nothing to stop the massacre." He looked at Amy with a sneer on his face. "Are you sure you still want to align with this worthless bunch?"

"But if the visitor was hidden, how could he—"

"Enough!"

The sergeant left the cell followed by the other two. As he walked down the hall, he called out over his shoulder. "Maybe the coward who reported the slaughter can confirm that you weren't at the camp at the time. You'd better hope so."

No one spoke until the sound of boot heels against stone faded away. Jandro was the first to move and he quickly grabbed hold of Licha before she collapsed. Amy helped him move her to an alcove with a bench on the opposite wall. Licha slumped against the inner wall with her eyes shut tight, although tears found a way out. Jandro sat on the floor at her feet and put his head in her lap. The numbness that held Amy upright faded, replaced not by fear but by overwhelming remorse. She turned to the apósto.

"This is my fault. Your people were killed because of me."

The apósto shook his head and began to pace. "No. This is all my doing. I foolishly believed everyone would be overjoyed by the news of the coming of *Lacáruna*. I am the one who brought destruction upon us."

Jandro lifted his head and wiped his black-ringed eyes with the back of his hand. "Why would they have killed *everyone*? Most of the camp didn't even know that she was among us."

"I don't know why everyone was killed. But I don't believe it was a member of the Carados who did it." Apósto Baruti looked at Amy. "We are peaceful and abhor violence."

Amy moved away from the others and looked out through the iron bars. "What about the apósto you said wanted to kill me? Doesn't sound like *he* abhorred violence."

Jandro wiped his cheeks with the back of his hand. "Who was he? What faction did he belong to?"

"He said he was from one of the small mountain factions, but I don't recall which."

Sniffling back her tears, Licha opened her eyes. "Mountain faction? If he was from one of the mountain factions, how could he have heard the news of *Lacáruna* so quickly?"

"He said he had been in the lower Outer Belt to spread the truth to firstborns coming through." Apósto Baruti stopped and intertwined his fingers, which he brought to his face. He pressed his hairy thumbs against his mouth. "But how could that be? The mountain factions don't spread the truth in the lower Outer Belt. They seek out the Isolationist Tribes in the mountains."

Amy turned to him. "Could he have been an imposter?"

The apósto stared at the stone floor and slowly nodded. "It would explain much. Three other apóstos arrived shortly after him and he knew them. I was so concerned with getting you out of the camp that it never occurred to me to ask the others where they had come from. All four were outraged when I told them that *Lacáruna* was gone. I had never seen such anger in an apósto's eyes. They really believed that you were *La Arañota*'s doing."

"And this didn't worry you?" Amy's question came out harsher than she'd intended.

Apósto Baruti looked up and dropped his hands from his face. He kept them clasped in front of him. "Of course it worried me. This is why I left that night instead of waiting another day as planned."

Jandro picked himself up off the floor and sat on the bench next to Licha. "But how could only four quimerté kill so many?"

"They couldn't have," the apósto said.

Amy's mind went to work. "You said that you didn't know any of the apóstos who showed up after you'd sent word. Were there other apóstos you knew who should have come?"

Apósto Baruti nodded. "I was expecting Apósto Anuli to be the first to arrive. Her camp is the closest to ours." He began to pace again.

"Maybe she never received the news about *Lacáruna*." The anger in Licha's eyes had dried her tears. "Maybe whoever slaughtered our faction killed the messengers you sent out."

"Possibly," the apósto said. "But how could they have known so quickly? I sent five messengers out at the same time. If someone were to have stopped them they would have had to have done so within a wheel of our camp, before the five had time to spread out."

As Amy tried to put the pieces together, she spoke aloud. "The sergeant said it was a visitor to the camp who reported the massacre. And the only visitors, as far as we know, were the four apóstos."

"*False* apóstos." Licha's eyes narrowed. "Even if they believed you weren't the true *Lacáruna*, apóstos would never kill..." She couldn't finish.

"But why would they report what they'd done?" Jandro asked. "Why wouldn't they have just left or come searching for us?"

Amy looked out between the iron bars of the cell. "Maybe they wanted help in finding us. By reporting it, the Fensoré would also be looking for whoever did it and question any Carados member they came across. What if it's one of those four who the sergeant said would be summoned?" She turned around and looked Apósto Baruti in the eye. "Here we sit, trapped behind these bars."

Jandro jumped to his feet. "We have to get out of here."

"Of course we do. But unless you are able to bend those bars, Jandro, or break down one of these walls, I'm afraid we're not leaving."

Amy sat on the stone bench. Sometimes an analytical mind wasn't much of a blessing. This wasn't like sitting in a boardroom making recommendations. All she'd done in trying to deduce who could have been responsible for the atrocity at the Carados camp was to remind her companions that they were sitting ducks.

No one spoke. The apósto continued to pace until, worried he would collapse from exhaustion, Amy asked him to stop. He sat on the floor opposite Jandro and Licha, who were sitting below the iron bars. An hour must have passed when they heard the sound of footsteps coming down the hall. Jandro jumped up and tried to look out between the bars but it was impossible to see more than a few feet from their cell.

"What do we do?" he whispered.

They had no time to formulate a plan. When the heavy iron door began to open Jandro quickly crouched down behind the metal portion of the wall below the bars ready to pounce. The other three stood. Jandro never had the chance to spring; a booted foot knocked him back. The fensoré in the brown tunic, the captain who had had them arrested, rushed in with his sword drawn. He looked at his captives for a moment, scrutinizing each of them, Amy in particular. He looked her up and down and, although he seemed unsure, she was certain they were about to be killed. He surprised her when he sheathed his sword.

"I'm here to help you. You must come with me."

No one moved. The fensoré was looking at Amy intently, but now she couldn't read the expression on his face. She averted her gaze and looked at the apósto, who seemed to be focused on the captain's hands.

"Fine. The three of you may stay here, but I'm taking *her* with me." He pointed at Amy, who was standing on tiptoe to see over the apósto's shoulder.

"Where she goes, we go." Somehow the apósto managed to sound humble, yet forceful.

A sarcastic smile spread across the captain's face. "Wonderful. Then all four of you will follow me. We must hurry and you must remain quiet."

Like dutiful schoolchildren they filed out of the cell behind the fensoré. Jandro walked directly behind him. Amy was next with Licha and Apósto Baruti behind her. She looked down the hall in the direction they had come when they were brought in and contemplated making a break for it. Without knowing the layout of the building, though, she knew that would be foolish. They had to trust that the fensoré who'd had jailed them in the first place was now aiding their escape. After passing six other cells, they turned to the left. The fensoré unlocked and opened a wooden door just a crack to peek in. Once he'd made sure it was safe to continue, he opened the door onto another, shorter hallway. Everyone had filed through and the fensoré locked the door on the other side. He led them only a few feet down the hall before stopping and unlocking yet another wooden door that also opened onto a hall. They went through three more doors in the labyrinth of hallways before coming to a stop. Amy realized that even if they could overpower the fensoré and escape on their own, there was no possibility they could find their way back to the initial hallway where they'd been held, much less out of the building.

In a niche to the right stood a perfectly smooth dark blue monolith about five feet tall. The fensoré told Jandro to help him move it and, side by side, with their feet pressed up against the inner wall, they pushed. Nothing happened until the apósto added his weight to the endeavor. Accompanied by the grinding noise of stone against stone the monolith slowly began to turn and with it, the back wall, revealing behind it a dimly lit room. As soon as there was an opening wide enough for them to fit through, the fensoré led the way. He stood by the entrance until everyone was inside and then, using a lever imbedded in the wall, closed the opening. The dim bulb overhead flickered.

"It's much easier to get out," he said to no one in particular, "than it is to get in."

The room was barely large enough for all five of them and the others had to squeeze against the wall so that the fensoré could pull up the trapdoor in the center of the floor. Below were stairs. The fensoré picked up a lantern that Jandro had kicked over while trying to get out of the way. Like the lantern Licha had used in the trinéot, it glowed with a green light. He went down the first few steps, lighting their way, before stopping to instruct the apósto to pull shut the trapdoor once passing through it.

They followed the captain down the spiraling narrow stairwell. When Apósto Baruti closed the trapdoor, they were enveloped by darkness except for the small area lit by the lantern. Amy hoped that the apósto was steady on his feet because one stumble would send them all crashing down the stairs. The stairwell spiraled downwards long enough for Jandro to complain of becoming dizzy before it opened up to a large, empty room. On the opposite end was a door outlined by light from the other side escaping around its edges. The fensoré hurried to the door and rapped his knuckles on it three times. He paused and then rapped again. Something clicked and the door moved outward a knuckle. The fensoré took the ring handle and pulled the door open. The room beyond it was so brightly lit he had to shield his eyes. He set the lantern on the ground.

"They're here." He stepped into the room and, a bit hesitantly, the others followed.

Unlike the hallways and the cell, the room that they entered was lit not by bare bulbs but by hundreds of candles that lined the walls in sconces, hung from the ceiling in glass tubes, and forested the floor on tall pedestals. The radiant array reflected off the polished marble tiles on the walls and floor like flickering starlight. Slowly, as Amy's eyes adjusted to the brightness, the circular room took shape around her. Approximately one hundred feet in diameter, the room's marble wall was light blue streaked with gold and the marble floor was dark blue like the monolith in front of the hidden passage. In the center of the room was a large round table that appeared to be made from obsidian. Atop it was a gold obelisk more than five feet tall.

Drawn toward the obelisk, Amy stepped around and through the many pedestals covering the floor. Even from afar she could see that there was a face stamped onto it, which, in the iridescent candlelight, seemed to shift from one image to another. The eyes never changed, however; only the features surrounding them did. Mesmerized by how the eyes appeared to follow her, to watch her, she was only vaguely aware of her surroundings until someone stepped in front of her and blocked her view of the obelisk. Amy looked up and saw—once again she almost used the word *man*—a tall, robust quimero in a purple tunic. His tan trousers were tucked into thigh-high black boots and the gold sash that crossed his chest was tied just above a black scabbard on his left hip.

The reason that the word man had come to mind was that on first glance his striking face looked no different than that of many handsome men Amy had come across. That thought was fleeting, however, because upon closer look it was obvious that the being in the purple tunic belonged to this world and not hers. While the shape of his face was no different from a human male, his skin tone was like none Amy had ever seen. His overall coloring was tawny, albeit on the yellow side, and his shoulder-length hair was only a shade or two more golden than his skin. His green eyes were lined with thick black lashes and above his brows were two rows of black markings that met in the middle in a lopsided arch. Three thinner black stripes began at both sides of his nose and moved out until they mingled with and ultimately disappeared into his white muttonchops. Mesmerized, Amy was unaware that the broad-shouldered fensoré was speaking even as she watched his full lips move and saw their pink inner lining and the tip of his equally pink tongue. Someone tugged at her sleeve and she looked down to see the apósto's hairy hand pulling her back.

"Forgive her," the apósto said without looking directly at the tall quimero. "We are all very confused by what has transpired."

When she noticed that the others, including the fensoré who had brought them here, were looking down, Amy did so as well. Her eyes seemed to have a will of their own, though, and continually drifted up so that she could look at the fensoré with the golden skin.

Ignoring the apósto, the tall fensoré addressed his obvious

subordinate. "These are the Carados believed to be from the massacred camp, Captain Tamezo?"

Unlike the captain who had no discernable accent, the colonel sounded distinctly British and, when Amy heard it, her head snapped up. Fortunately, the two fensoré were looking at each other. When Amy glanced to her left, she noticed that again the apósto seemed to be looking at the quimero's hands.

"Yes, Colonel. They claim to have been in Esterenas when it took place."

With long, sure strides, the Fensoré colonel came forward and stood in front of the apósto. "Why are you here?"

Although Apósto Baruti could have been eye to eye with the colonel, he hunched a bit so that he was lower and had to look up. He repeated what he had told the captain before they were taken into custody. "We are on a humble learning expedition."

The colonel put one hand on his hip in an oddly awkward position. "What is it you want to teach these"—he sneered as he said the next word—"círcudito of yours?"

The apósto glanced at the colonel's hand and when he looked up, the colonel backhanded him across the face and the apósto staggered from the blow. "Now tell me the real reason you have come to my outpost."

Certain that there would be another slap across the face, or something worse, if he did not answer truthfully and quickly, Amy spoke for him. And because she'd always hated when anyone danced around the topic, she got right to the point.

"We're here to find someone belonging to the Trotéjo." Unlike the apósto, she didn't cower when she looked at the colonel, who was only a few inches taller than she.

The colonel turned to her with a slight bemused expression on his face. "And what makes you think that you'll find one here?"

The question was one Amy didn't know the answer to and she wanted to look at the apósto to ask him what exactly were the signs he said he'd look for. If she did, though, she knew she would lose whatever advantage she may have gained by speaking up. Using a tactic that had served her well as CEO, she turned the question around.

"What makes you think that we won't?"

Out of the corner of her eye she saw the captain take a step toward her, and she fought the urge to flinch. Apósto Baruti, however, did.

The colonel retained his bemused expression. "Because it is my understanding that the Trotéjo have not existed for thousands of years."

His coloring and stripes aside, Amy knew his type well and had seen that bemused look hundreds of times. Usually it was on a male face, but not always. The expression, no matter whom it was on, always indicated the wearer was lying and knew that the person he was talking to knew that he was lying.

"If that's your understanding, then why did you have your captain sneak us out of our cell down a dozen hallways and through a hidden passage to get here? Something tells me a room filled with candles isn't the typical headquarters for a colonel." That was an assumption, of course, but it seemed plausible—even for this world.

The colonel smiled. "Fair enough." He rocked on his feet for a moment while he gazed at the floor. When he looked up, he crossed his arms over his broad chest. "Perhaps a better question would be: Why do you want to find someone belonging to the Trotéjo?"

Maybe it was because she was tired, or hungry, or that her bowels were irregular, or her feet and legs ached from all the walking, but whatever the reason, the colonel's charming and very familiar accent notwithstanding, Amy was quickly losing her patience.

"Because we have something to tell them ... or him." Amy crossed her arms as well.

"Tell them … or him … what?"

Amy's arms flew up. "Oh for heaven's—"

The apósto quickly cut her off. "We believe that the prophecy has come to pass and we believe that *Lacáruna* has been delivered to us."

The colonel's raised brows created furrows between the stripes on his forehead. Though he spoke to the apósto, he kept his eyes on Amy. "Is that so? Where is she?"

Even with the raised brow, his expression hadn't changed, and Amy knew that he was still playing word games. He knew exactly where Lacáruna was and she found his feigned obtuseness infuriating. It was time to fully accept what she'd been resistant to before.

"You're looking at her," she said. When the colonel said nothing and continued to gaze at her with contrived incomprehension, Amy held up her left arm and pulled up her sleeve so that he could see the bracelet the Carados had a name for. It was all she could think to do.

With little more than a glance at the bracelet, the colonel shrugged. "There is a vendor in Tripod Square who sells bracelets just like that one."

Amy continued to hold out her arm. "Are you sure? Are you sure they are *just* like this one?"

The apósto, still hunched over in deference to the fensorés, pointed at Amy's feet. "Look at her shoes."

The colonel's eyes moved slowly down Amy's body until settling on the bottom of her brown robe. She wanted to laugh; it wasn't as if she were wearing magical ruby slippers, only a pair of expensive, well-worn, running shoes. Feeling like one of Cinderella's ridiculous stepsisters, Amy lifted the hem of the robe so that he could see her feet. That he seemed unimpressed came as no surprise.

"Those are why you believe yourself to be *Lacáruna*?"

Amy let the robe fall. "No. That's why *they* believe me to be Lacáruna." She nodded toward the seguidosts.

Although she had covered her running shoes, the colonel continued to look down as if he could see through the brown fabric. His silence was unsettling and made her want to slink away and hide behind the apósto, but it was too late to back down. When he told her to take the shoes off, she didn't argue. She did what he demanded and held both shoes out for the colonel to take. He studied them for a bit while she held them out. The apósto pointed to the tongue of the nearest shoe, which had the manufacturer's name stitched onto it.

"Look there."

The colonel slapped the apósto's hand away. "I'll grant you that I have never before seen shoes constructed with that type of material. I've never seen a floating srudas either, but I know they exist in Maseprada. And you sound Masepradan; perhaps those shoes are the latest in fashion there." He smiled sardonically. "There has to be something more than unusual footwear and a cheap bracelet sold everywhere that brings you in search of the mythical Trotéjo."

"She was found alone in the sands of Esterenas," the apósto said. "From her appearance, her clothing, we knew that she wasn't Carados. More than any of that, including the shoes and the bracelet, it is that she remembers the world she came from. Just as the Primeróte did."

Shaking his head, the colonel walked away. "Not enough. Many insane quimerté have claimed to come from or see into a world other than this one." He reached the black table where the gold obelisk stood and turned back to them. The candlelight reflected off the shiny table he leaned against. "There has to be something more."

Amy held her shoes at her side. The captain seemed fixated on them.

The apósto stood taller. "There is one other thing." Everyone looked at him.

"What is it?" The colonel pushed himself up off the table, but remained standing beside to it.

The apósto's eyes darted from the colonel to the captain and back again. The captain seemed uninterested in what the apósto had to say while he continued to stare at the running shoes. Apósto Baruti reached into the folds of his blue robe and pulled out a small rectangular object, which he then held up. In his raised hand was Amy's driver's license. She'd forgotten that he had kept it.

The colonel came toward him. "What is that?"

"When she was discovered lying in the dunes, she had that with her. On it is the writing found only in the Extiguos."

No longer interested in shoes, the captain lunged for the card in the apósto's hands. Only because Apósto Baruti was a foot taller was he able to keep it out of the captain's reach.

The colonel stepped between the two and held out his hand. "I'll take it."

The apósto eyed the captain suspiciously as he gave over the license. As soon as the tall colonel looked at the face on the plastic card in his palm he inhaled sharply. He held the card out for the captain to see and the smaller fensoré gasped as well. They both looked at Amy with entirely different expressions, only one of which seemed to be awe. The look on the colonel's face mirrored that of all three Carados when they'd first seen the license. The captain looked almost angry, but only briefly. Immediately she worried that the apósto had spoken too soon and the two fensoré weren't Trotéjo at all.

The colonel held the card between his thumb and forefinger. "Do you know how to read this writing?"

Amy nodded. "I do."

The colonel looked at the captain, but the captain was focused on the license, his expression now neutral. The colonel told Amy to follow him and she did. The captain was close on her heels and the apósto on his. Licha and Jandro kept a respectful distance. Once at the obsidian table the apósto slowly inched his way closer to Amy. The tabletop looked as smooth and reflective as glass. The colonel splayed his fingers along the edge. He struck a match taken from a box on the table and bent slightly. Amy leaned back and saw that he was lighting a large candle below the tabletop. When he blew the flame out he must have pressed a switch because the candle under the table began to move in a circular fashion. As it did, the light illuminated blue glass embedded in the table. The glass wasn't decorative, but informative, creating three words that were repeated around the circumference of the table.

"Can you read what has been carved into the ventégra?" the colonel asked Amy.

She looked at what was written in blue glass. "If ventégra is that table, then yes."

"Ventégra is what the table is made out of." The colonel stared at her intently. "What does the writing say?"

Amy looked back at the tabletop. "It says—several times—*the finder protects.*"

The colonel and the captain stiffened at the same instant, but while the captain's eyes narrowed, a smile spread across the colonel's face.

"Then it *is* true. You are *Lacáruna.*"

"That's what they tell me." Amy suddenly felt a bit coquettish, like a schoolgirl flirting for the first time. "I still don't know what that means exactly, other than having something to do with a prophecy that was supposed to have happened a few hundred years ago. Sorry I'm late."

The colonel pointed at the gold obelisk with the image of the seemingly changing faces in the center of the table.

"That is *Dendos.* He is the originator of the Trotéjo. He carved those symbols into this table."

Amy squinted as she looked at the image reflecting the flickering candlelight. "I see two faces." *Human faces,* she almost added.

"Your eyes do not deceive you. Before the *Morphósis* he was two and after the world expanded, he was one."

"It's similar to this." The apósto he reached into the collar of his robe and pulled out the pendant with the two faces imprinted on it.

"That is the image of *Dendos* before the *Morphósis*," the colonel said. "Ours is *Dendos* after."

"Ours, huh?" Amy smiled a tad smugly. "So you are part of—"

With uncharacteristic vigor, the normally obsequious apósto knocked Amy from the table and she fell. He took her place just in time for the dagger held by Captain Tamezo to sink into his barrel chest. Licha screamed. The captain seemed to be as surprised by the action as the apósto, but his surprise was quickly replaced by rage as he shoved the larger quimero away and yanked out the dagger. The sound of the blade pulling out of Apósto Baruti's chest was sickening. The captain turned toward where Amy lay sprawled on the marble floor. She saw the hatred in his eyes, which so surprised her that she didn't have the sense to scramble backward. Not that it mattered because, as unexpectedly as the apósto had shoved her to the floor, the captain's head fell from his shoulders. For a moment his body stood over Amy with the dagger raised in one hand, ready to plunge into her. Then it crumpled to the ground, spraying blood across her robe. When the body fell, the colonel was standing behind it. Blood dripped from the sword in his hand.

◉　◉　◉

Jandro assisted the colonel in dragging the headless corpse of Captain Tamezo into the dark outer room. The colonel carried out the severed head himself and placed it on the captain's carcass. He closed the door and returned to the others, attending to the apósto as best they could. Because there had been nothing else to use, Amy had torn off part of her robe to press against the wound in an attempt to staunch the flow of blood pouring from the apósto's chest. It was doing little good and she was now covered with blood from both the attacker and his victim. The dagger that had been meant for *Lacáruna* lay on the ground only a few feet from where the apósto had fallen. The colonel called it a stiletto when he picked it up by its short metal handle. Amy thought he would wipe the blood from it with the bottom of his tunic as he had done his sword before returning it to his scabbard, but he simply held the handle between his thumb and forefinger in the same manner he had held her driver's license. The apósto seemed to know that, unless a surgeon was waiting in the wings, nothing could be done for him. He also seemed to know the reason why the colonel shook his head when Amy demanded he send for a doctor.

Apósto Baruti's voice was ragged and his breathing labored. "He cannot."

"Why?" Amy looked up at the colonel who stood over them. She couldn't read his expression. He seemed neither concerned nor compassionate, but somehow disconnected. Rather than fault him for it, Amy wondered if he had become numb as she had after learning of the slaughter of the Carados, or maybe detachment was inevitable after lopping off someone's head.

"There are no Trotéjo physicians here," the colonel said.

"So?" Amy didn't quite comprehend his meaning. "What about a Fensoré physician?"

The colonel shook his head. Amy felt the apósto grip her arm and she looked down at his hairy face that was now nearly as white as Licha's.

"No one can know about this place," he whispered hoarsely.

Amy leaned in and wiped his brow with her fingers. "You knew what he planned to do before shoving me away. How?"

"He never gave the sign."

"What sign?"

"This one."

When Amy looked up, the colonel demonstrated what the apósto had been looking for by again placing a hand awkwardly on his hip. She hadn't realized before that it was the placement of his fingers that made it look awkward. His thumb and forefinger formed a circle with the other fingers splayed out below.

Jandro and Licha were on the opposite side of the prone apósto, both gripping the same large, hairy hand. Apósto Baruti turned his head slightly so that he could look at them. When he spoke, his spittle was tinged with blood.

"You must stay by her side always until the prophecy is fulfilled."

As they consented with a nod, the young quimerté began to weep.

Apósto Baruti rolled his head in Amy's direction. She saw the light in his eyes dimming.

"You must ..." His words faded.

"What? I must what?" She leaned her head close to his and placed her ear just over his mouth, yet could barely hear him.

"You must expand the world again."

Amy remained crouching over the apósto with her hands pressing down on his blood-soaked chest and the side of her face close to his mouth until she could no longer feel his breath on her cheek. Only then did she sit back on her heels and allow her hands to fall into her lap. Her head down, she studied the blood that coated her arms up to the elbow and realized something fundamental. Despite their odd appearances, the beings called quimerté had the same kind of blood running through their veins as she did. The insight comforted her enough that she could look at the others. Licha ran her hand gently across the apósto's face and closed his eyes while Jandro planted tender kisses on the hand he held. That they hadn't fallen completely apart after all that had happened on this day alone amazed her and she knew that was Apósto Baruti's intent. He'd given the two a purpose to fulfill and, while it wouldn't ease their grief, it would make it more bearable. At least for a while.

Keeping his grasp of the apósto's hand, Jandro's watery eyes were filled with childlike confusion as he looked up at the colonel. "Why did he do this? Wasn't he Trotéjo like you?"

The colonel stared at the dagger swinging between his finger and thumb like a pendulum. He seemed to be lost in thought even while answering Jandro. "Yes, we were tapped together."

"Then why would he want to kill Amy?"

"It seems he was something more." The colonel squatted and placed the stiletto on the apósto's chest atop the strip of Amy's blood-saturated robe. "For years there have been rumors within the Trotéjo that the Arañalianza had returned, but there was never proof." His gaze never left the weapon. "Gossip feeds on tedium and I always assumed it was idle speculation brought about by boredom. Seems I was wrong."

Amy had no idea what he was talking about. "What is ranali—"

"Arañalianza," the colonel corrected. "They are the ancient foes of the Trotéjo from before the *Morphósis*. They are said to have aligned with *La Arañota* when she battled *La Reina*."

Licha started to speak but her voice cracked and she stopped. She took a deep breath and tried again. "How do you know that the *captain*"—she all but spat out the word—"was one of them?"

"I don't. As I said, I wasn't convinced that the Arañalianza had returned or reformed. I'm still not completely convinced."

Gone was any sort of deference, as Licha coldly looked at the colonel. "So you think that what has happened here is—what—simply someone intending to kill *Lacáruna* to keep the prophecy from happening? Maybe if you hadn't been so skeptical the apósto would still be alive."

Amy worried how the colonel would respond, and she could see that Jandro worried as well. He put a hand on Licha's shoulder as if to stop her from saying more, but she shrugged it off. The colonel seemed to take her accusation in stride while he continued to stare at the dagger.

"Perhaps. And perhaps this is the evidence I've been looking for." Without elaborating, the colonel stood and straightened the sash crossing his chest. He then looked at Licha. "You are not going to like what I say next, but it has to be done and I expect you to adhere to it."

Licha said nothing. The colonel continued.

"The Carados who were taken into custody earlier today escaped their confinement. The apósto was killed while struggling with Captain Tamezo who in turn was decapitated by one of them." He looked at the three seated around the body of Apósto Baruti. "In a fury, an unknown fensoré killed the remaining three seguidosts after they were taken to a separate cell. Tomorrow morning, four bodies will be burned on a pyre, but only the apósto will be uncovered. Word will spread that the four dead Carados members were those responsible for the slaughter of their entire faction. No one will ask questions, because no one will care."

"You're going to kill us?" Jandro didn't sound afraid, only confused.

The colonel didn't bother to answer him. "The three of you will be given new identities and when I feel it is safe to do so, you will leave Winter Outpost."

Amy couldn't believe that he was just going to send them on their way. "And do what? You're the one who is supposed to help us with the prophecy."

"I am helping you. But we cannot do anything about the prophecy here."

"Helping by sending us off?"

He seemed only then to understand what she meant. "You will not be alone. I will be with you. Until then, you will have to remain hidden. I will send my personal guards to retrieve the bodies and escort you someplace safe."

"You're sure you can trust *them*?" Amy stood and faced the colonel. Blood was smeared across his cheek and into his white muttonchops.

"I have no choice." His gaze lingered on Amy before breaking away. He pointed at Jandro. "You will help me put the apósto out with the captain. Then the three of you will remain there until my guards come for you. Is that understood?"

Jandro looked at Licha and waited for her to nod. Once she did, he followed suit, as did Amy. The young quimerté stood and Jandro helped the colonel drag the apósto through the maze of candle pedestals across what had to be years of wax drippings. Licha and Amy walked ahead. Outside the circular room the colonel told them to be patient. He shut the door and left them in darkness.

The wait wasn't long, which was what Amy had hoped for. As much as she had come to like Apósto Baruti, she didn't cotton to being in the same dark room as his dead body. She refused to even think about the headless captain lying beside him. Curiously, the lantern that the captain had left outside the door was gone. Better to hide the carnage that way, she supposed. In perhaps fifteen minutes they heard footsteps on the circular stairs that led up to the hidden passage. The three huddled close, waiting for the spot of light to discover them. The colonel must have prepared his guards for what they would find because when the three fensoré in beige tunics came into the room, they wasted no time. Two of the guards were male and the other female. One of the males was the sergeant who had questioned them in their cell. While he and the other male unrolled tarps they'd brought, the female told Amy and the others to follow her. She had the same slight Mexican accent as Licha. Leaving the males to place the bodies of the captain and the apósto on the tarp, she led the others up the spiraling stairs. There was no looking back, and no one tried to.

Halfway up the stairwell stood a door that Amy had not noticed on the way down. The female fensoré opened it and stepped through. The others followed her into a constricted passageway and down to the other end where another set of spiraling stairs waited. At the top was a stone room reminiscent of the cell where they'd been confined. While the room had no windows and only bare bulbs in the high ceiling like the cell, there were no bars and it was three times as large. The defining feature of the room was at the far end where water cascaded from an opening at the top of the wall and filled a pool below. The fensoré pointed to it.

"You will bathe there."

As her eyes adjusted to the brighter light, Amy got her first good look at the fensoré and was surprised to see that she was as hairy as the apósto had been. In fact, if it weren't for her obvious bosom and the timbre of her voice, Amy would never have known that that the fensoré was female at all.

"I will return with fresh clothing and something for you to eat," the fensoré said. "But first, you must give me what you are wearing."

Jandro and Licha had no qualms about stripping off their robes. They were naked and headed for the waterfall at the other end of the room before the fensoré had finished her sentence. Feeling the prude, yet again, Amy turned around and removed what was left of her robe. She handed over the blood-smeared garment over her shoulder but told the fensoré that she was keeping her footwear. The fensoré insisted that the colonel wanted *all* the clothing, but Amy adamantly refused. Finally, the guard gave up and left. Amy crossed the floor and kicked off her running shoes before stepping into the pool. The water was refreshingly cool and, as she joined Jandro and Licha under the fall, Amy let it rinse away the day's events. Wishing that she had some of the soap they had used while bathing in the river brought a smile to her face. In her mind's eye she saw the apósto washing his exceptionally hairy body; he had seemed so content when he had left the river to lie on an outcrop to dry. Until that moment she hadn't realized how much she had depended on the large quimero and how much she was going to miss him. She was grateful for the water pouring down her face as it hid her tears from the others who had to miss Apósto Baruti much, much more.

The female fensoré returned with garments that looked to Amy like muslin pajamas. She also brought three pairs of the moccasin-like shoes similar to what the seguidosts had worn. After dressing, Amy slipped on a pair (which fit surprisingly well) but kept a tight grasp on her running shoes, which she had cleaned off in the pool. The fensoré led them from the bathing room through a side door and up another flight of stairs. The room at the top was small, but furnished with a table, three chairs, and two beds. Amy longed to sleep, but even as tired as she was, the bed would have to wait. Food had been laid out on the table. Jandro was the first to reach it and didn't wait for the others. He bit into what looked like a peach and juice dribbled down his chin.

The fensoré informed them that they were to remain in the room until further notice. When she left, Amy checked to see if the door she'd gone through had been locked. As she'd expected, it was—from the other side. Although the room was a thousand times more pleasant than where they had been jailed before, it remained a cell nonetheless.

Occupied with filling their empty stomachs, the young quimerté didn't seem to mind that they'd been imprisoned once again and Amy followed their lead. A large fruit platter sat in the center of the rectangle table and beside it a cheese plate and a loaf of brown bread. Below that was a bowl of what looked and smelled like creamed spinach. What really made Amy's mouth water, though, was a large tray filled with grilled white meat. She leaned down, took a whiff, and her stomach rumbled. With her fingers, she picked up a chunk and took a small bite. The meat was delicious. She pulled up one of the three chairs and sat at the table directly in front of the meat tray. As it had been when they'd traveled in the trinéot across the sand, they had no utensils or plates. They had no bowls of pulabaza broth, either, which delighted Amy to no end. Her jaws had longed to chew on something substantial and though she hadn't eaten red meat in years, she would have gladly have sunk her teeth into a thick steak. The white meat on the tray was nearly as satisfying. She asked what kind of meat it was.

"I think it's ..." Jandro stopped and glanced sheepishly at Licha before reaching across the table for a chunk of the meat. He quickly popped it into his mouth.

Licha admonished him. "Seguidosts don't eat meat. You know that."

With his mouth full, he answered Amy's question. "It's pomalvado meat. Pomalvados are what I was on the lookout for. Remember? Pomalvado flocks?"

Amy remembered that she had imagined them to be giant, angry quail. They didn't taste like quail, though. Despite that the meat was white, pomalvados tasted a lot like beef. That really threw off her mental image of them.

Licha adamantly refused to even look at the pomalvado meat while she sat at the table. She dined mostly on fruit, but ate a healthy portion of cheese and bread. Jandro favored the meat and the spinach. Amy ate a little of everything. They'd been supplied with a pitcher of water and a carafe containing something that Jandro said was wine, but for Amy smelled like lemonade and tasted like oranges. Her senses were having a difficult time when it came to food and drink in this world. The three ate until they were stuffed and Jandro complained that his stomach hurt. Perhaps it was the so-called wine, or that she was wearing pajamas, but Amy's eyelids grew heavy and she worried that she would fall asleep at the table. She struggled to push herself away from it to stand momentarily before she fell onto the nearest of the two beds in the room. For a brief moment she thought she should ask what the sleeping arrangements would be, but sleep seemed more important than speech. She closed her eyes.

When she woke, Amy had no sense of the time. She felt rested, though, and suspected she'd been asleep for hours. Jandro and Licha were curled up on the other bed. Jandro had his arm draped across Licha's waist as they spooned. His skin looked all the more blue-gray compared to hers. Lying on a white bed beside a white wall and wearing off-white pajamas, the two looked like a black and white photograph. Amy scanned the rest of the room and when she saw that the table had been cleared she began to panic until she sat up and saw that her running shoes were on the floor beside the moccasins she'd worn after bathing. She propped up her pillow and laid back on it.

The light bulbs on the ceiling had been dimmed, presumably by whomever had taken away the remnants of their meal, which meant the lights were controlled from outside because the interior walls lacked switches and dimmers. As she looked up at the bulbs, Amy noticed something that she hadn't before. Opposite her bed were four vertical window-like openings, each about a foot high and two feet wide just below the ceiling. The openings were too high to see through from a prone position, but standing on the bed didn't put her high enough either. She crossed the room to the table where they'd dined. The seats of the chairs were no higher than the bed, but she thought the table might be just the right height. Slowly, so as to not make noise, she dragged the table closer to the wall. When it was near enough, she climbed atop it and, standing tiptoe, craned her neck. She could just barely see out, so she gripped the window ledge and pulled herself up for a better view.

It was dark out, but she could see a large white stone building to the right as well as a courtyard directly across. Judging by windows on the opposite building, she guessed they were being held on the fourth floor. Between the two buildings the wet courtyard reflected light from streetlamps lining it. A faint clattering noise caught her attention and by anchoring her bare feet against the wall, she was able to pull herself up a bit more. In the far corner of the courtyard a hooded carriage, pulled by a team of four pájastias, came through a tall archway. The pájastias looked fairly large so she guessed them to be avestrandés, although they could also have been the hybrids that Jandro had pointed out. Sitting at the front of the carriage a single driver drove them across the wide courtyard. Light from the streetlamps and from the full moon glinted off the black surface of the carriage as it came to a stop in front of the building to the right of the window. A fensoré ran down some stairs at the front of the side building and opened the carriage door. With an outstretched hand, he assisted three quimerté down from the carriage. Despite the full moon and the streetlamps Amy couldn't get a good look at the quimerté because they wore cloaks with hoods covering their heads. Two of the cloaks were a dull taupe but one had a dark green sheen. The cloaked quimerté followed the fensoré into the building. The driver then flicked the reins and drove the pájastias around the courtyard and back through the archway.

"What are you doing?"

Startled, Amy lost her grip and fell to the table. Fortunately, she was able to land on her feet and she turned around to see Jandro looking up at her.

"Good heavens, Jandro. You shouldn't sneak up on someone like that."

"Sorry. When I woke up, I saw you climbing up the wall. I thought you were trying to escape." He helped her down just as the fensoré unloading the carriage passengers had done.

"There will be no escaping through that." Amy pointed at the opening above. "We're much too high up. I was only looking out the window."

Jandro nodded. "What did you see?"

"Not much."

"Maybe you should wait until the sun comes up."

If he hadn't been a teenager, she would have snapped at him. He excelled at stating the obvious. "Help me move the table back."

They had just managed to return the table to its original position when the door to the room opened. Amy felt her pulse quicken when three hooded figures entered. From the color of their cloaks alone it was clear to her that they were the carriage passengers. The figure wearing the green cloak threw back the hood and revealed the hairy, female fensoré that the colonel had said was a personal guard. Amy relaxed.

"Come with us," the guard said.

Licha must have heard the door open because she was up and scurrying across the floor to stand with them as they watched the other two figures remove their cloaks as well. The sergeant and the other male, who had taken care of the bodies of Captain Tamezo and Apósto Baruti, gave over the taupe cloaks to Licha and Jandro. The female handed Amy the green cloak and told her to put it on. Everyone was told to keep the hoods up.

"If we encounter anyone as we move through the halls, they may bow." The female guard led the way out of the room. "If so, only you will acknowledge them with a slight nod of the head. I doubt there will be many about because it is so early."

"My shoes!" Amy started to turn back, but the female fensoré stopped her.

"They will be safe. I promise you."

Feeling foolish for worrying about a pair of running shoes when her life was in danger Amy continued down the hall. Fortunately, the cloak she wore was long enough to cover her bare feet because she'd forgotten to put on her moccasins. The cloak's hood hampered her vision even more than the robe hood had because it had no structure and hung limply over her face. She managed to keep from stumbling over anything, however, including the fensoré ahead of her. As it had been with every instance of traveling through what had to be a sizeable building, they went down several hallways, turning left and right, and up an equal number of stairs. When they came to a stop, the fensoré told them they could remove their hoods.

Amy was surprised to discover that she and the seguidosts had been brought to a lavishly appointed sitting room, larger than the room they had left and infinitely more extravagant. Ornate wooden furniture covered the floor and intricately designed tapestries and gilded mirrors the walls. On a long credenza against the wall, clothing had been laid out.

The female fensoré looked at Amy, as she pointed at the credenza. "You are to dress in those." She crossed the room to one of the velvet sofas where more clothing lay. "These are for the other two." She returned with what looked like a cyan-colored turban, which she handed it to Licha. "You will have to wear that until your hair grows out. Only seguidosts shave their heads and you are no longer one of them."

Licha glumly accepted the turban, but she didn't put it on.

The hairy female joined the other two fensoré at the door. "Get dressed and Colonel Sangcertigre will come for you shortly."

The fensoré left the room. Amy checked the door and found it locked from the other side. This was going to have to stop. If there were no way out of the room they were as vulnerable as they'd been in the cell. She looked around the room for something she could use to defend herself should it come to that.

"Sangcertigre." Jandro said the name with a hint of reverence.

After deciding that her only option would be to break a leg off of one of the chairs, Amy turned her attention to the clothing left for her. She picked up what she at first thought was a dress but seemed turned out to be a Bolero-style, long-sleeve jacket with a bustle-like tail. "Do you know the name?"

"Only that it means he has Primeróte blood." Jandro had already removed his muslin pajamas and was standing naked with no attempt at modesty.

Amy held up the dark green jacket in front of her face so she wouldn't have to look at him. "You can tell that by his name?"

"Surnames of all of those who are direct descendants begin with *Sang*," Licha explained, as she too disrobed. "Those who are of mixed descent end with *ezo*, like the apósto. Quimerté with no relation to the Primeróte end with *ode*, like Jandro and me."

"I thought Baruti was the apósto's surname."

"No, that was his given name. You don't remember when he introduced us to you in the tent?"

Amy shook her head. "I don't remember much about being in the tent, except there was an odd smell."

"That was—"

"His last name was Tigrezo." Licha wrapped a long, blue skirt around her waist.

"So, he was a mixed descendant?"

"Yes," the still naked Jandro said. "From the same line as the colonel probably, since they share part of a name."

Amy found it interesting that the quimerté would continue to be so concerned with their founders that they would denote who had their blood and who didn't. Keeping track of a family tree over three thousand years had to be an arduous task.

Along with the dark green jacket with the bustle was a black short-sleeved top, a pair of black stirrup pants, black knee-high boots, and a gold bustier. She glanced at Licha who had finished dressing and was adjusting her short-sleeved top that matched the color of the turban she'd yet to try on. Jandro had managed to dress in a shirt and didn't seem all that anxious to put on anything more as he admired one of the tapestries on the wall.

"Licha, might you give me a hand?" Amy asked.

"Of course." Licha stepped into a pair of black shoes that looked more like ballet slippers than moccasins and crossed the room to stand at Amy's side.

Amy held up the bustier. "Did you get one of these?"

"No."

"So you're not wearing anything underneath?"

Licha shook her head.

Amy lowered her voice. "How do you handle your periods?"

"My what?"

Amy lowered her voice even more. "Your monthly flows. Your menstrual cycle."

"Oh that. We have special garments for it. Are you in need of one?"

Although it couldn't be far off, Amy shook her head. "I was only curious because I see that you never wear any under ... things."

"Except for when the monthlies are needed, seguidosts never wear anything under their robes." Licha looked over at Jandro who was finally putting on his trousers. "We weren't given any so maybe it's only the ocático who wear them."

"Ocático?"

Licha thought for a moment. "Someone higher, someone like the colonel, but not because he's a colonel. Someone with Sang at the beginning of their name, but others too sometimes."

"You mean nobility?" Licha didn't seem to understand, so Amy tried again. "Um, upper class? High society?"

Licha nodded.

"What makes you think that this would belong to the ocático?" Amy looked at the bustier.

Uninterested in the bustier, Licha picked up the dark green jacket and turned it around. "This." She pointed to the bustle-like piece at the back. "This is what ocático quimera wear in Primerabrigo. We see them traveling Trade Road in route here quite often."

"I see." Amy examined the bustle's construction. It didn't seem to have any ribs within it, only fabric and something that felt like a pillow. "I wonder why they want me to wear this? I would think that looking like ocático would draw attention."

"I don't know, but I can help you dress if you'd like."

Amy looked over at Jandro who was putting on the same kind of shoes that Licha wore. "I think I can handle it myself. Why don't you keep Jandro occupied."

Licha grinned knowingly. "Of course." She left Amy to undress. When she stood in front of Jandro, she turned him so that he was facing the opposite direction and unhurriedly buttoned his cyan-colored long-sleeve shirt.

The gold bustier proved to be easier to put on than Amy had guessed. The knee-high boots had been difficult to get into until she found a pair of thin stockings that had fallen beside the credenza. Once they were on, she had no trouble pulling on the boots. After fastening the long gold chain that connected the jacket's facings, Amy stood in front of the mirror next to the cold fireplace and thought she cut an interesting figure, if she did say so herself. The way that the cropped jacket flared out in the back was reminiscent of open-faced dresses popular in the 1950s that were most often worn with capri pants. She sighed. Her capris, tank top, and presumably her panties, were now ashes somewhere on the edge of Esterenas. At least she still had her running shoes. The boots were almost as comfortable as her shoes, although they would take some getting used to. She turned to the side so that she could see the bustle part of the jacket. The bustle didn't stick out as far as some bustles she had seen in historical movies—nor was it very long as it came only to the back of her knees—but it stuck out enough that she wondered why anyone would find the look attractive. She thought it looked as if she had a sofa cushion stuck to her bottom.

Without any warning the door to the sitting room flew open, startling everyone as it banged against the interior wall. Amy whirled around just as the colonel stepped into the room and closed the door behind him. He was dressed in his purple tunic and thigh high boots, as he had been when she'd seen him last, but there was no blood on his clothing and he no longer wore the scabbard or the sash. His long golden hair was pulled back, making his white muttonchops stand out all the more. When he saw her, a smile spread across his face, stretching out the stripes on his cheeks.

"Good morning, cousin," he said with his odd, but unmistakable British accent. He bowed deeply and with flourish.

"Cousin?"

"Yes." The colonel stood. "You and your iado arrived from Navercío only an hour or two ago."

Amy looked to Licha, who had put on the turban when the colonel entered, for a translation of what the quimero had said.

"Iado are servants. Navercío is the capital of Primerabrigo."

Colonel Sangcertigre nodded. "Where my relations reside."

"I take it that you don't have any family members here."

As he strode across the room the colonel looked her over with a critical eye. "None. I'm the only firstborn of my extended family at Winter Outpost."

"Is that who I'm supposed to be? A firstborn?"

The colonel laughed as he circled her. "No. Firstborns do not arrive in Pliada in a carriage. Even ocático have to walk."

Out of the corner of her eye, Amy saw Jandro nodding in agreement.

"So what is your cousin doing here?" Amy faced the mirror again and the colonel stopped just behind her. Only the obvious number of legs, arms, and eyes could possibly link them as being part of the same family. She wondered what he had planned.

"She's come to inform me that I am needed at home and must take temporary leave of my post."

"She has?"

"That is what she is telling me right now." The colonel's

demeanor was considerably different from what it had been down in the candlelit room. He almost seemed happy.

"How will you respond?"

"I will go. Family is vital to the Sangcertigre." His smile faded when he met her eyes in the mirror and he spoke softly. "It's the only way I can keep you safe. I have to get you out of Pliada."

Jandro suddenly came forward. "But she has to fulfill—" He stopped and dropped his head submissively when the colonel looked at him. "Forgive me, señor."

The colonel shook his head. "You must stop speaking and acting like a seguidost. Is that understood?"

Though he kept his head down, Jandro looked up. "Yes … Colonel."

"I understand that she has to fulfill the prophecy, which is why we must get her out of Pliada quickly. Until we know more about the forces trying to stop her, *Lacáruna* must be kept hidden."

Amy turned so she could face the colonel. "I have a name, you know. It's Amy. Please don't call me *Lacáruna*."

"Of course not, cousin. And you must call me Dack."

"Sure thing, cousin." Amy smiled. "Cousin Dack."

"Dack is sufficient." He stepped back and looked her over once more. "I'm glad to see that everything fit. Siphiwe is adept at judging sizes, it seems."

"Who is Siphiwe?"

"One of my personal guards. The quimera who has been assisting you."

"Oh." Amy looked down at her outfit. "Tell her that she did a good job. The trousers are a little tight, but everything else fits well."

"The trousers are supposed to be tight." The colonel looked at the other two in the room and pointed at Jandro. "She'll have to get you another shirt. That one is much too big."

Amy thought the shirt fit well enough and wondered why he would need another. Jandro seemed to be a bit confused, as well, but said nothing.

The colonel dug a hand into his trouser pocket and pulled out a small jar that he handed to Amy. "You need to cover your exposed skin with that."

"What is it?" She took it from him. "Sun block?"

"I don't know what that is. What's in the jar is a cream that will tint your skin a more suitable color."

Amy looked at the back of her hand. "What's wrong with the color of my skin?"

"Nothing, except that no one in my immediate family has it. Since you have no other markings, you need to tint your skin appropriately."

When she opened the small jar, she expected to see a tawny-colored cream that was close to the colonel's skin color, but it wasn't what she found at all. "This is pink."

"And it will look nicely on you, I think." The colonel turned and headed for the door. "Put that on and when Siphiwe returns with a proper shirt for the quimero, we will break the fast together in my dining hall."

"Wait."

Colonel Sangcertigre stopped and turned to her.

"Don't lock that door again. We're not going anywhere. If you want us to trust you, then you must trust us."

The colonel nodded and without further ado, he left.

⊙   ⊙   ⊙

The pinkness of her skin was subtle. When Amy had rubbed the cream onto the back of her hand to test it, she'd been afraid that it would leave her looking raw but, once the cream had time to sink in, it looked more like she was blushing slightly—*everywhere*. To be sure that she didn't inadvertently expose her normal skin color, she'd taken off her clothing except for the bustier. Licha assisted her in covering the parts of her body that she couldn't reach. As the young quimera rubbed the cream on her back, Amy mentioned the similarity in accents between Siphiwe and her.

"That's because she is Pliadalé. We all sound like that. I don't really hear it myself. It's everyone else who has accents."

"So that explains why the sergeant said I didn't sound like I was from Pliada when he questioned me."

Jandro was sitting nearby unabashedly watching what Licha was doing. "You sound like me. Like you came from Maseprada." He looked away as sadness fell across his face. "Like me and Apósto Baruti."

Before Amy could question them about the colonel's accent the female fensoré named Siphiwe returned with Jandro's new shirt. While the colonel had said Jandro's shirt was too big, Amy (and mostly likely Jandro as well) had assumed he meant it was too long or the collar was too wide. Apparently, however, he had been precise in his choice of words. The shirt Siphiwe brought was no bigger than the cropped jacket Amy wore, minus the bustle. Its sleeves came down just past the elbow and the bottom of the shirt fell just below the ribcage, leaving a broad band of blue-gray skin above Jandro's belt. He didn't find it nearly as funny as did Licha, though. Amy thought he looked kind of cute.

"This is a quimerito's shirt," he said. "Someone has made a mistake."

"I don't think so." Licha adjusted the collar. "The shirt fits well in the shoulders."

"I don't like it." Jandro tugged on the shirt as if he could stretch it out over his stomach.

"I'm surprised at you, Jandro." Amy grinned. "You certainly

didn't seem to mind showing some skin when you took your time getting dressed."

"That's not the same. This is just silly looking. I've never seen anyone, quimero or quimera, wearing this."

Licha suggested it must be how the iado in Navercío dress.

Whatever humble qualities Jandro had learned from the Carados were currently nowhere to be found. "Why do we have to be iado, anyway?"

"Obviously, the colonel couldn't say that all three of us were family members. This way he can keep *Laca* ..." Licha stopped and glanced apologetically at Amy. "I mean, this way he can keep Amy close to him and close to us at the same time." She turned to the mirror, took off her turban, and rubbed her bald head. "I don't like how I'm dressed any more than you do. I no longer recognize myself."

"Tell me about it," Amy muttered.

Jandro seemed to forget his grievances. As he took Licha by the shoulders and spun her around, he looked into her eyes. "You're still Carados." He took the turban from her and placed it on her head, tugging it into place. "No one, not even the Fensoré can take that from you."

Licha smiled as she held his face in her hands. "Thank you, Jandro. You'll make a fine apósto someday."

Before Siphiwe escorted them to the colonel's dining hall Amy took one last look in the mirror and like Licha, she could hardly recognize herself. Unlike Licha, she liked it. As she followed Siphiwe out with Licha and Jandro behind, her stomach unexpectedly knotted with nerves. Until she'd stepped out of the sitting room she hadn't considered how sheltering the robe and cloak hoods had been. They had afforded her a small semblance of safety as they shielded not only her face from view but also her eyes from the unfamiliar and, until very recently, hostile surroundings. Nothing impeded her vision now, nothing to retreat into, and she fought to keep her nervousness at bay.

Although she had seen little of her environment when they'd gone through the labyrinth of hallways and stairwells, Amy had seen enough to recognize that she was in a more lavish section of the building. The stone floors had been replaced with marble and the stark stone walls had been plastered and were decorated with large medallions embossed with a shield and two crossed swords. Stationed between the medallions on alternating sides of the hallway were more Fensoré guards, each holding at their sides a staff tipped with a silver spike. On their heads each wore a metallic helmet oddly reminiscent of the nipple on a baby bottle. Amy did her best not to stare, although she easily could have done so with impunity because each guard focused on the medallion that hung on the wall opposite them. She noted that most of the guards looked like Siphiwe and were covered with hair. Some had black hair like Siphiwe's, while others had blond hair, or red hair, or all shades of brown. She felt as if she were walking down a hall staffed with werewolves from different parts of the globe.

Rather than bare bulbs on the ceiling, light came from the electric sconces on the wall in the shapes of large flames. The sconces were lit, but were hardly needed; every ten or so feet were tall multi-paned windows. Siphiwe escorted them through double arches into a long, narrow room with a vaulted ceiling. Wooden pew-like benches lined the walls and above them hung more tapestries. Rather than the decorative, patterned tapestries like those that had covered the walls in the sitting room, these tapestries portrayed various events including battle scenes that wouldn't have been out of place in a medieval castle—if not for the armored pájastias the armored warriors rode. Hanging at the farthest end of the hall was a dark bronze medallion three times as large as those that had lined the hallway with a more ornate silver shield crossed with two gold swords. Around its circumference were the indecipherable symbols that seemed to be the written language of this world. Directly below the medallion was a long table that stretched nearly the entire the width of the room. Sitting at the head, on the left end, was Colonel Sangcertigre and next to him on the side closest to the wall were three other fensorés, wearing dark brown tunics. All four stood when Siphiwe approached with her charges.

The colonel raised a hand, gesturing to Amy. "Allow me to introduce my first cousin, Señora Sangcertigre."

Unsure of whether to bow or curtsey, Amy did neither, choosing to simply nod her head.

"To my left," the colonel said, "are Captain Cebrode, Captain Osezo, and Captain Zorrode."

Living with her stepmother for several years had one advantage: Amy was able to mimic Alice's British accent with ease when she addressed the captains. "A pleasure to meet you." She noted that the colonel seemed a bit surprised by her feigned accent.

When she looked at those with him she was once again confronted with the startling awareness that she was in another world. Captain Osezo was an older quimera with the flattest pug nose Amy had ever seen. She had brown skin, long curly silver hair, and large wide-spaced brown eyes. Captain Zorrode was the least odd-looking one of the bunch, except of course for his calico skin that made him look like he'd been pieced together from a few different sources. And until she met Captain Cebrode, she had never quite understood the term, *horse-faced*. He was the darkest quimerté at the table, almost the color of milk chocolate. His eyes were green and were a pleasant diversion from his long face.

The colonel gestured to the seat to his right. "Please sit." He looked at Jandro and Licha. "Your iados are welcome to break fast as well."

"Thank you." Amy was relieved. She'd worried that they would be taken someplace else and didn't want to be separated from them. The two were seated several chairs away toward the center of the table where it was obvious that they weren't part of the honored guests.

When Amy sat, the others followed. In front of every chair, including those unoccupied, was a silver plate, two silver goblets (one empty and one filled with water), a silver knife, and fork. More than anything, Amy was delighted to see the utensils; she never felt sanitary enough when eating with her hands. The sergeant and the other male fensoré that had been with them from time to time entered through a side door carrying trays of food and a silver carafe that they placed at the head of the table in front of the colonel. More fruits and vegetables and cheeses and bread. Amy was hoping for another plate of the pomalvado meat but there didn't seem to be any. There was, however, something that looked like huge brown hard-boiled eggs. The colonel was first to fill his plate and he began with one of the giant eggs that were large enough to have spanned his hand from fingertip to heel. Using a set of tongs, he offered one to Amy and she accepted it. She also accepted a bit of cheese, some fruit, and a slice of brown bread. Once the colonel, the captains, and she had taken what they wanted, the trays were brought to where Jandro and Licha sat. Jandro seemed to be excited about the eggs. Licha only ate fruit and cheese.

"Colonel Sangcertigre told us you were raised in Maseprada and only recently returned to Primerabrigo," the horse-faced captain said. "I'm surprised you still sound very much like a Primerabrigite."

Amy kept her gaze on Captain Cebrode. "Oh, well I've been back long enough to acquire it again."

"Again?" the female captain asked.

Colonel Sangcertigre picked up the silver carafe that had been placed on the table. "My cousin was born in Primerabrigo. She and her family moved away when she was young, but not so young that she hadn't yet learned to speak." He turned to Amy and filled her empty goblet with what was in the carafe and placed it on the table.

"I've informed my captains of your request. Unfortunately, I won't be able to leave for a day or two. I need to attend to the consequences of an incident that occurred yesterday when one of my captains was ferociously butchered by rogue seguidosts."

The clattering of a dropped goblet echoed through the hall and he looked down the table where Jandro was using his napkin to sop water from in front of Licha, who made no attempt to right the goblet she had knocked over.

Returning his attention to those nearest him, the colonel continued. "Actually, we don't think they were authentic members of the Carados and were, in fact, imposters."

"It's entirely unheard of." Captain Osezo shook her head. She sounded as if she hailed from the Southern United States. "Who would want to impersonate seguidosts?"

"How else do you explain their actions?" Captain Zorrode had the same British-sounding accent as the colonel. "For seguidosts to slaughter their kin…" He shook his head. "And what they did to Captain Tamezo, is even more unheard of."

Amy didn't dare look down the table and draw attention to Licha and Jandro, whom she was sure would give themselves away. "I don't understand. What happened?"

The colonel explained what she already knew, although the captains didn't realize it, about the massacre of a Carados camp and how three seguidosts and an apósto had been taken into custody. While being interrogated, the seguidosts had overpowered Captain Tamezo and brutally murdered him, but not before he had impaled the apósto on his knife.

"The tragedy, besides the captain's death of course, is that we'll never know who the false Carados really were because the remaining three committed ritual suicide while being held in custody."

That was something new. "They did? How?" When the colonel looked at her Amy realized too late she really shouldn't ask questions.

"It's too gruesome to discuss while eating." The colonel filled his goblet and passed along the silver carafe.

"And nothing was learned of who they were while they were in custody?" Captain Cebrode, who had to be Pliadalé because he had Licha's accent, asked.

The colonel shook his head. "If there was information gained, Captain Tamezo took it to his grave. That is why I called for the three of you. I must go to Primerabrigo and this cannot wait until my return. You will have to run the investigation in my stead. I want you to start by learning what happened at that Carados camp and perhaps that will lead us to uncover the imposters' identities. I will send a mensáneo to the major general to inform him of my plans and that the three of you are to be left to the orders I have given you."

The captains nodded.

"Very good, Colonel." Captain Cebrode spoke for all of them. "We will have answers by the time you return."

"I'm certain you will. Enough business." Colonel Sangcertigre picked up his knife and sliced into the giant brown egg. "Let's enjoy our meal before the procession begins and we must be solemn."

When the colonel's knife easily sliced through what she'd assumed was a shell Amy wondered if it was an egg at all until a portion fell away and she saw the cooked yellow yolk inside. The colonel folded the piece he'd sliced off, stabbed it with his fork, and put it in his mouth. He smiled as he ate it. A believer in trying anything once, Amy cut a small piece from the egg and tentatively tasted it. A bit on the rubbery side, the egg had a smoky flavor while the yolk had a hint of cinnamon. Though one of the oddest tasting combinations she'd had so far, it was one that she liked very much. So did everyone else, including Jandro, apparently, because in no time the eggs vanished from all plates.

The colonel kept the conversation going throughout the meal, twice steering it to safer pastures, when one of the captains asked Amy about Primerabrigo. He saved her from the awkwardness of having to talk about a place she'd never been or seen, but when Captain Zorrode asked Amy how she and the colonel had gotten along as youngsters, the colonel's mouth was full and Amy was compelled to answer.

"As well as can be expected from cousins of the opposite sex. I teased cousin Deck—" The instant she said the name Amy realized she'd made a mistake. The colonel didn't look at her, but the other three did, each with a quizzical expression. "That was my nickname for him when we were young—Deck." She placed a hand on his forearm and looked at him with as much fondness as she could muster. "I won't embarrass Dack by telling you why I called him that. Some things should remain private, I believe."

Captain Osezo smiled. "We all have our secrets."

Captain Zorrode's mottled coloring gave the illusion that his left eye was larger than his right and Amy found herself looking from one eye to the other as she spoke with him. "What about you, Captain? Where are you from?" Again, she realized she'd made a mistake; she should have known where he was from by his accent alone. "I mean, of course, what part of Primerabrigo are you from."

"I grew up in the southeastern portion of the Lagosla Region."

As badly as she wanted to look at the colonel for explanation, she knew that it was inadvisable. "Really? What was the name of the town?"

Finished swallowing, the colonel cut in before the captain could answer. "My cousin enjoys travel. With the exception of the Lagosla Region. She thinks it's too swampy. Of course what that really means is that she hates to get her boots wet."

The captains laughed appreciatively, especially Captain Zorrode.

"Indeed," he said. "I'm sure I wasn't the only firstborn from Lagosla who was delighted to leave it."

Amy took a sip of the liquid the colonel had poured for her. She didn't care for the taste and quickly exchanged it for the goblet filled with water. The colonel was finished eating and the moment he tossed his napkin onto his plate, his guards were there to clear the table. Amy hadn't finished her egg, but she dropped her folded napkin onto her plate and nodded that it should be taken away. Before the table was entirely cleared, the colonel stood and everyone, including Licha and Jandro, followed his lead.

"I'm going to give my cousin a tour of the outpost before the procession begins. If you'll excuse us, captains, I will join you later."

The three captains nodded and came around the table. Each expressed his or her pleasure at meeting the colonel's cousin before leaving the long hall through the double arches at the front. The colonel waited until they were out of sight before calling over the seguidosts. Standing in front of the imposing colonel, the young quimerté looked like children expecting to be chastised. In that, they weren't disappointed. The colonel's eyes narrowed and his brow furrowed.

"If you are bloody well incapable of hiding your affiliation to the Carados, then I will have one of my personal guards escort you a safe distance from the outpost and return to you your robes. You may join another faction or do whatever it is you wish. I don't care what happens to you. If you choose to stay, however, then there will be no more gasping, no more knocking over goblets, no more exchanged looks every time Carados is mentioned. Is that understood?"

The two nodded.

"So which will it be? Do you wish to stay or go?"

Simultaneously they both said, "Stay."

"Splendid. Then you must rid yourselves of your past. You must behave as do most quimerté and not give the Carados any acknowledgement whatsoever. Do not forget, they are the lowest of the low especially outside Pliada. Is that clear?"

They nodded again, but when Licha looked down, the colonel lifted her chin with a finger. "I'm speaking to you in particular. If you find yourself incapable of truly masking your emotions, then you must leave; otherwise you put *Lacáruna* in great danger."

Licha kept her eyes locked with his. "I understand. I will do as you ask."

Colonel Sangcertigre took his hand away. "I'm not the one who asked you to do this. Your apósto did. I will, however, add this coda to what he said: If I catch either of you responding to anything that has to do with the Carados with something other than disdain, I will kill you myself."

Hearing this, Amy stepped between the colonel and the seguidosts. "Hold on. There's no need for—"

Gently, the colonel pushed her aside. "They understand why I would do it." He looked at the shorter two. "This is your last chance to leave under your own volition. Do you take it?"

Squaring her shoulders, Licha looked up at the colonel defiantly. "We said we wish to stay."

"I assumed you would. Just keep my warning in mind."

When the colonel turned to go, Amy looked at the companions that had been with her from the beginning. She wanted to apologize for the colonel's harsh words, yet she understood that he had said what needed saying. With nothing to add, she turned and pursued the colonel. Jandro and Licha followed.

Colonel Sangcertigre offered to have one of his radamia saddled for her, but Amy quickly declined, preferring to ride in one of the Fensoré vehicles. The stable guard brought out an open buggy that was little more than a driver's box with a backward-facing bench for passengers, pulled by a single large radamia. Amy sat next to the colonel in the front while Licha and Jandro sat in the back. She'd noted a difference in how Licha carried herself since the talk with the colonel and was surprised to see such a quick change in the quimera, who kept her head high and no longer avoided eye contact. Licha's face remained expressionless, however, in contrast to Jandro who looked like a youngster in a candy store, big eyes and mouth slightly agape while the buggy crossed the cobblestones.

"You handled yourself well in there," the colonel said quietly. "Had I known you had the ability to mimic accents—not many quimerté do—I wouldn't have told them you were Masepradan, but I suggest you ask fewer questions when we're around others."

As they moved through the arch on the western side of the courtyard the colonel raised his voice while he explained the edifice that had been both Amy's prison and sanctuary was the Fensoré garrison. Even larger than Amy had guessed it to be, the garrison was a fortified city within a fortified city. The walls surrounding the vast stronghold were made of stone, rather than timber as was the wall surrounding the entire outpost. Although only a quarter as tall as the wooden partition, the garrison walls were topped with perforated parapets. Spear-wielding guards wearing the nipple helmets patrolled the battlements. Spaced evenly along the wall were defensive towers with embrasures, slits with the business end of what had to be a cannon sticking through them. The colonel explained that the garrison was the original Winter Outpost.

"How long has it been here?"

"More than eight hundred years. There have been many outposts in Pliada since the time of the *Morphósis*, three thousand years ago. Most of them have either fallen into ruin like Naclaquí or were destroyed in one of the hundreds of wars that have taken place in this nation."

The buggy passed through several smaller courtyards within the garrison, leaving Amy confused as to which one she had seen through the window early that morning. "All the wars have taken place in Pliada?"

"Not all, but most."

"Why is that?"

"It is what was agreed upon shortly after the *Morphósis*. In exchange for protecting each nation from the other, Pliada controls the commerce between them. Periodically, one of the nations will try to take that control for themselves and they will send in their military. The first major battle was the War of 333 when Pliada was nearly lost. After it, a congress was formed in which it was mandated that every family would send their firstborn to serve the Fensoré. The ocático, including those belonging to the ruling families, were not exempt. After the decree was implemented, no nation was so anxious to go to war against some of their own.

"Of course that didn't end all the wars, but it cut them down considerably. Most skirmishes these days are with the tribes in the Outer Belt." Despite that no one could hear them over the rattling of the buggy, he lowered his voice. "Some within our ranks have whispered that has to do with the return of Arañalianza."

"You think that the Arañalianza come from these … tribes?" She recalled the topless quimera they'd come across on their way to Winter Outpost. Could she have been Arañalianza? Was there a way to tell, as there was with the Trotéjo?

"They come from somewhere," the colonel said. "After all, there wasn't anything in the prophecy about *them* dropping into the world."

Amy held onto the seat to keep from bouncing off. "What can you tell me about prophecy? The apósto wasn't particularly clear about that."

"Because the Carados don't know. They've never read it."

"Yes, I know. Have you?"

"No."

That didn't surprise her at all. Disappoint, yes, but not surprise.

"But I hope to when we reach Navercío, the capital of Primerabrigo."

"Is that where it's kept?"

"It's where the first three of the Extiguos are kept. We believe the prophecy was sent to Primerabrigo along with them." He pulled on the reins to slow the radamia. "I want to get to them before anyone else realizes you are here."

Before it passed through the garrison gates, the buggy was joined by six radamia-riding fensorés to escort it into the outpost. If not for the escorts they might have escaped attention, but the moment they left the garrison, every quimerté they passed stopped to stare.

The colonel explained that the populace wasn't used to seeing him driving a buggy. "Neither are they used to seeing a quimera at my side."

Amy laughed half-heartedly. "The gossip mill will be grinding overtime tonight, I imagine." The colonel's explanation as to why everyone was looking at them was surely meant to put her at ease but only added to her apprehension. Not only had he just reminded her that *Lacáruna* was in serious danger, his early insistence that she add a pink hue to her coloring now had her worried that it wasn't enough to hide that she was an interloper. Certain that any one of the quimerté standing on the brick sidewalks or moving along the cobblestone streets could see that she wasn't one of them, she longed for a hat with a veil.

After passing through a short tunnel cut into the center of a large building, the colonel slowed the radamia. Without knowing the precise layout of the outpost, Amy didn't try to venture a guess as to where they were in relation to where they'd originated; although, recalling the stench they had passed through on their way to the garrison, she knew wherever they were it had to be far from the outpost gate. While the garrison had smelled faintly of dust and dung, the area beyond the tunnel smelled delightfully of palm dates.

Colonel Sangcertigre pulled on the reins, stopping the buggy. "This is the Primerabrigo Plaza, home to the Primerabrigo Trading Guild."

The expansive plaza was awash with activity. Quimerté rushed about loading and unloading large flatbed carts filled with a sundry of crates, sacks, bales and miscellaneous containers. Most of the buildings surrounding the plaza were of considerable size and looked to be warehouses rather than residences, but the shingles hanging over the entrances of some smaller buildings seemed to indicate a few shops as well. While the writing on the shingles was incomprehensible to her, Amy recognized many symbols such as an ear of corn and what was unmistakably a steaming bowl. Quimerté of all shapes, sizes, and hues hurried in and out of shops and warehouses taking care of business. Most were dressed in simple, unadorned clothing in muted colors, but many quimeras wore bustles similar to the one attached to Amy's jacket. Several quimeros wore variations of the cropped shirt that Jandro found so objectionable. Sadly, few had his taut stomach, and their tops began to resemble brassieres as shirts rode up over rounded bellies. From what Amy could surmise, the cropped shirt-clad quimero were in charge of loading and unloading the flatbed wagons and seemed to be assigned to or associated with either a bustle-wearing quimera or a quimero wearing a jacket that was as short in the front as the cropped shirts but tapered to a long coattail in the back. When she inquired, the colonel explained that the latter were either ocático or fellows of the Primerabrigo Trading Guild monitoring transactions.

"I take it you don't get many tourists," Amy said.

"Unless you're interested in pomalvado hunting in the Límitotas there is really no reason for anyone but merchants and Guild fellows to come to Winter Outpost."

"Do the people ..." Amy stopped and corrected herself. "Do the *quimerté* traveling from one nation to another come through here?"

The colonel shook his head. "No, we're far too north for anyone other than Masepradans."

"If you're so far north, why use this outpost as the trade center? A more centralized outpost would make more sense."

The colonel dipped his head in appreciation of her observation. "You are right, of course. At one time the trade outpost was in a central location in the Ocaflu along a trade road that no longer exists."

"Why was it moved?"

"As punishment." The colonel adjusted one of the gloves he'd put on back at the garrison. "Seven hundred years ago, Primerabrigo and Rescatazo—that is the nation to the west—banded together and brought their military might into Pliada to wrest control. Like every prior attempt to overthrow the Fensoré, they were defeated, but not before causing many fatalities and much destruction. In the distant past, those who fought against the Fensoré would have been put to death, but the major general at the time decided that a better tactic would be to punish the trading guilds. He decreed that the trading outpost would be moved so far from the defeated nations that it would be impossible for their armies to march into Pliada without notice."

She guessed the tactic went beyond invader detection. "And by punishing the trading guild you hit the nations in their pocketbooks, helping to ensure that it wouldn't happen again."

"Pocketbooks?" The colonel was clearly confused by the word.

"Their coffers," Amy explained.

Colonel Sangcertigre nodded. "Indeed. That is why, for the most part, only merchants and the trading guilds travel Trade Road. Not only is it out of the way, Trade Road passes through the Outer Belt, which can be dangerous. Nearly all quimerté not engaged in commerce choose to travel Chorgo River; it spans from the western mountains to the eastern sea."

Amy turned so that she could address Jandro where he sat at the back of the buggy. He and Licha were silently watching the crowded plaza. She tapped him on the shoulder "Jandro, did you have to pass through the Outer Belt when you were sent to Pliada?"

"Of course. There is no other way to get here except through the

Outer Belt. It runs along all of Pliada."

Turning back to the colonel, Amy asked him why, if the Outer Belt is too dangerous for miscellaneous travelers, are the firstborn sent through it on foot.

The colonel flicked the reins and the radamia began to pull the buggy slowly through the plaza. "That is the way it has always been. Seldom has any firstborn come to harm; to do so is considered an extreme transgression that would bring penalty not only on the quimerté who committed the crime, but also on their tribe or family. Sending a firstborn into Pliada is considered an honor and we take it very seriously. Also, the firstborns travel Trade Road, which is heavily patrolled by the Fensoré. Only when a firstborn strays from the road is there trouble."

Amy could smell dates more strongly as they moved farther into the plaza. "Why would they want to stray from the road?"

"Adventure, it seems. Some seek out the Isolationist Tribes, some just want to do a little exploring on their own before their induction is finalized."

Amy glanced over her shoulder again. "But not every firstborn becomes Fensoré."

"No. A few are deranged enough to join the Carados."

Surprised that he would say such a thing, Amy scoffed. "Yet you belong to a secret society that has a connection with—"

"Never speak of that out in the open," the colonel quickly cut her off. "Never speak of it in closed quarters, either, unless you are certain not to be overheard."

The smell of dates became the strongest when they passed a storefront displaying a shingle embossed with a palm tree. Amy pointed at it to draw the colonel's attention.

"What is that?"

"It's part of a date depot. Dates are one of Primerabrigo's largest exports."

"I love dates." Amy began to salivate from the smell alone. "May we go inside?"

The colonel seemed to weigh his choices before deciding to pull the buggy to a stop. He signaled to the escorts, as he stepped down, and offered his hand to Amy. She took it and climbed off the driver's box. Jandro hopped down from the bench in the back.

"What are we doing?"

"My cousin has a fondness for dates, it seems," the colonel said.

He offered Amy the crook of his arm. She hadn't been on the receiving end of such an act of chivalry since before she was married. The lack of gallantry wasn't the fault of her ex-husband or those before and after him, though. More than once she'd bristled at the idea of not being able to open her own door or walk down the street without clinging onto a man, and she'd always made sure the men in her life were aware of that. Yet something about how the colonel held out his arm was different, something beyond his exotic looks. His offer seemed not to come from a desire to shelter her but rather to be at her side. She took his arm and, as they walked toward the shop, he reminded her that she was a citizen of Primerabrigo where dates grew abundantly.

Amy was unsure why he would feel the need to tell her that until she stepped across the store's threshold. Barrels and baskets filled with dates of varying sizes and colors filled the interior of the building and if not for the colonel's reminder, she very well may have squealed in delight. Maintaining her composure, she strolled the aisles looking at all things date-related and marveled at what she saw. The dates were enormous, some as large as a football. The smallest she could find was the size of her favorite kind of date, Medjool, which she'd always thought were the largest dates around. Not so here. Not even close.

A quimero in a red coattail hurried toward them through the maze of date barrels and baskets. He had a slightly sienna hue to his otherwise unremarkable face. What distinguished him from most of the quimerté Amy had seen were the horns that grew out the sides of his forehead just above the temple. They weren't the bone-colored horns that she had seen on other quimerté, nor were they pronged like the others had been. The quimero rushing toward them had dark brown horns that were more flat than round with notches along the rounded top.

The quimero bowed with flourish. "Colonel Sangcertigre, what an honor it is to have you in my shop. What may I do for you?"

"My visiting cousin smelled your goods and wanted to have a look."

The shop owner bowed again before he addressed Amy. "Señora, I am at your disposal. Whatever you wish is yours to have."

What she wanted was to pick up one of the large dates and bite into it like she would a slice of watermelon. That probably wouldn't have been in keeping with the pretense that she was ocático from Primerabrigo, so she refrained. She let go of the colonel's arm and looked about the room as if she had been in such an establishment hundreds of times. "You have quite a selection, but I'd like something new. What can you show me that I can't get at home?"

A wide smile spread across the quimero's face. "Oh, I have many things that you can't get in Primerabrigo, even in Navercío. Follow me."

For someone with such large feet, the shop owner scurried quite well while he maneuvered around his displays. Amy and Colonel Sangcertigre didn't attempt to keep up. Licha and Jandro remained at the door. The proprietor darted around a counter, behind which were rows and rows of what looked like wine bottles, and took a box from underneath. "These are made special for me right here in the outpost." He placed the box on the countertop. "The quimera who makes them said the recipe comes from her great-grandmother, who was the curandera of an Isolationist Tribe."

*Curandera,* another word Amy recognized. She wondered if it had the same meaning. Her recollection was that it meant healer or shaman, something along those lines. Maybe here it meant baker.

The shop owner opened the box to reveal several dark brown cubes the size of a child's building block. "They're called tuercacha cakes. Many dates are reduced to their essence, which takes an extremely long time. That is why they are so expensive." He quickly glanced at the colonel. "Of course for you it is free. You may have one." He looked at the colonel again. "Or you may have the entire box if you'd like."

"She doesn't need the entire box. One will suffice. Wrap it for her, would you?"

"Of course, Colonel. Of course."

The smell of dates surrounding her was intoxicating. She didn't want to have to wait to taste the tuercacha cake and said so to the colonel. He leaned in to whisper.

"Believe me, you don't want to eat it here. Wait until you're back at the garrison alone in your room."

She looked at the carton of tuercacha. The large cubes were moist and dense, almost gelled. As rich as they appeared to be the little cakes certainly didn't look like something she needed to refrain from eating in front of others. Still, she took the colonel's advice and smiled when the shop owner handed her a small box tied with a ribbon. She thanked him, keeping her eyes off his antlers, and left the building as the colonel followed. Licha and Jandro hurried after them and climbed into the back of the buggy. The escort guards had remained mounted and one of them blew a whistle while the colonel turned the buggy around. The crowd nearest them parted to give him the space to do so.

"Where are we going now?" Amy asked.

"Back to the garrison. We must return for the procession for Captain Tamezo."

"I thought you were going to show me more of the outpost."

"I'm afraid we won't have the time." With a roll of his head, he indicated the plaza surrounding him. "There are two more plazas just like this one, each belonging to a guild from one of the other two nations. The only difference between this one and those are the commodities and the quimerté."

He flicked the reins and the radamia trotted off. Licha and Jandro seemed to be as anxious to return to the relative safety of the garrison, or perhaps they were simply glad to be away from the crowds. Amy doubted the Carados camps held even a quarter as many quimerté as had filled the Primerabrigo Plaza. The colonel's three personal guards waited for them outside the main building and, Siphiwe, the hairy female, escorted the señora and her iado to their quarters. She explained that the wing also housed the colonel's apartment and that their rooms would be nearby.

"He wants you close." Siphiwe opened the door to a more sumptuously appointed and even larger space than the sitting room had been. Amy laughed when Jandro pointed out that the canopied bed within was bigger than the entire cell they had been confined to when first brought into the garrison. Every piece of furniture in the room was oversized, as if to remind the occupants of the importance of the garrison and, perhaps, of the Fensoré. Even the fireplace, which was large enough for someone of Jandro's height to stand in, was massive. The walls from the wainscoting to the high ceiling were covered in a dark, textured fabric and the floor was covered with a multitude of decorative rugs each designed to incorporate a different sitting, sleeping, or dining area. Yet despite that there was ample room for all three of them within the main chamber, Licha and Jandro would have to share an adjoining room with separate beds. For appearance's sake, Siphiwe justified. Obviously trying to distract Amy from objecting, the fensoré pointed to a long claw-foot tub to the side of the fireplace and offered to have it filled with hot water so that she could bathe before the procession. The thought of soaking in warm water was too good to pass up and Amy gladly accepted the offer. Out of the corner of her eye, she saw Licha shake her head and retreat into the adjoining room she would share with Jandro.

Siphiwe opened a tall wardrobe with doors embossed with the shield and spear emblem. Inside was Amy's clothing for the procession as well as a nightgown, another blouse, and another pair of trousers. The garment Amy was to wear to the procession particularly entranced Jandro. Although Siphiwe called it a jacket, it looked more like a ball gown. Jandro found the high gold collar and the enormous mauve bustle beautiful, but Amy thought it looked like a fashion show reject.

Holding the tail end of the bustle, Jandro stretched it out almost five feet. "It's a shame this is going to get so dirty dragging along behind you."

Siphiwe shook her head and pushed past the hanging clothes until she disappeared from the waist up. When she reappeared, she had in her hands what looked like a wire topiary frame. "The hem won't touch the ground at all. This attaches at the waist and the bustle drapes over it." She demonstrated by holding the frame to the small of her back and buckling the leather straps at the front around her waist. The straps were thick to keep the frame aloft.

"That's not a bustle. That's a parade float." Neither Siphiwe nor Jandro understood the reference and rather than explain, Amy just shook her head.

Siphiwe took off the wire frame and returned it to the wardrobe. Jandro offered to help her fetch water for Amy's bath and when they left, Amy sought out Licha. The young quimera was sitting on one of the two twin beds in the small, sparsely furnished adjacent room. The turban she'd been instructed to wear to hide her baldness was on the floor. Though she hadn't seen it happen, it was clear that the turban hadn't gotten there by accident.

"Licha? Is there something wrong?"

Although she shook her head, Licha had tears in her dark blue eyes. "No."

Amy sat on the bed next to her. "Is it this room? You and Jandro can sleep out there on one of the sofas if you'd like, or I can ask Colonel Sangcertigre to put the two of you somewhere else."

Licha shook her head again. "It's not the room."

"Then what is it?"

Leaning down, Licha scooped up the turban. "Why are we still here? If the colonel wants you out of Pliada, why are we still here? What is he going to do? He doesn't know any more about the prophecy than we do."

With her elbows on her knees, Amy cupped her chin with her hands. She could see Licha's frustration, but wasn't sure where it came from or why it was there. "The colonel believes the prophecy is in the Primerabrigo capital. That's why he's taking us there, but he can't leave until this procession, or whatever it is he wants me to see, is over."

"*Why* do you have to see it?" Licha asked, loudly. "*Why* is he putting on this show of you being his cousin when we should have left the outpost yesterday? He said himself that you are in danger here."

"He also said that he has to be the one to take us to Primerabrigo." Amy sat up. "Licha, he can't just leave without causing suspicion. I think he's setting up a plausible reason for his absence, as well as our reason for accompanying him."

"I realize that. I just …"

She didn't seem to know how to finish her sentence, but Amy did.

"You miss Apósto Baruti's guidance."

Licha nodded. "The colonel has given us none. Except to tell Jandro and me to stop behaving like seguidosts."

Amy stood and took the turban from Licha's hands. "He's not anything like the apósto, I'll grant you that. Apósto Baruti said time and time again that we needed the leadership of a Trotéjo. And since the colonel is one, we have to trust that he knows what he is doing." She placed the turban on Licha's head.

Despite what she'd said, Amy wasn't as accepting of their

circumstances as she'd led Licha to believe. Just as she'd done with the apósto, she'd been following the colonel's lead and that bothered her. Perhaps it was time to gain some control, even if it was only to demand that he tell her his exact plan. Although she was all for leaving the outpost, she wanted to know why he believed she'd be safer in Primerabrigo. Did no one know of *Lacáruna* in Primerabrigo, even though the prophecy was there?

When she heard Jandro's voice, Amy looked into the main chamber. The grayish, blue-skinned quimero had returned with one end of a pole on his shoulder and Siphiwe had the other end. Between them they carried two large buckets filled with steaming water. The colonel's male guards followed with more. Jandro was obviously straining under the weight; he collapsed to the floor when Siphiwe and he set the buckets down.

"I hope you don't need more than one bath," Jandro said as he dramatically threw himself onto the carpet surrounding the claw-foot tub, huffing and puffing.

Amy walked into the room. "I'm not sure I'll be taking this one."

Jandro sat up. "What? You mean we—"

Ignoring Jandro, Amy addressed Siphiwe. "I want to talk to Colonel Sangcertigre immediately."

Siphiwe seemed surprised not only at Amy's request but also her tone. "I don't understand. Are you displeased with something?"

"Not at all. I simply need to speak with the colonel."

Siphiwe gestured to the tub that the other two guards were now filling with the steaming water. "Then once you've bathed and dressed—"

"I'm not doing *anything* until I speak with the colonel." As she had done with Jandro, Amy cut her off. "So either you take me to him or bring him to me. Now."

One thing that she'd learned as CEO was that there was never a reason to raise her voice. As long as she kept eye contact and a blank expression on her face, as long as she didn't flinch in any way, she preserved her authority. Siphiwe seemed to understand that Amy meant what she said and bowed slightly.

"I will inform Colonel Sangcertigre of your request." Snapping her fingers, she indicated that the other two guards should follow her. They quickly dumped out the last of the buckets and gathered what they brought in before hurrying after her.

As they left, Jandro stood and looked into the water-filled tub. "You're really going to give up this hot water?"

With her eyes locked onto the closed door that the guards had retreated through, Amy sighed. "That's going to depend on the colonel. I want you to go into the other room and stay there with Licha until I call you." She expected Jandro to argue, but he nodded and did as she asked. He even closed the door between the rooms.

Slowly, Amy walked to the front of the chamber and sat in the nearest chair that faced the door. She waited. Her veneer of calm determination notwithstanding, she was a bundle of tingling nerves. Sometimes that was the best way to be, especially when making an impromptu decision, and she hoped that would be the case when the colonel arrived. She didn't have to wait long to find out. Flinging open the door, the colonel marched angrily into the room demanding to know why Amy refused to get dressed.

"I want to know what your plans are."

He looked at her as if he couldn't believe what she was asking of him. "We will discuss this after—"

"No." She stood abruptly forcing the colonel to take a step back. "We will discuss this now or I'm no longer going to be a willing participate in this … game of hide and seek you seem to have put me in."

The colonel bit back whatever his initial response was going to be. He paused and a smile spread across his tawny face. "And if I refuse? What will you do then?"

Amy absolutely abhorred a smirking male. "Tell the next person … I mean, *quimerté* … I see that you are Trotéjo."

She could see that he wasn't used to having someone challenge his authority and appreciated that. Though she was loath to think it about the apósto, blind adoration was useless.

Though the smile never left his face, Colonel Sangcertigre responded through clenched teeth. "Without my assistance, you would be dead sooner rather than later. You almost couldn't get through the morning meal without giving yourself away."

"And if I'm dead, where will that leave *you*? What happens if the world doesn't expand?"

"It will wink out of existence."

"You believe that?"

The colonel took a long breath through his nose. "This is ridiculous."

"It is." Amy crossed her arms. "What will you do now?"

The anger in his large green eyes softened into resignation. He stepped around her and sat in the chair she'd been seated in when he arrived. "I will answer your questions. But, please, do make this brief. We have a procession to attend."

"Will they start without us?"

"Of course not."

"I didn't think so." Amy sat in a chair opposite his. "I need to know the agenda. I'm tired of being in the dark about all of this, which is what I have been from the start. Please do shed some light, won't you?" She could smirk with the best of them.

The colonel snorted. "As I've explained to you before, we are all in the dark when it comes to *Lacáruna*. Until we read the prophecy in its entirety we will not know exactly how you fit into it or what you're supposed to do to fulfill it."

Exasperated, Amy gripped the arms of her chair. "I know *that*,

Colonel."

"Please call me Dack."

"What I'm asking is what happens next? Besides taking us to Primerabrigo."

Leaning back in his chair, the colonel crossed his long legs. The tops of his thigh-high boots were very supple. "I don't have an agenda. Not exactly and I think that is to our advantage. Tonight, you will accompany me to the procession and the feast that will follow. Then tomorrow morning you and I along with your iado will return to Primerabrigo in the carriage that brought you here."

She caught the look in his eye and kept from reminding him that she hadn't arrived in a carriage.

"We will travel Trade Road, which will take several days until we cross the Outer Belt to Summer Outpost on the northern side of Chorgo River. From there we will cross the bridge into Primerabrigo and on to Navercío where it is my intention to seek audience with the viceroy."

His plan was vague and it occurred to Amy his reticence in explaining it wasn't because he didn't want her to know the details, but that he didn't want anyone *else* to know them. She glanced about the room. Although the building had electricity, she didn't think that the Fensoré was sophisticated enough in technology to have bugged it. Still, it was often prudent to believe that the walls had ears.

"How will this keep me safe? What if, like your captain, the moment someone learns who I am they try to kill me?"

"No one will know because we won't tell them."

"Some already know, and I'm not speaking of whoever did that to the Carados camp. I'm speaking of your guards."

The colonel looked at the floor and shook his head. "I don't know what more I can say to assure you."

Amy understood that further questions regarding what her part was in all this and how she would return to her world couldn't be answered until the prophecy was read. She decided to give him a break and sat back in her chair. "Thank you ... Dack."

The colonel stood. "Now, if you'll excuse me I must return to my duties." He looked to the back of the room where the claw-foot tub stood. "I'm afraid you won't have time for a bath. The procession will begin shortly, so you must dress. I will send Siphiwe for you in twenty minutes."

"I will be ready."

"Splendid." Dack turned to leave, stopping only when he reached the door. "Your servants will not be needed this evening."

Glancing over her shoulder at the door to the adjoining room, Amy started to protest.

"Trust me on this. They won't want to be there."

He left the room.


Although Licha and Jandro were worried about not being able to accompany Amy during the procession, they didn't argue long when she said that the colonel insisted they remain behind. Jandro was the first to give up because Amy told him that Licha and he could use the bath. Without hesitation, he quickly stripped and hopped into the tub, explaining that he didn't want the water to get cold. While there was plenty of room for the both of them, Licha opted to help Amy dress instead of joining Jandro. Amy needed the assistance; putting on the wire frame and draping the long, black-with-dark-green-trim bustle was more than she could handle alone. Unlike the bustle-jacket she had worn earlier, her new attire took some getting used to. The dress was longer in front than the jacket had been and came down almost to her knees. She could have gotten away with forgoing trousers, but since she was unsure whether that was the style, she kept them on along with her knee-high black boots. She found that, because her back half stuck out so far, it was difficult to walk about the room without knocking something over.

"I hope we don't have to turn any corners," she said when Siphiwe arrived to fetch her.

"Do not worry." Siphiwe took no notice of Jandro splashing about in the claw-foot tub, even when he momentarily hopped out to chase after a bar of soap he'd let slip out of his hands. "There are plenty of open spaces."

When Licha finished attaching the long bustle to the wire frame, she followed Amy and Siphiwe to the door. She seemed reluctant to stay behind, but accepted that it was what she had to do.

"I'll be fine. I'll be at the colonel's side the entire time. Besides, I think it's best you stay here to keep Jandro from drowning."

That elicited a slight smile from Licha. "Be careful." She clutched the edge of the door as Amy and Siphiwe crossed the threshold.

"I will be."

Siphiwe led Amy down several flights of stairs, the bustle jarring her as the tail end of it bumped down them as well, threatening to throw her off balance. Colonel Sangcertigre waited for them at street level. He bowed slightly at Amy's approach and took to her side as they continued through the hall and out onto a wide portico to join several fensorés in brown tunics, including the three she had already met. At first, she expected at least one of them to snicker at her outfit, but when no one gave her more than the most cursory glance, she remembered that what she wore was outlandish only to her. The quimerté gathered on the portico had, no doubt, seen it all before.

"Señora Sangcertigre and I will follow," the colonel told one of captains.

*Señora, La Reina, El Hámster, La Rata.* So many words she recognized interspersed with those that she didn't, although they sounded Spanish. The various accents were just as familiar. Throughout her life she'd heard the accent Licha had and Dack had the same accent as her stepmother. Even the southern accent she'd heard—

A gentle tug on her arm brought her out of her contemplation. She looked up as a cart with a low, flat bed pulled by four small radamias and driven by another hairy fensoré in a beige tunic appeared.

The colonel took Amy's hand and guided her onto the cart, which was reminiscent of a Roman chariot. He indicated that she should hold onto a bar just behind the driver, who was seated and therefore lower, and stepped onto the vehicle beside her. When the colonel was in place, a squashed-face captain blew a whistle and all the captains, including himself, boarded similar vehicles, four captains to a cart. Another puff on the whistle and the procession began to move slowly across the courtyard. The fensorés patrolling the battlements high up along the walls stopped and stood at attention while the procession left the courtyard under a bridge connecting two wings of the building. In the expansive enclosure on the other side of the bridge the carts moved from cobblestone to hard packed dirt. Ahead, forming a path, were rows and rows of fensoré wearing the nipple helmets, all standing at attention. Because the colonel kept his gaze forward, Amy did as well. She wanted to look about if for no other reason than to count how many soldiers stood in formation. Hundreds of them faced straight ahead.

Once past the Fensoré regiments, the two carts at the front of the procession parted to reveal a large bonfire near the far garrison wall. The colonel's cart pulled forward so it was now at the lead and moved close enough to the bonfire that Amy could hear the crackling of the burning wood. The six carts filled with Fensoré captains came to a halt slightly behind and to either side of the colonel's cart. From across the field, a piercing horn blared and Amy jerked her head in the direction of the sound. A gate opened at the side of a small wooden building far from the main edifice. Once the horn's reverberation died out, only the squeaking of the gate hinges broke the stifling silence. A single avestroté appeared, pulling behind it a small wagon. From the darkness within the wooden building marched four quimeros. Dressed entirely in black, their faces were hidden behind black mesh that hung from their helmets. Like a metronome, the synchronicity of their footsteps matched the gait of the avestroté and seemed to guide it.

"Now you'll know why those two had to be left in your quarters," the colonel whispered. He didn't look at Amy or turn his head in the slightest. His eyes remained on the crackling bonfire that licked the air far above the garrison wall.

Not possessing the colonel's restraint, Amy's eyes sought out the wagon. Despite his warning and although she thought she had prepared herself for the worst, when the wagon passed directly in front of her, she gasped so deeply her lungs sucked in enough air to take a deep plunge into a bottomless pool. She was unable to exhale though and stood with her mouth agape.

"Do not make a sound," the colonel warned her, barely moving his lips. "Keep your face neutral, and do not look away."

Her body obeyed him even as her mind reeled.

Lying across the slowly passing wagon was the splayed, naked body of Apósto Baruti. The obscenity wasn't his nakedness but that his extremities had been separated. Amy's heart stopped when she saw that his arms and legs had been pulled, not cut, from his torso. His head was separated as well and it sat on the apósto's less hairy belly, as if it had popped out of his navel to see what the fuss was all about. Except that it couldn't see anything. The eyes had been gouged from the skull.

Desperately, Amy wanted to turn her head and look away. She wanted to scream. She wanted to let loose the flood of tears brought on by the rage that welled up deep inside; instead, she kept her gaze forward but unfocused. With all her might, she concentrated on breathing again. The technique had worked before, although she'd never had to use it while experiencing something so abhorrent. The closest she had come was when Peter had told her he wanted a divorce. She had froze then too, but she used it to her advantage; she wouldn't give him the pleasure of seeing her become undone in the middle of their favorite restaurant. She wouldn't give him anything. She wouldn't give the surrounding fensorés anything either. She gripped the bar behind the driver's head so tightly her knuckles whitened and her fingernails dug into the wooden dowel.

When the black-clad quimeros came to a halt, the avestroté pulling the wagon stopped. The pájastia was close enough to the bonfire that it bobbed its head back from the heat, but it was exceedingly well trained and remained in place while the hooded quimeros stepped up to the wagon, two to a side. Each guard grabbed a corner of a canvas tarp the dismembered body sat upon. The quimeros on the left tossed their end over the carcass and then the quimeros on the right did the same. Together they took hold of the corners of the death shroud and stepping backward, pulled it up and off of the wagon. Slowly, they walked toward the bonfire. As her eyes began to focus once again, Amy saw that there was no blood on the canvas tarp and reminded herself that the apósto had been dead long before his body had been torn apart. Even so, it was of little consolation. When the quimeros in black reached their destination, they tossed the canvas-wrapped body into the flame. Although not one of them faced the fire, somehow the fensoré standing at attention knew what had happened and they erupted simultaneously with what sounded like an agonized growl. When they did it a second time, the colonel and the captains did the same. The deep guttural sound shook Amy to her core and she nearly lost her composure. She was only able to keep it by reminding herself that the apósto wouldn't have minded the subterfuge she witnessed. He would have welcomed it if he knew it meant that she and the seguidosts could leave Winter Outpost alive.

So intent on the tarp smoking atop the bonfire, she hadn't noticed that another wagon had come out of the small wooden building pulled not by an avestroté, but by two quimeros in civilian garb. The shackles on their legs kept their strides short. Still they moved faster than the avestroté had and quickly pulled the cart past the officers. On the wagon, stacked like sacks of grain, were three bodies already wrapped in canvas. While Amy understood that the bodies were supposed to be the three Carados imposters who had committed suicide in their cell, she chose to believe that the tarps contained something other than bodies, something else that would take to the flame.

Once all four tarps had been disposed of, the colonel's cart turned from the bonfire and wheeled back down the fensoré-lined path. They left the dirt field through another underpass into another cobblestone courtyard where a hooded carriage festooned with black ribbon and white flowers waited. The captains' carts stopped so that the ribbon and flower covered carriage containing the body of Captain Tamezo could fall in line behind the colonel. Four members of what Dack called a Ceremonial Squad escorted the carriage, two to a side. They wore helmets with black fringe around the lip and black feathers that looked to be sprouting from the top. The radamias they rode had longer necks than the other radamias ridden by miscellaneous fensorés following behind.

In single file, the procession slowly proceeded out the garrison gates.

The abject horror she'd been subjected to would remain with Amy for a very long time, but she had done what Colonel Sangcertigre had demanded of her. It was easier to detach herself from the funeral procession into the outpost.

Unlike during her trip into the Primerabrigo Plaza, she didn't care if the quimerté lining the streets stared at her as they paid their respects to the fallen fensoré. It wasn't that she retreated into some dark recess of her mind, however; Amy was present the entire time. She simply chose not to be aware of her surroundings except as if it were a film projected on the screens that were her eyes. The colonel's cart led the procession only as far as the entrance of the outpost, where it pulled to the side. The cart containing Captain Osezo took the lead. The funeral carriage followed it out and, behind it, rode several fensoré dressed in regalia unlike any others and mounted on long-necked radamia.

Once the rest of the procession returned to the garrison for the funeral feast, the colonel tried to engage Amy in conversation but she had little to say. She smiled politely and graciously whenever introduced to someone and even engaged in a bit of small talk, although the moment the words left her mouth she'd forgotten what they were.

The feast began somberly enough, but when the wine was poured the gathering quickly turned into a rambunctious melee punctuated by loud laughter and angry voices. Because the movie playing out before her was in Technicolor, she was aware that besides the purple tunic of the colonel and the brown tunics of the captains, the fensorés wore blue and red tunics as well. The only beige tunics were on the guards standing at the door. Civilians from the outpost were in attendance, mostly as servants, but a few sat at the tables with the officers. Various Trading Guild fellows joined the revelry, spurred on by fensorés who behaved as if a war had been won and they were the victors. The wine tasted like butterscotch and was too sweet for Amy. She had no desire for the food that had been piled on her plate, but at the colonel's urging she nibbled on a few bland crackers while he did his best to explain why there would be a celebration following the death of one of their own. She understood. She knew about wakes, although that wasn't the word the colonel used. What she found odd was that the fensorés were not celebrating Captain Tamezo's ascension to the afterlife, but his journey to Runakopolis, the capital of Pliada. There he would be given a hero's welcome before being interred alongside the honored dead.

When the guests at the feast were long past noticing her absence, the colonel escorted Amy back to her quarters. Though the hour was very late, he told her to try to get some sleep because they would leave the following morning before sunrise, only a few hours away. Prior to departing, he asked whether she was all right. He seemed genuinely concerned. She had nothing to tell him and closed the door. Licha was waiting up for her. Jandro had tried but his hot bath must have worn him out because he was curled up, naked, on one of the many sofas. Amy was grateful that Licha never asked for the details of what had transpired. Maybe she could see in Amy's eyes that it wasn't something that she wanted to discuss, or maybe Licha didn't want to know at all. She helped Amy separate from the protruding bustle and pulled off her boots. Too tired to remove anything else, Amy crawled into bed in her bustier and trousers.

◉    ◉    ◉

Siphiwe shook her awake.

Feeling groggy and a bit light-headed, Amy sat up slowly. Most of the lamps scattered about the large room were on and through the uncovered windows she saw that it was still dark outside. She felt as though she hadn't slept at all.

Licha rose from the sofa she must have slept on, stretched, and padded across the room to where Jandro lay snoring loudly. She shook him awake, as Siphiwe had done Amy, and when that didn't work, she slapped his bare thigh soundly. Jolted, he woke.

Siphiwe told Amy to dress. "I've already packed your belongings." Indeed she had; several crates and a few cloth bags sat in front of the now empty wardrobe. "The colonel is waiting."

Amy crawled to the side of the bed and put her socked feet on the floor. "What do I wear?" Although she hadn't taken more than a few sips of the butterscotch beverage the colonel called wine, she felt slightly hung-over. A couple of pieces of nearly burnt toast would quiet her stomach, but she doubted there was time. She hoped there would be something to eat waiting in the carriage.

"I've laid it out." Siphiwe indicated the clothing lying on the end of the canopied bed. "Do you need help dressing?"

Amy shook her head.

"I'll see to your belongings then."

Jandro, naked and mumbling something about not wanting to wear that stupid shirt again, lagged behind Licha as she pulled him along into the room where they were supposed to have slept. Amy roused herself and staggered to the end of the bed and dressed in the clothing lying on the end. She looked around for a brush to take the tangles out of her long hair and found one on the vanity. With the brush in hand she sat down before the mirror and wondered whether there were something to tie back her hair with. Licha came out of the adjoining room and must have known what Amy was searching for because she held up a small piece of ribbon in her hand. She tamed Amy's brown hair with the brush and then gathered it into her hand so that she could tie the ribbon around it.

"You have beautiful hair."

"Thank you." Amy yawned and looked at the quimera through the mirror. Licha had returned to her servant garb, including the turban. "What's your hair like?"

"I don't remember." Licha handed Amy the brush and turned to help Jandro, who had tottered into the large room claiming that his shirt was even smaller than it had been the day before.

Siphiwe came to his rescue by handing both Licha and him cloaks to wear against the chill of the early morning. They were the same cloaks that had concealed the guards' identity when they had acted as the colonel's cousin and her two iado to fool anyone who had observed their arrival; although, anyone who had seen them when they'd first arrived might wonder what had been done to shrink two of them.

"You'll need those," Siphiwe explained. "It's very cold out this morning and has begun to snow."

Amy wasn't sure why she found it surprising that it would snow in a city called Winter Outpost. Maybe it was because she'd caught the slightly amazed tone in Siphiwe's voice.

She swung the long dark green cloak over her shoulders. "Is that unusual?"

Siphiwe nodded. "The cold months seem to come earlier every year."

"The world is shrinking," Jandro said.

When the fensoré looked at him as if she didn't understand, Amy wondered how much Colonel Sangcertigre had divulged to his personal guards. Did they know that she was the supposed *Lacáruna*? Maybe not. Or maybe they hadn't heard of the Carados belief that the world stopped expanding when the prophecy hadn't taken place three hundred years earlier. She wasn't going to ask because the colonel probably didn't want them to know the entire story.

Several fensorés that Amy didn't recognize came into the room and Siphiwe instructed them to carry down the crates and bags containing clothing and whatever else she had packed into them. Cloaks securely tied, the rest of them left the room as well. Siphiwe led them to the main courtyard where Colonel Sangcertigre stood giving final instructions to captains Cebrode and Zorrode. Snowflakes fell softly on the ground and quickly melted. The colonel and captains wore short cloaks that came down just past their waists and were colored to indicate their rank. The captains greeted Amy with a nod and when she asked after Captain Osezo they reminded her that she had accompanied the body of Captain Tamezo to Runakopolis. The colonel took their attention from her to tell them that he would send word if he was to be gone longer than expected.

"But if you learn of anything important in your investigations that you believe I should know, I may be reached at my family estate."

The captains nodded and the colonel clapped them on the back. He said goodbye and they bowed to him first and then to Amy before returning to the building. The colonel turned to his faux-cousin and asked if she was ready to leave.

"I suppose so."

The fensorés had secured what they had brought down from her chambers onto the back of a large carriage. Four avestroté were harnessed to the front. The colonel ushered everyone down the steps to the carriage and Jandro and Licha climbed in first. As they did, Siphiwe and her male counterparts came out of the building wearing short beige cloaks. The sergeant and the other male guard climbed up to the driver's box and Siphiwe sat at the back of the carriage beside the baggage. The colonel gestured to the open door of the carriage. "After you, cousin."

She looked up into his green eyes and realized that, although she would never admit it to Licha or Jandro, she was glad it was the colonel who was aiding her and not the apósto. While she had enjoyed Apósto Baruti's company, once she'd begun to accept her fate, he had seemed more of a teacher than a leader. Now that there had been two attempts to take her life, she wanted to be with someone stronger in both spirit and will. As a colonel in charge of such a large outpost he had to have skills and knowledge the apósto couldn't have had. And as a soldier, he wouldn't yield to others the way the apósto had to do because of his vocation. She accepted the hand he held out, as she stepped up and into the carriage. He called out to the drivers and the carriage began to move across the courtyard. The colonel hopped in and closed the door.

The carriage interior was dark, but with the window shades up enough, light streamed in to reveal between the cushioned benches at either end a table upon which sat a basket of bread and cheese and a pitcher of water. Her stomach had settled enough that she no longer wanted burnt toast, but she longed for one of the large brown eggs she had tasted the day before. She had to settle for a soft brown roll. The colonel sat at her side on the back cushioned bench, Jandro and Licha across from them.

Once outside the garrison, the carriage moved quickly down the streets, which, wet from melting snowflakes, glistened in the moonlight. Looking out the window at her side, Amy saw a few quimerté on the sidewalks. No one seemed to take notice. She understood then that the ruse of disguising the same three currently outside the carriage as cousin and servants had been necessary not for the outpost's general population but for the fensoré in the garrison. She couldn't have been the only one looking out a window when a carriage unloaded three cloaked passengers.

But there had been four.

"What happened to the driver who brought your cousin to the garrison?"

The questioning look the colonel gave her was brief. He knew what she meant.

"Why isn't he with us now?"

He picked through the basket of cheese until he found something to his liking. "He's dead. So are the two who accompanied my guard when you were placed in the cell." When he sat back, his face was in shadow. "As I said before, I know whom I can trust and whom I cannot."

Amy could hear him gnawing on a chunk of hard cheese and it chilled her. No longer able to convince herself that the three canvases thrown into the fire along with Apósto Baruti hadn't actually contained bodies, she winced.

"It had to be done. They saw your faces."

Amy returned the roll to the basket—she wasn't hungry anymore—and looked out the window.

Jandro and Licha had fallen asleep by the time the carriage passed Lake Miracle. Through the thick forest of giant pine trees Amy caught glimpses of moonlight reflecting off its placid surface. The colonel and she remained awake for another couple of hours, as the sun rose. At the junction where the portion of Trade Road coming from Maseprada joined the east-west portion, a fensoré in a blue tunic, surrounded by four others in beige tunics, stopped the carriage and demanded to know where it was headed. The colonel stepped out and when the fensoré saw him, he began to apologize.

"No need, Sergeant," the colonel said. "You're doing the job you were given."

They seemed surprised that he wasn't riding in an official carriage until the colonel explained that he had personal business in Primerabrigo. The sergeant, a mottle-skinned quimero with heavy jaw, nodded vigorously and waved the carriage on. The colonel thanked him and climbed back on board. The minor excitement hadn't lasted long enough to keep Amy's eyes open and before the carriage started to move she closed them.

When she opened them again, the light pouring through the windows had heated the interior considerably and she no longer had a need for her cloak. The colonel had his long legs stretched out in front of him. With his head lolling on the rear wall as he slept, his thick, golden blond hair fell away from his face in soft waves. He must have felt the rising heat as well, because his purple cloak had been tossed over his shoulders revealing a white shirt underneath instead of his usual purple tunic. The shirt was halfway unbuttoned, exposing much of his broad, muscular chest, the skin of which was slightly lighter and a bit more yellow than the skin on his face. Drawn to the contrasting skin tones, Amy wondered if it were due to never going about shirtless in the sun. Neither Jandro or Licha had tan lines and if Jandro's behavior was any indication he had been more than shirtless a time or two. Maybe it was just the natural color of the quimero's chest, or perhaps the tiny hairs that covered it, which were caught in the sunlight that streamed through the window, that accounted for his coloring. Squinting so that she could see the miniscule hairs more clearly, she really couldn't tell if they had any coloring at all.

The carriage hit a bump and fearing she'd been caught, Amy sat up quickly. Fortunately, the colonel remained asleep. She relaxed and, once she figured out how to detach the pitcher from the table, poured herself a mug of water and drank deeply. Her throat slaked, she found the roll she had earlier returned to the basket and nibbled on it while she returned her attention to the view out the window. The passing landscape seemed to have returned to the barren stretch the three Carados and she had walked through directly after leaving Esterenas, except it was filled with more of the scraggly mesquite-like trees. She noticed the carriage was slowing down considerably. It seemed unlikely that there would be another Fensoré checkpoint so soon, but without a window at the front of the carriage she couldn't tell. She shook Colonel Sangcertigre by his arm until he opened his eyes.

"I think we're stopping."

Seemingly unconcerned, the colonel yawned. If Licha hadn't been curled up on the front bench he would have kicked her when he flexed his booted feet. His cloak fell from his shoulder as he sat up and looked out the window. The carriage had come to a complete stop.

"We're at the end of our line." The colonel noticed that his shirt was open and quickly buttoned it.

"Already?" Amy leaned across him and looked out his window. "You said it was going to take several days to reach Primerabrigo."

"I did say that. But we're taking an alternate route."

He opened the door on his side and stepped out. As the cold air rushed into the carriage Amy tried to scramble after him but the bustle on her jacket caught on the table and jerked her back. Rather than disentangle the bustle, she took off the jacket before hopping out of the carriage. Her flailing about woke both Jandro and Licha. The colonel stood talking to the male guards at the front.

"What route are we taking then?" Amy asked as she approached.

Shading his eyes with one hand, the colonel used the other to point in a direction that the road didn't go. "That one." He moved to the rear of the carriage. "West for a day or two and then we'll turn south."

Recalling what they had done when they had left the sand of Esterenas, she asked if they were going to leave the carriage where they'd stopped.

The colonel laughed. "No. It will continue on to Summer Outpost where it will wait for our return."

Jandro stuck his head out of the carriage. "Why aren't we going with it?" He jumped to the ground.

Stopping to address both Amy and Jandro, Colonel Sangcertigre said, "Because that is where everyone knows we are headed. Not only the fensorés of Winter Outpost, but also the fensorés back at the junction. There will be another checkpoint at the junction where the Rescatazo end of Trade Road meets the Primerabrigo end. The fensorés there will have already heard that I am in this carriage, so when my guards tell them I am sleeping within, they will let the carriage pass. No one will know the carriage is empty until it reaches Summer Outpost."

The sergeant Amy had once thought looked like a clown without the makeup climbed down from the driver's box, while the other male guard climbed atop and stood on the hood of the carriage. Licha stepped out of the carriage, tying her cloak around her neck. In the crook of her arm she held Amy's cloak.

"What's going on?"

Jandro pointed in the direction that the colonel had. "We're going to have to walk."

Licha looked at Amy with a perplexed expression. At the back of the carriage, Siphiwe and the sergeant were unloading the baggage.

"I'm not sure I understand," Amy said to the colonel, who was supervising. "Do you think someone may try to attack the carriage on the road?" The air was chilly; she wrapped herself in the long cloak.

"It's not the road that worries me." He helped Siphiwe with a crate. "What worries me is what may be waiting for us when we cross into

Primerabrigo. It's there we would have to change drivers and carriages."

"Why?"

The sergeant answered. "Fensoré of lower ranks are not allowed out of Pliada unless under special provision only the major general can give. Someone else would have to take you through Primerabrigo."

"And," the colonel added, "what better place to plan an assault?"

When Amy said she still didn't understand, the colonel pulled her aside. "If there is even the slightest possibility that someone may have learned who you really are"—he glanced at his guards—"then the moment we're out of Pliada and away from the Fensoré we're vulnerable."

Amy glanced at the guards as well. "I thought you knew who was trustworthy."

"This is just a precaution."

Siphiwe opened the crate that had been taken from the bedchamber. When she saw what was inside she looked over her shoulder at the sergeant with a confused expression. Instead of being filled with the clothing that had been in the wardrobe, the crate was filled with several large dark canvas bags. The colonel reached into the crate and tossed one to Jandro and another to Licha.

"The knapsacks have been packed with what provisions we can carry. Your two have traveling clothes to change into. Do so now." He pulled out the last two bags, gave one to Amy, and set the other at his feet.

The colonel told Amy to leave her bustle-jacket behind, as he traded his short purple cloak for a longer black one with a hood. He nodded at Jandro and Licha. "From this point forward I am no longer a Fensoré colonel. If we happen to come across anyone, you will address me as señor; otherwise you may call me by my given name."

Amy turned to him. "Am I to call you señor as well?"

"No. Dack will do."

He handed out what looked to Amy like a tool belt with several pouches hanging off it and demonstrated how to attach a canteen. Siphiwe opened another of the crates. This one contained several swords and knives. Everyone received a sword. Amy stared at hers, which looked razor-sharp.

"Um, I have no idea how to use one of these. Got anything else in there?" She looked into the nearly empty crate. "Like a gun, say?"

"A what?"

"A gun that you can hold in your hand. " She held up her right hand in pistol fashion, forefinger out and thumb raised, and mimed shooting it. Because he still didn't seem to know what she was talking about, she cocked her thumb again and accompanied the action with the closest approximation of a gunshot that she could manage.

"Oh," Dack said. "You mean a esacueño. No. They're more trouble than they're worth. The range is short and not very accurate. You'll do fine with that." He pointed to the sword Amy held away from her body. When she didn't move, he took it from her and slid it into the scabbard that was attached to the belt she had put on.

"I'll teach …" He looked at Jandro and Licha who seemed to be as unaccustomed to swords as Amy. "I'll teach all three of you what you'll need to know to get by, but I doubt you'll have to use it."

"Good," Jandro muttered as he stowed his sword.

The crates and bags were closed and returned to the back of the carriage just in time. The guard on the driver's seat called out that he could see someone heading their way from the direction in which they'd come.

Dack instructed the guards to go and without a word of farewell, the three climbed back to their previous perches. The carriage lurched as it continued down the road. Amy waved at Siphiwe, who sat at the back. The hairy quimera didn't return the gesture.

Like the avestrotés pulling the carriage, Dack took off at a trot.

"We have to hurry."

# PART THREE

They ran until they were out of breath. With nothing to hide behind, Dack found a dry shallow ravine and bid the others to lay in it. He didn't want to risk being seen even though they were now far from the road. On his stomach, he rose just high enough to see over the edge and took from a pouch on his belt a round copper-colored object about four knuckles long. He held it up to his eye.

Jandro, who was lying beside Amy, tapped her on the shoulder. "He's got a lupita. They can see very far."

Although she had never actually seen one before, Amy waited for Dack to extend the monocular like a telescope. He didn't pull on it, but he did twist it. After a few minutes, she crawled next to him, keeping her head low.

"Do you see anything?"

"Nothing to worry about. Two trader carts, but no Fensoré." He returned the lupita to its pouch. "I wanted to be certain the carriage wasn't being followed."

She stood when he did and dusted off the front of her cloak. "Do you suspect someone within your ranks?"

Dack dusted himself off as well. "I suspect everyone."

His surreptitious glance at Jandro and Licha didn't escape Amy's notice. "There is no need to suspect them."

"There was no need for me to suspect Captain Tamezo, either. But if Apósto Baruti hadn't gotten in the way, you would be dead."

Dack stepped out of the ravine and held Amy's arm to help her out of it. "I had known Captain Tamezo for more than twenty years. We came into Pliada at the same time, he from Maseprada, and I from Primerabrigo. We bunked together during training. I considered him not only a friend, but also a brother. I would have given my life for him and I know he would have given his for mine." He paused and looked to the east, where a small dust cloud was all that remained of the carts that had gone by. "We were brought into the Trotéjo at the same time. Raiquen …" He paused to clear his throat. "Captain Tamezo gave no indication he was anything but dedicated to the cause."

"Which was what?" Amy asked. As they headed west, she kept to his side while the other two trailed a few feet behind yet remained close enough to hear what he had say.

"To fulfill the duties that the Trotéjo were created to fulfill. *Dendos* established the Trotéjo to search for and protect *Lacáruna*— you—and keep the world expanding."

Amy recalled the glowing words that repeated around the table in the room filled with candles. "The finder protects. Except you didn't find me." She glanced over her shoulder. "Those two did."

"The meaning of the phrase isn't that whoever finds *Lacáruna* is going to protect her. It means that she will be revealed to the Trotéjo who are obliged to protect her as she fulfills the prophecy."

"You've said that no one knows exactly what's in the prophecy, but I keep hearing that the time it was supposed to happen came and went. Clearly someone knew at least a little about it."

"What has been known, and passed along to all Trotéjo, generation after generation, was the year when *Lacáruna* would arrive."

"So basically then, the Trotéjo was just a secret club for"—she did the math—"two thousand seven hundred years. That's a really long time just to have to wait. What did you do in the meanwhile?"

He looked at her with a slightly annoyed expression. "I don't know; I wasn't there."

"Oh come on. There had to be something. Annual luncheons, or something."

"I don't know what a luncheon is, but if you're asking if we came together, the answer is yes. Every nine years."

"All of you?"

"No, only those you tapped and who had tapped you, usually not more than a dozen or so. We would reaffirm our commitment to the cause."

She could have asked how they reaffirmed it—she had images of college fraternity initiations floating through her head—but chose another question instead. "And then the time of the prophecy came and went without finding anyone to protect."

"Correct. Allegedly, we lost many comrades after that."

"Apósto Baruti said something similar happened to the Carados."

"No doubt. But unlike Carados factions, those who remained were dedicated with an unwavering belief that the prophecy would come to pass and the Trotéjo became even stronger than before. I believed it and I would have staked my life that Captain Tamezo believed it just as fervently." He glanced over his shoulder. "I hope you'll understand why no one will ever escape my suspicions."

Licha surprised Amy by saying she agreed.

Dack stopped and turned around to look at her. "I'm glad you understand."

"So what's going to happen when the empty carriage reaches Summer Outpost?" Amy asked. "How are your guards going to explain that?"

"Only my sergeant was aware of the plan. I gave him a letter that he will hand over to the colonel in charge explaining that I am on a covert mission and was dropped off at an undisclosed location. The letter also states that my guards are to wait for me and I will join them at Summer Outpost in a fortnight."

Amy was surprised he was so certain of when he would return. "Two weeks? You think we'll find the prophecy and expand the word by then?"

"I have no idea, but I had to give a timetable of some sort for it to be plausible."

He slapped his hands to his hips and looked north. Though they were far from them, the Límitota Mountains remained almost as imposing as the first time Amy had seen them on the way to Winter Outpost. Now, however, their tall peaks were hidden under thick dark gray clouds. While he gazed at the mountains, Dack removed his canteen from his belt and took a swig. "Drink up if you need to. I suspect those clouds will be on us by morning and we won't have to worry about our water supply." He returned the canteen to his belt.

Only Jandro followed his advice about taking a drink. He picked up his pace when they began walking again so that he was side by side with the larger quimero.

"Why are we going west? Why not just head straight south for Primerabrigo?"

Dack looked down at him. "How long have you been a seguidost?"

"A little over a year."

"Then you should know the answer."

"He means the Ocaflu," Licha said. She looked up at Dack. "Jandro hasn't been out of Esterenas since he joined us."

"What's the Ocaflu?" Amy asked.

Licha explained it was a large expanse of rough rock that is extremely difficult to traverse.

"It's directly south of here and we need to go around it," Dack added. "Circumventing it will add a couple of days to our journey, but the route is far less dangerous."

Jandro still seemed not to understand the necessity of it. "Why didn't we just travel farther down Trade Road?" We could have avoided the Ocaflu altogether."

"Enough!" Dack shouted at him. "Quit asking questions."

When Jandro flinched, Amy stopped. Licha stopped as well but it took Jandro a moment to realize that they had fallen behind. Dack took even longer and he was a good five threestrides ahead before he realized he was walking alone. When he turned back and shouted for them to hurry up, Amy didn't budge. Jandro and Licha remained with her. Stomping angrily over his footsteps, Dack backtracked.

"What is this?"

Having discovered a long time ago that there was often a need to put a distance between a question and an answer, Amy paused just long enough to take the upper hand. "I understand why you don't trust these two. I accept that, as do they. But you told them you are no longer a Fensoré colonel not even an hour ago and I won't have you speak to them in such a dismissive manner."

Dack grunted with indignation. "Just because I told them not to address me as colonel, doesn't mean I have to suffer the questions of a seguidost."

With a vehemence that shocked everyone, Licha took a step forward and yelled at him. "You took that from us!" Her hands were clenched in tight little fists and the tendons in her white neck stood out. "We agreed to your terms because it is what Apósto Baruti would have done, what he would have wanted us to do. You demanded it of us and we agreed, but you cannot take something away and then throw it back whenever the mood strikes."

When the large quimero's back stiffened and he brought up his hands, Amy was prepared to throw herself in front of Licha to keep her out of harm's way. Instead of lunging for the smaller quimera and wrapping his hands around her throat, Dack began to clap.

"Splendid. Your point is well taken, Licha." He turned to Jandro and bowed slightly. "I apologize for my rudeness."

Jandro seemed a little embarrassed and couldn't meet Dack's eye. "That's all right. The apósto always used to say that I ask too many questions."

Dack looked at Amy expectantly. "Was that to your satisfaction?"

Amy began to walk. "I suppose."

When he caught up to her in a few strides of his long legs, Amy brought up what he'd said earlier.

"Even though you keep trying to convince me of your guards' trustworthiness, you don't really think they are; otherwise, you wouldn't have only informed the sergeant of your plan."

When he confirmed her suspicions, he did so softly. She doubted it was because he didn't want Jandro and Licha to hear; they were still too far behind. She guessed he did it because he didn't want to believe it himself.

"It's Siphiwe you suspect, isn't it."

Dack looked surprised. "How did you know? Did you see something?"

"Not anything suspicious."

"Then how did you know it was Siphiwe I was concerned with?"

Although she knew it would sound silly, Amy told him anyhow.

"She didn't return my wave. She'd been nothing but kind, even a little warm, so it seemed odd to me that she wouldn't wave back when I waved goodbye to her."

Dack thought it over. "An interesting observation. My reasons for suspecting her are less abstract. She was absent from her post several times the last two nights, which is not something she's prone to do. Also, she was very flustered not only when the carriage stopped earlier than had been planned, but also when she saw that the trunks she'd packed with clothing had been replaced. Last night I had Sergeant Aulnode—"

"That's the driver?"

"Yes. I had him obtain four knapsacks with provisions along with a few weapons, to replace what Siphiwe had packed, and to tell no one."

"So he's the most trustworthy of them."

"He's who brought you to my attention. Captain Tamezo had you lot arrested, but he didn't know what he had on his hands. The sergeant informed me there was an"—with a slight smile on his face, he glanced apologetically at Amy—"older quimera with a full head of hair acting as if she was a seguidost, when it was quite clear that she wasn't. I then informed Captain Tamezo."

"*Lacáruna* was prophesized as being older?"

"Not at all. *Lacáruna* has never been described as being anything other than female. We never knew what to expect, so we Trotéjo are always on the lookout for the unusual. An older female with full head of hair traveling with Carados disguised as a seguidost is unusual."

"So the sergeant is also Trotéjo?"

"He is not, but as my personal guard he knows to inform me when something is amiss. Normally, someone being arrested wouldn't have come to my attention at all. But I had heard about the decimation of the Carados camp from Captain Tamezo, who thought it would be wise to search the outpost for any Carados to question. I had the sergeant join in the search."

"How did Tamezo find out about what had happened at the camp in the first place?"

"I don't recall." He pondered this for a moment. "Actually, I don't believe he said how he'd come by the information."

"Do you think he knew who he had arrested?"

"I don't believe so. If he was part of Arañalianza—as it seems he must have been, though it's still difficult for me to comprehend—he would have killed you in the street."

"He never saw my face until he came for us to take to you."

"My guess is he planned to question all of you but that was thwarted when I told him I wanted you brought to me."

"Did you tell him you thought I could be *Lacáruna*?"

"No, but he must have surmised that because I wanted you brought to the secret Trotéjo room. He could have killed you, yet he brought you to me."

"Maybe he just wanted to be certain."

"Yes. And now that I think about it, Captain Tamezo always thought that *Lacáruna* would be a quimerita. Perhaps that's why he waited."

"He thought she would be young, you mean."

"Very young. It was just a theory he had. Based on what, I never knew." He sighed.

Amy didn't really want to talk about the quimero who'd tried to kill her. "Back to Siphiwe. Do you think she'll be able to let anyone know where we were dropped off?"

"Not until they reach Summer Outpost and by then sending someone after us would be pointless because they'd be too far behind."

As she looked back the way they'd come, Amy hoped he was right.

By nightfall, the temperature had dropped twenty degrees and only Jandro seemed immune to the cold. Fortunately, the knapsacks had been loaded quite carefully. Each included a thin, yet sturdy straw mat to lie on and a tightly woven blanket that retained the warmth while they slept. Dack suggested that the others lay side-by-side so that their body heat would assist the blankets. He, however, chose to sleep on the other side of the fire he had built. Although she didn't want to think it of him, Amy had the notion that, despite supposedly taking Licha's point, he didn't want to sleep so near a seguidost. Jandro, however, thought it was a strategic move that would keep Dack more observant.

"Staying a bit chilled will keep him from sleeping too deeply."

At first sign of dawn, everyone was awake. Licha made porridge from a grain packed in Jandro's knapsack. The porridge was as bland as the pulabaza broth they'd slurped down on the way to Winter Outpost, but far more satisfying. A small portion was all they needed to fill their stomachs. As much Amy missed it, she was reluctant to ask if coffee actually existed in this world; even if it did, there was no telling what it would taste like. She would have to subsist on cold water and hot porridge, at least until they crossed Chorgo River into Primerabrigo where Dack said they would procure more supplies.

"When do you think that will be?" she asked.

Dack held the lupita to his right eye and scanned the western horizon. The dark gray clouds that had hovered over the outpost had yet to reach them, but it wouldn't be long before they did. He returned the lupita to a pouch on his belt. "Foreseeing no unknown obstacles, we should reach it in five days."

Amy tied her bedroll to her knapsack. "Are there any *known* obstacles?"

"Not on this side of the Chorgo, but we'll be crossing into the Lagosla Region, if I'm heading us in the right direction."

Jandro packed Dack's bedroll for him. "What's in the Lagosla Region?"

"A large swamp. Didn't you attend school in Maseprada? I should think you would know that."

Amy recalled the region being mentioned when she sat at the colonel's table with his captains. "Can we go around it?"

"Doing so would keep us in Pliada where *Lacáruna* is believed to be. We shouldn't spend any more time here than absolutely necessary." He thanked Jandro for repacking his knapsack and slung it over his shoulder, slipping an arm through a strap. "Besides that, Lagosla is the best place for us to enter Primerabrigo unnoticed." He kicked apart the remnants of the fire and stomped out a few glowing embers. "It's a difficult place to police and is the only province in Primerabrigo that openly does business with the black market."

"Because it's a difficult place to police?"

"Yes."

"Is that because it's a swamp?" Licha asked.

"That's the general belief, yes. I think it has more to do with the Centación benefiting monetarily from the black market."

"Centación are the Primerabrigo military," Jandro said to Amy. He was the last to put on his knapsack, but the first to cover it with his cloak. He grinned at Dack. "See? I did learn something in school."

Dack took another look at the dark clouds progressing steadily toward them. "We should move along. If we're lucky, we can outdistance that storm."

They weren't so lucky.

The clouds had blocked out the sun by noon and the temperature dropped to nighttime level. Nonetheless, their steady but rapid pace kept them warm. Amy wanted to remove her cloak because she had begun to sweat, but Dack told her to keep it on lest she chill too quickly and get sick. She considered informing him about the latest scientific studies that proved *being* cold didn't lead to getting a cold, but it took too much breath to speak and walk at the same time. And who knew? Maybe that's how it worked in this world.

By mid-afternoon, the clouds burst. The four had come down in altitude enough that there was little chance of snow, but not so far that it kept the rain from turning to sleet. The mesquite-like trees offered no shelter from the downpour so they kept moving. Their cloaks were waterproof, fortunately; so were their boots. The hard rain continued well into night, making it impossible to start a fire to keep warm even if there had been a place to seek refuge. So despite encroaching exhaustion, they kept moving. Worried about flash floods, Dack warned everyone to keep away from even the shallowest ravine, a difficult task not only because the ground was rife with gullies but also because with the overcast sky there was little light to see by. Apparently, the *Eye of Dendos* had closed.

The night was by far the darkest Amy had experienced and although she'd complained, to herself if to no one else, that the constant full moon was disconcerting, she certainly missed its brightness while trudging over the increasingly muddy ground. The lack of moonlight was fortuitous in one way, though; Dack lost his bearings and rather than continuing in a westerly direction, he slowly steered them south—right into the very area he'd been trying to avoid. He was the first to recognize his mistake when the squashy ground slowly solidified underfoot until they were walking through puddles of water instead of mud. During a sudden flash of lightning Licha saw something in the distance.

"Over there!" She pointed at the silhouette of something large jutting from the ground. Thunder blocked out anything else she had to say.

Another lightning flash revealed what she was pointing at. Dack seemed to recognize it and yelled for everyone to hurry. Even though he had waited for the thunder to subside, his voice could barely be heard above the din of the rain.

Fatigued beyond exhaustion, Amy began to run, stopping only to grab Jandro's arm to keep him from slowing down. Licha must have had a fensoré's stamina because she was hot on Dack's heels. They pounded across the rocky, uneven plane toward the tall silhouette, which protruded diagonally from the surface like the tail of an airplane. Lightning slashed across the sky at an increasing rate, cutting through the darkness.

"This must be the Ocaflu," Jandro shouted to Amy between loud claps of thunder as she pulled him along. "How did we get here?"

"I don't know. But I'm glad that we found it."

"I think it found us."

One lightning bolt, so close it seemed to be directly behind her, was bright enough that Amy could see Dack and Licha darting under an outcrop of a large rock formation. The thunder that followed the bright flash was deafening and seemed to sweep across the landscape like a bomb blast, knocking both Jandro and her off their feet. Jandro fell first, somehow careening in such a way that he toppled in front of Amy and she fell over him. The stars she been missing in the night sky appeared in her eyes when her head hit the hard ground. As her senses returned, she saw, in another flash of dazzling light, that Jandro was face down in a puddle and not moving. Lunging, she shoved him over, but it made little difference as the unrelenting rain fell on his upturned face. Before she could throw herself over him, he suddenly rose off the ground. Amy looked up and saw Dack gathering the unconscious young quimero in his arms. Dack reached out to help her up but she pushed his hand away and stood on her own volition. Once she was on her feet, they hurried to the overhang where Licha waited.

When Dack knelt and lay Jandro on the dry ground under the outcrop, the snow-white quimera asked if he were all right.

"He had the air knocked out of him." Dack leaned down and

placed his ear near Jandro's mouth. "He'll come to in a bit."

Amy dropped to her knees next to them. "He knew where we were."

Dack pushed back his hood as he sat back on his haunches. "I'm glad someone did."

"You didn't bring us here?" Amy asked.

"No. I thought we were too far west to be anywhere near the Ocaflu. We must have traveled farther south on Trade Road then I'd thought."

"It's a good thing we did; otherwise, we'd still be out there in that." Amy pointed to the rain that was coming down in sheets so hard that it seemed as if they'd taken refuge behind a waterfall.

Licha had Jandro's head in her lap, smiling down on him. "He's awake."

Dack leaned in close. "Do you know who I am?"

Jandro blinked several times and then glanced at Licha before answering. "You're not a colonel."

Slowly, a smile spread across Dack's face. "Splendid."

The shelter they found themselves in was less a cave and more of a recess within the rock, open on three sides and slanted sharply toward the back. The roof was high enough for the others, but Dack had to stoop a bit when he stood to inspect their refuge. The lightning that had spurred them on outside was of little use in illuminating the long, narrow alcove. Tossing his cloak over his shoulders, he removed his knapsack and let it fall to the ground. He knelt and began digging through it. After dumping out the knapsack's contents, he still hadn't found what he was looking for.

"Don't tell me the sergeant forgot to pack one." He held up the bag and began squeezing it all over as if were wringing it out. "Aha!" he said, feeling something in an unnoticed pocket just below the right strap. He dug into the pouch and pulled out a long cylindrical object that in the darkness looked like a small baton. Holding the object vertically, he twisted the top end. The baton began to glow.

"A paluz," Licha said. "I didn't know we had them."

"This may be the only one. It would draw attention if more were missing from the equipment depot."

The greenish light emanating from the paluz was bright enough to illuminate a five-foot radius. Dack held it out while he slowly searched the rocky ground surrounding them.

Amy had seen where Dack had found the hidden pocket in his knapsack and discovered that she had a pocket there as well. "Hey, I have one too." She pulled out the cylindrical paluz and twisted the top. When that didn't work, she flipped it over and twisted again. The paluz came to life and she laughed. "I can't remember the last time I used a glow stick."

With the aid of the paluz, she examined Jandro for injury. He had a nasty bump on his forehead and the side of his face was scraped, but was otherwise all right. Once she was sure he wasn't near death, Amy stood and moved to the opposite end of the alcove where Dack continued his search of the floor.

"What are you looking for?" she asked.

"Medorocas."

"Is that something we can use to build a fire?"

"They probably wouldn't burn well, although I have heard that they are good on a grill."

"You mean it's something to eat?"

"Only in Maseprada, as far as I know. Masepradans have strange tastes."

"What does it look like?" She needed to know what to look for.

"Medorocas are long and have many legs. Those that make the Ocaflu their home are stronger and the most dangerous of their kind. They have mandibles powerful enough to dig through this rock."

If the roof of the recess had been any higher, Amy would have climbed onto Dack's shoulders. "How big are these things?"

"They can grow up to three feet long; although, I believe the Ocaflu medorocas are smaller by a foot or two." He must have sensed Amy's unease as she stepped even closer to him, her paluz held high. "I don't see any indication that there are medorocas around, so you may relax. They probably don't dwell in the outskirts of the Ocaflu where they would be easy prey for pálas."

If it could eat what sounded like a three-foot long centipede, Amy didn't want to know what a pálas was.

They had no supper that night because there was no fire to cook with. Sergeant Aulnode hadn't thought to add any fruit or other food that could be eaten raw, which was just as well since everyone was too tired to do much more than spread out their bedrolls. Whatever Dack's reason for not sleeping next to them the night before must not have seemed important any longer because he slid his mat next to Amy, who was lying next to Jandro. Licha was at the other end. Draping their cloaks over their blankets didn't keep out the cold, but it was enough to stop the shivering. Believing that her paluz would keep the medorocas away, Amy was reluctant to shut it off and did so only because Dack said it was keeping him awake. In the darkness, she lay listening to the far off thunder as the storm moved on.

When Amy woke, she smelled smoke. The quimeros on either side were still asleep, but Licha was gone. A flash of panic almost had her waking Dack and Jandro, but when she lifted herself to her elbows she saw Licha sitting before a fire only a few feet outside the overhang. Carefully, Amy slid out of the makeshift communal bed. The sun was out, but it was still rather cold. Her cloak, however, was currently covering much of Jandro so she wrapped her arms around herself and made her way out of the alcove. Licha sat cross-legged by the fire, hands on her knees, her face up and her eyes closed. Though Amy did her best not to disturb the meditating quimera, Licha must have heard her approach because when Amy squatted by the fire, she opened her eyes.

"Good morning." Licha's boots stood beside her and she moved them out of the way so that Amy could sit.

"I didn't think we'd have a fire today," Amy said. "At least not until the sun was out long enough to dry the wood."

"Wood doesn't have to be completely dry to start a fire. I found a patch of dead árbont shrubs just over there." Licha pointed west toward the mesquite-like trees that were pervasive in Pliada. "I dug to the bottom for branches that weren't soaked through. I just had to cut off the bark."

The fire was small but it gave off enough heat for Amy to feel it down to her bones. If the rocky ground hadn't been dotted with puddles of clear water, she would have stretched out before the flames. "Is there enough wood to cook with?"

"Yes. I was just going to go get the pans and grain."

"You tend the fire, and I'll get them."

Amy stood and puddle-hopped her way back to the alcove. Dodging rainwater rivulets dripping from above, she crossed under the outcrop and searched for Licha's knapsack. When she heard rustling, she assumed that either Dack or Jandro had woken and she turned towards the sound. Her heart skipped a beat when she saw, crawling between the slumbering and unaware quimeros, a monstrous centipede that had to be at least two feet in length and nearly a foot wide slowly making its way over the spread cloaks. Its segmented body was a deep red-brown, almost the exact color of the surrounding rock its dozens of long legs skimmed across. The huge insect had what looked like antennae at both ends and if not for enormous mandibles that clicked menacingly, she wouldn't have known which end was the head. Dack had said only that their mandibles were strong enough to cut through rock, but Amy knew that centipedes were poisonous, and one this size probably had enough venom to kill.

The medorocas was nearing Dack's head when Amy's paralysis

broke. Her belt with the scabbard attached to it was too far away, but Licha's was not. She grabbed the sword handle and yanked it from the scabbard. As quickly as she could, not only to save Dack from being bitten, but also so she wouldn't have to think about what she had to do, she ran to the mats. The centipede-like medorocas either saw her or sensed danger. Like a cobra, it began to raise its front half threateningly. Amy didn't wait to see what it was capable of. Holding the sword with both hands, she stabbed downward with all her might. She felt the tip penetrate the shell-like casing, just below the creature's head, and pass through the flesh underneath. What she had forgotten, however, was that the surface below the centipede, under the cloak, blanket, and mat it writhed on, was solid ground. The jarring of sword meeting rock nearly caused her to lose her grip. So did the surprise of hearing the medorocas scream, a shriek that would put an eagle's cry to shame. Jandro and Dack woke. Dack was on his feet in an instant, but it took Jandro a moment to get his bearings. Then he did his own imitation of a shrieking eagle.

The medorocas writhed as it tried to dislodge itself from the sword by bucking its back end. The antennae there whipped around and struck Amy on her left forearm. The slap stung terribly and she nearly dropped the sword, but before the medorocas could strike again, she used all her weight and bore down on the sword, twisting and rocking it back and forth until something popped and the creature stopped moving. If she hadn't been so sickened by what she'd done, she would have found the astonished expressions on the quimero's faces rather amusing.

Dack looked down at the headless segmented body that lay where he had been sleeping. "You could have woken me."

"I thought you said those things wouldn't be in the outskirts." Panting, Amy wanted to drop the sword but her hands seemed welded to it and wouldn't let go.

"Apparently, I was mistaken," Dack said.

Jandro pulled his sword from his belt scabbard, which he'd kept beside him through the night, and used it to flip the body over to expose its underside. "I bet this one has a lot of meat."

Amy thought she might vomit at the thought of eating the monster she'd killed, but Dack was willing to give it a try.

"Who knows if we'll come across anything edible between here and Primerabrigo. I don't know about you, but I don't look forward to several more days of eating nothing but porridge." He pried Amy's hands off Licha's sword, stuck it through the inert medorocas' body, lifted it up, and shoved it toward Jandro.

"You're from Maseprada. How do we cook this?"

Jandro frowned. "The only medorocas I've ever eaten were a lot smaller than that."

"So? How did you cook those?"

"I … guess we just threw them on the fire."

"We better make a fire then," Dack said.

"It's already done." Amy pointed out to where Licha sat.

"Looks like it's time to break the fast." Dack strode from under the outcrop.

Licha jumped up when she saw what Dack had on the end of the sword. She seemed to be as put off by it as Amy had been, but after a few words from Dack, she took the sword and held the dead medorocas over the flame. Dack turned and waved the other two over.

"Hope it tastes like chicken," Amy said.

Jandro looked at her. "Like what?"

Amy shook her head. "Never mind."

Soon the four were sitting around the dying fire with segments of cooked medorocas on the ground before them. The underside had been cut away revealing white flesh that could easily be pulled out with their fingers. Jandro dug in without hesitation, while Amy and Dack took their time. Apparently, insects were included in the Carados vow to eat no meat, because Licha refused her share. She didn't admonish Jandro for eating his, though, and even encouraged him to eat what she wouldn't. Amy watched Dack's expression turned from skepticism to delight when he popped a bit of the meat into his mouth.

"Tastes like cénarra," he said.

It was difficult for Amy to overlook that what sat on the ground in front of her belonged to something she was sure would cause her nightmares—that is, if she ever had any. Finally, her rumbling stomach overruled her squeamishness. She gingerly sampled the meat, and nearly swooned. Medorocas tasted exactly like lobster. If there had been melted butter to dip it in, she would have been in heaven.

After eating, they packed up and filled their canteens from the many puddles covering the rocky terrain of the Ocaflu. The ground outside it had been so parched that it had soaked up nearly all the rain from the night before, leaving only a damp surface that dried as soon as the sun beat down on it. The dampness dried up even more quickly and eventually they were kicking up dust as they walked along.

In the light of day, it was easy for Dack to regain his bearings. By nightfall they'd reached the southern end of the Ocaflu. Amy objected when Dack suggested they look for another outcrop to sleep under, so they continued on a while longer until they reached a spot where the hard packed ground gave over to tufts of dry grass and trees that twisted like mesquite but were thicker and taller with uneven, tooth-edged leaves like an elm's. Dry wood and grasses were abundant and they were able build a roaring fire. The day had warmed up considerably, but as the sun went down the temperature dropped with it. The night wasn't so cold that they needed to sleep huddled together as they had at the Ocaflu, although Amy slept near Jandro and Licha. Like he had done the first time they'd made camp, Dack chose to sleep on the other side of the fire. He sat up for a while, however, after the others had lay down. Finding it difficult to fall asleep, Amy watched him through narrow eyelids. For the longest time he simply sat on a rock he had found in the field surrounding them and had brought near the fire to use as a stool. He stared up at the full moon making its way across the otherwise empty sky. When he lowered his head, she thought that he was nodding off until he raised his clasped hands and held them below his chin. His lips moved slightly. As he looked out into the darkness, he could have been praying or simply muttering to himself. Maybe he was repeating a Trotéjo motto over and over.

The connection between the Carados and the Trotéjo confused Amy. She wasn't sure if the Trotéjo were auxiliary to the Carados or vice versa. Both touted *Dendos* as their creator, but as far as she could tell the Trotéjo seemed to be more of a fellowship than a full on religion, which was just as well. She'd never been a comfortable with religion as topic. She rarely engaged in a religious conversation beyond stating that it seemed to cause more strife than peace. She had vague recollections about going to church with Meemaw, but had never been to services with her father, who claimed to be a lapsed Catholic. Her stepmother Alice was an avowed agnostic and loathed any talk about religious doctrine, one of the few things upon which she and Amy agreed. Both believed that it was extremely presumptuous to claim to know who God was and what God wanted, but while Alice saw no real evidence of God in the world around her, Amy believed it was there, though she'd never actually seen it. The only true faith she had was her belief that God existed. Somewhere. In some form. Her ex-husband Peter had called that a copout.

Dack hadn't changed position and was still moving his lips ever so slightly. Feeling that she was intruding on a private moment, Amy rolled over, facing away from him. She listened to the crackling fire until she fell asleep.

The next morning, she discovered that her left forearm, just above the Cocúlta on her wrist, was red and tender and there was a strip of tiny blisters running along it. She assumed she had been bitten by something and hopped up from the ground to frantically shake out her bedroll. When Jandro saw what caused her distress he told her that it was the result of being struck by the medorocas' rear antenna.

"They're poisonous," he said as if she should have already known this.

"Really? I assumed it was the mandibles that were poisonous."

Jandro nodded. "Those too."

Licha examined Amy's wound and said that it was healing itself nicely, but that Amy should take off her bracelet so as not to further irritate it.

"I don't think I can," Amy said. She tugged on the bracelet until she was able to pull it over the thickest part of her hand. "What do you know? I hadn't been able to do that before." She wondered if it had to do with weight loss but it wasn't as though she'd had fat hands to begin with. She hadn't been able to get it off in her world, which was why she had it on in this one.

Or was it the other way around?

Amy looked closely at the bracelet, turning it over in her hand.

"What is it?" Licha asked.

The bracelet looked no different than it had when she'd examined it in her office. "Do you really believe this has something to do with me being *Lacáruna*?"

Both Licha and Jandro said yes. Dack wanted to know why she'd asked.

"Because if this was brought into my world that has to mean there is a two-way door between us."

"Maybe it was always in your world," Jandro suggested.

"I can assure you that this hasn't always been under the sofa in my office, and if it was taken from here to there then I can get back there too." She saw the worried look on Licha's face. "After I fulfill the prophecy of course."

Licha smiled.

Dack held out his hand. "Perhaps you should give that to me for safe keeping."

"Why? You've said that these are sold at every marketplace."

"They are. Cheap trinkets, which are not what an ocático would wear."

"Is that what I am? Ocático?"

"Of course you are, cousin."

"How are you going to pass me off as your cousin in your hometown?"

"Obviously, we will have to come up with another persona. But whatever it will be, you will remain ocático and you'll have to play the part." He nodded at the *trinket* she held.

Amy looked at the gold bracelet again. Despite all that she had put it through since first slipping it on, the bracelet remained untarnished. Even more surprising was that it remained as smooth and unblemished as the day her assistant had discovered it lying on her office floor. She found that a bit strange; while gold didn't tarnish, it was a malleable metal and should have been rather banged and scratched up by now. Yet it wasn't, and that likely meant that it wasn't entirely gold. But if that were true shouldn't it have been even the slightest bit tarnished? It gleamed in the sunlight. Maybe she was wrong, but if the bracelet was her ticket home, she wasn't giving it to anyone. She slipped it back onto her left hand because that's where she'd always worn it. The medorocas wound be damned.

"Maybe I'll set a trend among the ocático by wearing it," she said as she continued with packing her bedroll. "In any case, I'm not giving it to you or to anyone else. I've already given up the only thing that proved I wasn't …"

She stopped what she was doing and looked up at Dack, who was standing over her with his hands on his hips, his cloak draped over his shoulders like some sort of super hero. "Where are my running shoes? I haven't seen them since we were given new clothing after ... Siphiwe has them."

Dack blanched, his tawny skin turning nearly as white as muttonchops. Licha saw it as well as she stepped between them, looking from one face to the other.

"What? What is it?"

Dack raised his hands in disbelief. "I'd forgotten about your shoes. I knew she had them, and I told her to keep them safe until it was time for us to leave." He looked at the others. "Are you sure they weren't packed in any of your sacks?"

"I think we would have discovered that by now."

"Maybe she did pack them," Jandro said. "But they were taken out when the knapsacks and stuff were put in the crate. Why are you worried about the shoes?"

Amy and Dack were too busy staring at one another in disbelief to answer. Licha, however, was not and she turned to Jandro.

"Because they are proof that Amy comes from another world."

Jandro shrugged. "I know that, but who cares if Siphiwe has them? Unless you think ..." His jaw dropped and for a moment it seemed as if he were going to join the staring contest. "No. She wouldn't ... She wasn't ... Why would they think Siphiwe would betray us?"

Dack's shoulders sagged as he looked at Jandro. "We don't know for certain that she has."

Amy wondered why he was fudging the truth.

"But you have your suspicions," Licha said.

He nodded.

"And if she has those shoes she could ... what?"

"I don't know what she could do. That's what worries me. Perhaps she could pass them along to the Arañalianza. She certainly wouldn't need them to prove to anyone else Amy's true identity."

"Hold on there," Amy held up her hand. "Amy *is* my true identity."

Shaking his head slowly, Dack looked at her. "Not in this world. Here you are *Lacáruna*." He stopped to think. His fingers tugged on his chin while he walked around the smoldering fire, looking at the ground. "Perhaps she did us a favor. If someone were to find them in our possession, we'd be at more risk than simply worrying about their current location. Those shoes would be difficult to explain and would only draw attention to us." His eyes traveled from the bracelet on Amy's wrist up to her eyes. "To you."

Suddenly the bracelet felt heavy.

Despite his worried brow, Dack smiled. "I think you have the right idea about starting a trend. When we get to Primerabrigo, we're going to buy more bracelets and we're all going to wear them."

"Even me?" Jandro asked.

Dack chuckled. "Even you. In fact, you're going to wear dozens of them. Both of you." He looked at the young quimerté. "The only way not to inadvertently draw attention is to purposely draw it. Why notice a single bracelet when there are dozens of others to see?"

"I don't understand."

Dack patted him on the shoulder. "As long as you do as you're instructed, you don't have to understand."

Jandro looked at Licha, who shrugged. When Dack snatched up his knapsack and began walking south, Amy hung back. She too patted Jandro on the shoulder.

"Sometimes I don't understand him, either."


With no roads or trails to follow, Dack's sense of direction was all they had to go by. The ground gradually sloped downward and while that made their journey less of a trudge, the landscape also began to crowd with vegetation. With more clumps of grass and small shrubs to step over and more thickets to go around by the end of the second day out of the Ocaflu, Amy felt as exhausted as she had when she'd traveled uphill from Esterenas to Winter Outpost. As they neared Chorgo River, trees became more abundant, starting with the mesquite-elm trees that no one in their party knew the name of. Farther south, the unnamed trees dwindled and were replaced by trees Dack did know the name of. The árbaguas were very tall with dark maroon leaves and branches that began high up on the trunk and spread out like an open umbrella. Sunlight filtered through the canopy enough that the vegetation below thrived, especially a shrub, the fruit of which looked like tiny apricots but tasted like cucumber. Those were plentiful and easy to pick and became a staple of their diet for the next two days, as they passed through a section of the Outer Belt. Jandro asked if they should be on the lookout for any Isolationist Tribes, but Dack said he'd be better off keeping an eye out for forest piónas. He kicked aside a shrub as if looking for something that might be hiding beneath it, before winking at Amy. She wasn't sure if he winked because he was pulling Jandro's leg or if he simply enjoyed unnerving her. Whichever it was, she kept her eyes on the ground ready to climb an árbaguas should anything come skittering out of the bushes.

On the sixth morning of their travels they came upon the Chorgo River. When Dack suggested that they bathe and rinse out their clothing, Amy was the first to unbutton her shirt. Dack stopped her and said he meant they would bathe *in* their clothing. Amy was sure she was more disappointed than even Jandro, but she didn't argue. She removed her cloak, scabbard belt, boots and socks and stood on the bank of the Chorgo. The river was a dozen times as wide as the Mika, where she had bathed before, so there would be no swimming across it. And it was much, much deeper; she could feel the strength of the current when she walked into the water and swam out past the reeds. Despite what Dack had said, and because no one else went past the reeds as she had, Amy removed her shirt and pulled down the top of her red bustier. She had no pulabaza soap to clean herself with but she rubbed her torso vigorously, especially her armpits and between and below her breasts where sweat gathered. She didn't feel very clean but she felt refreshed when she pulled up her bustier and put on her shirt. She swam back through the reeds to the bank and when she stepped onto the bank, she considered removing her shirt and trousers to wring them out, but suspected that if Dack wanted them to wear their clothes in the water he probably didn't want them taken off once out of it. She wondered if he was a prude or if the seguidosts were a little more free-spirited than the average quimerté. She suspected it was a bit of both. Dack was, after all, the only one who made sure to go far off whenever he had to relieve himself. While everyone else remained close enough that they could be heard if needed, Dack would find a spot off in the distance where he was merely a speck on the horizon. Amy was sure he was thrilled when they reached the forest where he could go off and not be seen at all.

The water didn't do anything about her increasingly greasy hair, so she kept it pulled back in a ponytail. Dack had his pulled back as well. Licha barely had more than stubble on her head and Jandro had no hair at all, so they didn't have much to worry about keeping clean. Licha was less than thrilled, however, that she had to cover her head again. She'd assumed that when given new clothing she would be able to go bare headed, but Dack reminded her that only seguidosts shaved their heads.

"And it's not cold enough unless we're out on the river to go about with your hood up," he added. "Here, use this." He tore out a piece of the lining from his cloak and used it as a scarf to tie around Licha's head. Everyone agreed that it was more flattering than the turban had been. Still, Licha wasn't happy about having to wear it.

While their clothing dried, Dack held the lupita to his eye and surveyed the opposite bank. Although he had managed to lead them in the right direction, he wasn't sure where along the river they'd come out.

He knew that they had to be fairly close to the Lagosla Region due to the thick reed beds on the other side, but the treetops were wrong.

"Going off course at the Ocaflu must have put us too far east. There are no árbaguas in Lagosla, only árbosgo." He turned to Amy, although he could have addressed the younger two as well, since they hadn't been to the region either. "Árbosgo grow in the water."

"Right," Amy said.

"They are significantly different from árbaguas, not only in how they look but where they grow."

Amy nodded. "Swamp trees, I get it."

"I don't," Licha said. "What makes them different?"

"You'll see." Dack slung his knapsack over one shoulder, opposite the hip where his sword hung. He held onto the strap with one hand and the sword handle with the other. "We'll have to do a bit of back tracking. But probably not for long."

The riverbank was no easier to traverse than the rocky ground of the Ocaflu had been. Often they had to go inland because the bank would drop off sharply or be so thick with vegetation that it was impossible to walk through. After several hours of weaving in and out of the árbagua forest, Dack told the others to stop and rest while he went on alone to find the quickest route to where they could cross the Chorgo.

Licha objected. "Let Jandro or me go. You have to stay with Amy and protect her."

"From what?" Amy didn't feel much in the need for protection, currently. With the exception of irritating gnat swarms, they hadn't come across anything but plant life.

"Neither you nor Jandro will know when Lagosla begins," Dack said.

"Yes we would." Licha put her hands on her hips. "It's where the árbaguas stop and another kind of tree starts."

Amy grinned at Dack. "She's got you there."

Dack asked Licha if she'd ever seen a swamp. Licha shook her head. Jandro must have anticipated that he would be asked the same question because he shook his head as well.

"I don't know what a swamp is but it sounds wet."

"It is," Amy said. "Where I come from a swamp is often called a wetland. They're usually adjacent to rivers."

Dack clapped his hands. "That's quite enough geography lessons. Suffice it to say that because I am more familiar with the region, I will go in search of it. Furthermore, getting us to the right area isn't all that needs to be done, I'll also have to procure transportation across the river to it."

Licha wasn't going to give up that easily. "We could find a route to the region and then come back for you and then you could ..." She trailed off when Dack began vigorously shaking his head like he had something in his ear.

"I don't want to discuss this."

Holding up her hands, palm outward, Amy put a stop to their conversation. "Let's all go. There is no need to separate and besides, if I sit down, I won't want to get back up." She looked at Dack. "Unless you want to camp here for the night, we're all going with you."

With a sigh, Dack surrendered. "If that's what you want, then let's keep moving."

Three or so hours later they came out of the forest near a wooden jetty, at the end of which was a rowboat. Seeing a small wooden shack on the bank, Amy had an idea why Dack had been so adamant about going on alone. Before heading for the shack, Dack informed the others that he would do all the talking. He kept one hand on the hilt of his sword and purposely shuffled his feet to announce his approach. Just before he reached the shack, someone stepped out of it. Amy had to quickly turn away to hide her shock.

The quimero who came out from the shack was the strangest one she'd seen yet. He had broad shoulders and a huge belly. His neck was short and thick and supported an incredibly wide head. His ears were large, especially the lobes, which nearly touched his shoulders and wobbled when he spoke. None of that, however, was as odd as his nose. Like his head, the quimero's nose too was wide, and it hung down in a fleshy mass that nearly obscured his mouth. He had more of a trunk than a nose, although it didn't seem capable of movement other than wobbling like his earlobes. He had pink coloring, which was much like the cream that Amy rubbed into her skin before presenting herself in the garrison, but his face was ruddy and heavily lined.

"Ho-ho there, friend," Dack said as he approached.

"A friend, indeed." The quimero sounded like an Englishman with a head cold.

"Are you the proprietor of that boat?" Dack pointed to the jetty.

"That I am." The quimero looked beyond Dack and eyed the others with suspicion. "You're not deserters, are you? Because I don't deal with Fensoré deserters." He threw a thick thumb over his shoulder, indicating the river. "And they sure as bloody blazes don't want any on the other side."

Dack squared his shoulders. "I've never heard of a Fensoré deserter."

Amy wondered if he were about to disregard all that he had said about no longer being a colonel. The wobble-eared quimero had to see that he had taken offense.

"Me neither," the quimero said. "Not until real recent."

"And you've come across one of them yourself?"

The quimero shook his head and his nose quivered distractingly. "No, but I've heard about it from reliable sources."

"How can you be sure it's not just rumor?"

The quimero leaned against the shack wall and folded his arms atop his considerable belly and shrugged.

Groaning, Dack dug into his knapsack. "All right. How much is it going to cost for you to pour the pisspot?"

That wasn't an idiom Amy had heard before, but she had a good idea what it meant.

The quimero shrugged again. "How much you got?"

Dack held up a silver coin. The quimero took a step closer to get a better look.

"That'll do."

He reached for the coin, but Dack closed his palm. "It better be worth it."

"You'll never know unless I tell it, now will you?"

Dack gave him the coin and the quimero dropped it in his shirt pocket. "I'll tell you how I know it's not rumor. I've rowed a few across the Chorgo myself."

"You just said you don't deal with Fensoré deserters."

The quimero shrugged. "I lied."

"How do you know they were Fensoré?"

"Theys in uniforms, of course. I first thought maybe theys just sneaking over to see family but no, theys doing something else."

"Doing what? Get to it?"

The quimero snorted through his sizable nose. A little trumpet blast. "Working with the black market, that's what."

"Why?"

"Don't know why. Maybe theys tired of being fensorés. I can tell you this, though. They ain't the only ones who've become venbado these past weeks. Black market is big business these days."

"Why?"

The quimero was quite good at shrugging. The two stared at each other saying nothing. Amy was sure Dack was going to pull out another coin, which he did, but not for more information.

"I wish to book passage on your craft for myself, my cousin, and her two iado. I assume your boat is for hire."

"That it is," the quimero said. "For a price."

With a flick of his thumb, Dack tossed the coin into the quimero's hand. "I'm sure that will do. The information you gave me was hardly worth the first coin."

Before putting the coin in his pocket the quimero bounced his hand slightly, as if weighing his payment and options. "What brings ocático to this side of the river?"

Dack folded his arms across his chest. "Why would that be your business?"

The quimero's mouth spread out from under his proboscis in a wide smile. "Not my business at all. It's only that I recognized a Sangcertigre the moment I laid my peepers on you. The name's Wystan, what's yours?"

"Señor Sangcertigre."

"That's how it's going to be is it?" Wystan nodded in the direction of the others. "Your cousin must not be full-blooded. I wouldn't have taken her as ocático."

"As they say, looks can be deceiving." Dack waved his hand impatiently. "Now if you would be so kind as to take us across the river."

Wystan put the coin in his pocket with the other. "Let me get the bloody oars."

Dack gestured for the others to follow, as he walked onto the jetty. He waited for them to join him at the end where the boat was tied. Amy walked faster than the other two so that she would reach Dack before they did. She stood close to him.

"You didn't want us to come with you because you thought that you may have to kill that man ... that quimero, didn't you?" she asked in a whisper. "I'm glad that you didn't."

Dack glanced at the shack; his green eyes narrowed slightly. "Then let us hope I won't need to. He's a bit dodgy."

"Because he knows your Sangcertigre? Does it matter? You said we'd be safer once we're out of Pliada."

"This business about the black market has me concerned. We can't afford to let our guard down until we're out of Lagosla."

Amy doubted Dack would ever let his guard down.

Wystan came out of the shack carrying four long wooden oars. "One of your iado is going to have to help me row you across." He thudded down the jetty toward them. "Otherwise, I'll have to take you two at a time."

"He'll help." Dack looked at Jandro, expressionlessly. "That's what he's here for."

Shoving two of the oars in Jandro's hands, Wystan told him to sit at the stern. When Jandro was seated, the quimero climbed in and ambled to the bow, stepping over two sets of benches. He sat down hard, rocking the boat. Dack's outstretched hand helped keep Amy and Licha steady while they boarded and sat on the bench closest to Jandro. He climbed aboard last and sat on the front bench facing Wystan, who untied the dock lines and pushed off the jetty. Seated, the quimero faced the stern and began to row. Jandro wasn't doing a very good job in assisting him, until Wystan shouted that he should turn around and face the stern as well. Jandro soon got into the rhythm.

Everyone faced the rear of the boat except for Dack. Curious as to why, Amy leaned back so she could hear the conversation between Wystan and him without having to look at them. She hoped it would be a genial exchange and that the quimero with the strange nose wouldn't cause them any difficulty. While she had no doubt as to Dack's abilities to protect them, they were in a narrow rowboat. If there was trouble someone was going to end up in the water.

"I'm a distant relative of yours, you know." She heard Wystan say to Dack while he rowed.

"Is that so?" Dack replied.

She couldn't lean so far back as to see his eyes, but she was certain that Dack kept them on the distant bank and not the rowing quimero.

"I am," Wystan said. "My family descends from a Primeróte secondborn."

Amy glanced over her shoulder. Wystan's ruddy face was growing darker from the exertion of rowing the boat.

"There have been many Primeróte branches since the time before the *Morphósis*," Dack said. "Anyone can make that claim."

"Sure, but with me, it's true." He snorted through his nose, a bit less trumpet-like. "This should be proof enough."

Just by hearing the tone of his voice, Amy was sure Dack was smiling wryly.

"Charvi wasn't the only one of her kind brought from another world. How can you be sure you're not descended from one of them?"

The quimero at the front of the boat snorted again. "How can you be sure you're a full-blood?"

"You recognized me as a Sangcertigre. You tell me how I can be sure."

As badly as she wanted to turn and see the expression on Wystan's face, Amy remained staring at Jandro's back while he struggled with the oars. Apparently, that was the end of the conversation at the bow. Nothing more was said until the boat reached the jetty on the opposite side of the river.

Wystan was the first out. Rather than tie the dock line to the cleat, he held onto it as the passengers disembarked. Once the boat was empty, the quimero stepped back into it and rowed off without comment. Dack stood on the dock watching him leave. Licha stood beside him.

"Who's Charvi?"

"The spouse of one of the Primeróte quimerito."

"An ancestor of yours?"

"No, but she married the brother of my ancestor."

Amy was less concerned about lineage than she was about what Dack had been saying before they'd crossed the river. "Why did you say we have to keep our guard up?"

"Because Wystan was venbado, which is someone who deals in the black market." He turned and headed up the long, empty jetty.

Amy caught up with him quickly. "Is that a problem? Do you think he was lying about Fensoré deserters becoming venbado?"

"He could have been, but I don't think so. He couldn't have known I was Fensoré so why make up something that sounds so outlandish?"

"Then what's worrying you?"

"Because now his *reliable sources* will soon learn that a Sangcertigre and three others passed into the Lagosla Region, and it won't take much deduction for anyone to guess it was the four of us. The black market trades in information even more than they do in goods. If the Arañalianza are looking for us, and most assuredly they are, word will get to them eventually. Sooner, if what we believe about Siphiwe is true."

"Maybe you should have given him more of those silver coins to keep him quiet."

"That would work until someone gave him even more coin to talk. What's done is done. No need to dwell on it."

They continued down the long jetty, which cut through thick, tall reeds. The Lagosla Region was indeed a swamp. Dozens of islets rose above the marsh, each connected by a series of narrow rope and plank bridges. The árbosgo, draped with large swathes of moss Dack had said only grew in the region, grew around the inhabited isles, but not on them and reminded Amy of trees she'd seen while spending a semester of her sophomore year at Tulane in New Orleans. Most of the islets had been cleared to make room for structures that were little more than shacks shoved against one another as if in a continual attempt to vie for space. The region had no avestrandés or radamias, not only because they were too large to traverse the network of bridges, but also there weren't any carts to pull. Everything was hauled by the resident quimerté on their backs or balanced on their heads.

Although Lagosla was free of mosquitoes, the gnat swarms were just as bothersome. The teeny bugs seemed to want nothing more than to fly into Amy's ear canal and up her nose. She noticed several quimerté wearing what she at first took for funeral veils over their faces but quickly realized was actually insect netting. She suggested to Dack that they procure some netting for themselves. Soon.

Crossing the rickety rope and plank bridges took a bit of getting used to, but their party managed without anyone falling into the slow-moving, murky water. As always, Dack led the way. Jandro seemed to be fascinated with, but not frightened by, their new environment while Licha, on the other hand, stayed so close to Amy that she may as well have been in the taller female's knapsack. Amy understood Licha's unease. She wasn't the only one who had been thrust into a situation so unlike what she was used to. Having grown up in Pliada and lived her entire life as a member of the Carados, Licha was nearly as unprepared for their new circumstances as Amy herself.

Dack followed signposts across several bridges and islets until he found what had to be the largest isle of the region. The isle was the only one they'd come across that had more than one or two narrow paths between the shacks and not only housed many Lagosla denizens, but also had a large marketplace. Stalls lined the center of the isle in row after row. Most of the wares seemed to be food or clothing, but several booths sold goods such as powders, ointments, and what looked like ordinary rocks. They stopped at one of the clothing booths that sold the insect netting called a cucabeza, which came in the form of a sack that was loosely placed over the head and tied around the neck. Dack bought one each for Amy and Licha, but Jandro declined, saying that the bugs didn't bother him at all. Amy thought it had more to do with the fact that Dack didn't buy one for himself.

They continued up and down several rows until Dack stopped in front of a stall that sold trinkets, including bracelets like the one Amy kept hidden under her shirtsleeve. He quibbled with the quimera behind the counter about the cost for a bit until she came up with a reasonable price, which was then lowered slightly when Dack informed her that he wanted all the bracelets. He thanked the quimera and took his purchase.

"Here." Dack passed around the bracelets, leaving a few for himself. "Put these on."

When the bracelets were on, Dack nodded approvingly. "Now no one will notice one bracelet because there are so many."

Amy looked at all the adorned arms. "And you really don't think this is going to draw attention."

"Of course it will, but only momentarily. Compared to some of the fashions in Maseprada this is mild."

"What about here?"

Dack gestured to their surroundings. "Do you see anyone looking at us? No one in this region wants to be noticed; therefore, no one notices anyone else." He looked down the row where they stood. "At least not overtly."

He held out a bent arm for Amy to take, which she did. "Let's see if we can find transportation to Edalés before nightfall. Otherwise we'll have to travel over these bridges in darkness to find a place to stay."

"What about the …" Amy struggled, and failed, to remember the word. "What about the glow sticks?"

"You don't want to use a paluz here. Trust me."

That was what Amy hated the most about being a stranger in a strange land; someone was always asking her to trust them.

The deeper into Lagosla they went, the more everyone they passed had their own business to attend to and paid scant attention to the travelers. Amy noted that only the gnats seemed interested in them and as the insects became more prevalent, so did the quimerté wearing the cucabeza. Jandro began to whine about not having a net and even Dack's stoic stance against the buzzing around his head cracked. Unable to stand it any longer, he asked a passerby where he could acquire a cucabeza for himself and his young portadores and was directed to a shop and eatery on another, smaller islet just ahead. Dack all but ran across the bridge to get there. Because it was the only building on the islet, they had no trouble finding the shop.

Unlike all the others they'd crossed, this islet was covered in vegetation, including trees bearing fruit that looked like small red gourds. They hurried toward the building, plagued by an increasing cloud of insistent gnats. Amy could hear someone, with a very good and very loud voice, singing. When she turned her head in that direction, she nearly jumped out of her skin.

"What the ..." She grabbed onto Licha thereby reversing their roles of guardian and ward.

Not two feet from where she stopped was yet another outlandish bird-like creature. Relatively smaller than any she'd seen so far, it resembled other pájastias in that it had feathers, a beak, and sharp talons. If she had stood next to it, it would have come up only to her breast. What made Amy want to grab Licha and make a dash for the building were the incredibly long claws growing out of the little beast's wings. The fore-claw was the longest, a foot at least in length, with two much shorter claws below. The pájastia used the long claw to pull down a gourd tree so that it could snag one of the small gourds in its beak. At first, Licha seemed confused why Amy suddenly wanted to hug her until she saw what Amy was looking at. She giggled and gently pushed the taller female away.

"Don't worry. That's a polloté. They're kept for their eggs. They're harmless."

Amy wasn't so sure about that. She made a wide berth around the creature as she hurried toward the building where the singing had come from. Dack and Jandro were already inside. Licha, giggling, hurried after her.

The screen door creaked loudly when Amy stepped into a shop that was considerably less bizarre than the creature outside. Reminiscent of the shops lining the streets of Tijuana, Mexico, the Lagosla shop was crowded from floor to ceiling with items for purchase. She saw some of the rocks she'd seen earlier and couldn't fathom why were there so many ordinary-looking stones for sale, even if they did have small blue veins circling them. Licha and she wound their way through the aisles until they stumbled upon Dack and Jandro, who were trying on several different styles of cucabeza. Dack settled on one that was attached to a hat called a cucabero, similar to a pith helmet although not so tall or wide of brim. Jandro settled for the plain black cucabeza that Amy and Licha wore. As Dack paid a somewhat normal-looking quimero for the goods, Amy wandered a bit and noticed the aforementioned eatery around the corner from the counter where the others stood.

"Do we have time to stop for a bite to eat?" she asked. "I'm sure we could all use something to drink."

Even though the gnats hadn't followed them inside, Dack's annoyed expression hadn't abated even slightly. "I don't think we—"

"Of course you do," a loud feminine voice rolled out from behind them.

Standing in the aisle was the largest quimera Amy had seen. Not only was she over six feet tall, the quimera had to weigh three hundred pounds. She wore a long, peach-colored dress with a very low neckline that pushed her enormous breasts up and out. Her coloring was similar to Jandro's, but more grayish, and her skin had a slight leathery quality. Though not heavily lined, her skin just seemed somehow thick like an orange peel without the dimples. Her deep red hair was piled atop her head like several scoops of raspberry ice cream. The quimera's face was huge, as was needed on such a large frame: wide mouth and nose; large, piercing blue eyes; and a double chin that almost concealed her neck entirely. She had an air of mischievousness about her, as if she would love to do something naughty at any given moment. Her cool blue eyes sparkled while she smiled at them.

"Of course you have the time," she said. "Stop for a moment to catch your breath and sample our fabulous food." She stepped forward, light on her feet considering her bulk, and swept past them as she went around the corner into the eatery.

Amy didn't wait to see if Dack wanted to take up the quimera's offer of some fabulous food. She found the quimera intriguing, to say the least. But when Dack saw Amy starting to follow her, he stepped in front to lead the way. She bristled, still uncomfortable with his insistence about being at the front. The large quimera stood in the middle of an empty café waiting for them.

"Ho-ho there, friend," she said.

Dack bowed. "A friend indeed. Thank you for the invitation. My cousin and I are in need of refreshment and I'm sure the youngsters would like something to eat as well."

"Good, good. Then you have come to the right place. Have a seat."

Dack chose a table closest to a door leading outside, where gnats swarmed. The quimera hummed disapprovingly, as she too looked out the door.

"The gnats are thick as thieves these shrinking days," she said.

As the others removed their knapsacks before sitting down, Amy saw Dack look at the large quimera sharply and quickly look away before she noticed.

The quimera smiled broadly. "My name is Maru Tamucier. This is my esteemed establishment. Allow me to get you something cool to drink." With flourish, she spun around and left through a swinging door.

Jandro leaned forward and whispered to Dack. "She's got to be from Maseprada. What's she doing owning a store in Primerabrigo?"

"We're in the Lagosla Region. The rules get broken here or, perhaps I should say, they get stretched."

"Why?" Amy asked as both Licha and she removed the cucabeza from their heads. "Quimerté from one country can't own property in another?"

"Not own property, but own any sort of mercantile."

Amy turned to Jandro. "How did you know she was from Maseprada? Is it the lack of accent?"

He shook his head. "No. I mean, yes that too, but it's her family name—Tamucier. That means she's descended from the Post-Primeróte."

"Post?" Amy lowered her voice so as not to be overheard, although there wasn't a soul around to hear them. "There's more than one set of Primeróte?"

"Actually, there are three sets, if that's what you would like to call them," Dack said. "Three separate couples. What Jandro is speaking of is heresy to many quimerté, at least those not living in Maseprada. The Tamucier lineage isn't considered a true Primeróte bloodline, because only the blood of one actual Primeróte is in it."

"When Hagos Tamus' first spouse, the Prophet Salama, passed on," Jandro said, "he married a quimera named Lilen. She was born in this world—"

"He means the pre-*Morphósis* world," Dack interjected.

"Yes, that. Lilen wasn't brought there like the Primeróte."

When the young quimero took a breath, Dack, who Amy thought seemed distracted, wrapped it up. "Because Tamuciers have some Primeróte blood in them their descendents don't have to use a suffix in the family name. But they're forbidden from using the prefix *sang*, which is only allowed for full descendants."

Finding their lineage as confusing as their religion, Amy wasn't disappointed that the conversation ended when Maru returned. She brought with her a tray of six cups, a glass pitcher filled with a honey-colored liquid, and a plate piled high with cheese, fruit, and bread. Rather than simply serve her customers, the large quimera set the tray in the center of the table, pulled up a chair, and sat with them. Maru gestured toward the food on the plate.

"Enjoy."

She picked up the pitcher and filled the cups while humming pleasantly. After passing the cups to her guests, she drank from hers, smacking her lips after she swallowed. Amy took a tiny sip of the honey-colored liquid and took an instant liking to it. The fluid was mildly sweet, but refreshingly clear almost like water. And it was delightfully cold.

Maru noticed Amy's obvious pleasure. "There is nothing as invigorating as libélosa nectar."

Jandro began to cough. He sputtered out his nectar all over the table and Licha.

"Jandro," Licha admonished as she wiped his spittle from her arm.

He pushed his cup away. "I didn't know libélosa made nectar."

Maru laughed loudly. "Oh, in this shrinking world, most everything has a dual use." She looked at Dack. "Don't you agree?"

Keeping her gaze while he nodded, Dack told Jandro to drink his nectar and stop acting like a quimerito. Jandro did as he was told, but Amy now had reservations about what it was that she was drinking. Because of Dack's earlier decree she had to act the ocático, she couldn't ask what a libélosa was or why Jandro was averse to drinking its nectar. So caught up in trying to keep from conjuring in her mind some disgusting creature that could be a libélosa, Amy didn't notice that Maru had begun to unbutton her dress starting at the plunging décolletage. When Licha nudged her with an elbow, Amy looked up and saw Maru pull open her dress to one side and present one of her enormous breasts, which had a salad plate-sized areola. Like the others at the table, she was too shocked to say anything when Maru lifted that breast to reveal three dark moles in a row, the middle mole higher than those on either side of it.

Stupefied, Amy managed to turn her head to say something (she didn't know what) to Dack and saw that he too was unbuttoning his shirt. If her jaw could have dropped any lower, Amy's would have fallen off completely while Dack peeled back his shirt to reveal three moles in the same configuration a few knuckles below his left nipple, which was considerably smaller than Maru's. As quickly as the two had exposed themselves to one another, they re-buttoned their clothing and returned to sipping their nectar as if nothing unusual had just occurred. Licha, Jandro, and Amy, however, sat frozen in place, not saying a word, although their eyes darted around the table as if looking for a safe place to land.

Dack picked up a piece of fruit. "We're looking for transportation to Edalés. Do you know where we could hire a boat nearby?"

Maru nodded. "Two isles over. I can send word to them, if you'd like, so that they can make preparations."

"That would be most kind of you."

He took a bite out of the fruit in his hand. His eyes never left Maru's until she stood and went around the corner into the store. Her absence instantly thawed the others and they began to whisper at the same time, asking the same question. Dack held up his hand to silence them. He glanced over his shoulder to be sure they were alone.

He leaned forward, bidding the others to do as well, and whispered. "She's Trotéjo."

"Is that what that was about?" Amy tapped her left breast.

"Yes. Those are the three points on the crown. We all have the marking."

"You mean you're born with it?" Jandro asked. He then bit his lip when Dack looked at him without answering.

Amy was confused. "But how did you know? Or, I guess I should ask, how did she know since she was the first to ... you know ... expose herself. I didn't see you give the hand signal the apósto was looking for."

"No, that's only for Carados. There are many small ways for a trotéjo to find a comrade, one of which is this button." Dack pointed to the top button on his shirt. "It is upside down and the third one below it is upside down as well."

Amy leaned in close, but for the life of her, couldn't see a difference between any of his buttons.

"And there are other things, such as her using the phrase, *this shrinking world.*"

"I've heard others say that," Licha said. "Back at camp we ..." She grew silent and sadness washed over her white face. Although her eyes momentarily shimmered, no tears fell.

"Of course the Carados would use that phrase. But it's when others use it—in conjunction with a number of other clues—that signals one trotéjo to another."

The gentle shaking of the floor announced Maru's return as she rounded the corner into the eatery. She bypassed their table and closed and locked the door next to it. When she sat down again, her face was damp with sweat.

"We don't have much time before my clerk returns. I sent him to inform the neighbors about your transportation needs and locked the door after him so no one can interrupt us." She took a deep breath and let it out. "My heart hasn't beat this quickly in ages."

"Nor mine," Dack said.

Amy wondered if that were another Trotéjo clue because Dack didn't look as if his heart were beating fast. In fact, he seemed calmer than she had seen him … Well, the calmest she'd ever seen him.

Maru fanned herself with her hand as she spoke. "Is it true? Has *Lacáruna* arrived?"

"So it's believed." Dack was careful not to look at Amy when he said it. "The time of the prophecy seems to be on us. We came from Winter Outpost where we heard tales about the destruction and murder of an entire Carados camp. They were said to have taken *Lacáruna* into hiding before it happened, but their camp paid the price."

Under the table, Amy squeezed Licha's leg. Licha kept her face as impassive.

"It was reckless for you to reveal yourself in front of these three," Dack continued.

Maru shook her large head and patted Jandro's hand. "When this one said he never heard of libélosa nectar I knew you had come out from Pliada. Anyone from Primerabrigo knows of libélosa nectar. Anyone from Maseprada, as well."

"Not in the north," Jandro quickly defended. "I ate a lot of things there but not libélosa nectar."

Maru looked from Jandro to Dack. "Are you Fensoré?"

Dack nodded.

"All of you?"

"Yes."

Maru looked around the table. "You're not defectors, I'm guessing."

"We're not."

"Then you've heard what happened at Winter Outpost. Did four Carados kill a comrade, a Fensoré captain, and were themselves killed after?"

"Partially true."

"They were imposters. I knew it." Maru slapped the table. "For months now I've been saying the Arañalianza is back and here's proof."

"That's not the part that's true. Three of the four *were* Carados and they didn't kill the Trotéjo captain. I did."

The news seemed to hit her like a blast of hot air. Maru's head snapped back and her eyelids fluttered. "Why?" She placed both hands on the table's edge, as if ready to flip it over.

"The fourth quimerté with the Carados was she who we've been waiting for."

"*Lacáruna.*"

Dack nodded. "When she revealed herself to us, the captain revealed himself not to be the comrade I thought him to be and he tried to kill her. I had no choice but to kill him instead."

This seemed to shock Maru more than anything. She brought a hand to her cleavage and shook her head. "A traitor amongst us? The Arañalianza have infiltrated the Trotéjo?"

"So it seems."

The large quimera stood. She rubbed the heels of her hands together repeatedly. "What happened after that? Where is *Lacáruna?*"

"She's with the three that took her away from the camp that was destroyed when the Arañalianza were looking for her. We still don't know how they knew *Lacáruna* was there. Right now she is hiding in Esterenas until we know what she needs to do to fulfill the prophecy."

"If she's there, why are you here? And why are you with these three, if they're not Trotéjo?"

It was only then that Amy noticed Maru had managed to maneuver herself very near a large butcher knife left on a counter. Her tone of voice left no doubt that the female trotéjo was suspicious of her male counterpart. Rather than have another version of what happened with Captain Tamezo, Amy spoke up, mimicking Licha's accent.

"Tell her the truth, Dack."

He looked at her sharply. "What?"

Amy turned to Maru, hoping that the quimera hadn't noticed the accent was missing when she'd spoken earlier. "We're not Fensoré." She nodded toward Licha and Jandro. "We're the three Carados who took *Lacáruna* to the outpost."

Maru looked at Dack, who nodded. "Then who's with *Lacáruna*?"

"She's under the protection of the Trotéjo," Dack said. "Tell me how you've heard what happened at Winter Outpost."

"Through a comrade, of course." Maru eased herself back at the table. "I heard about the three supposed Carados who were killed from a venbado. The same venbado who told me about Fensoré defectors joining the black market."

"Do you think that has anything to do with *Lacáruna's* arrival?"

"I hadn't thought so. There's been a lot of movement in the black market as of late. I'd suspected that the defectors were just venbado firstborn returning to their roots to get in on the action."

"Do you know why there's been a lot of movement?"

"Not for certain, but I believe it involves the military."

"Which military?"

"All of them." Maru looked at the other three. "Tell me about *Lacáruna*. What's she like?"

Jandro was the first to answer. "She's beautiful."

"And smart," Licha said.

Although he hadn't been asked, Dack added, "And very strong willed."

Amy had something to say as well. "She's also very confused because no one seems to know why she's needed for the prophecy."

Dack cleared his throat loudly. "That is why we're here. We believe the written prophecy is in Navercío."

"You know where it is?" Maru asked.

"Not exactly, but from what I've learned the prophecy is with the first three Extiguos in the viceroy's possession. I plan to seek audience with him when we get there."

Maru took Dack's hand in hers. "Stay vigilant when you reach Navercío. There have been strange stories coming from there about the viceroy's behavior."

"What stories?"

"It's rumored he is about to declare himself king."

Dack responded with such surprise that Amy almost asked what was wrong. She glanced at Licha and Jandro and when she noticed their shocked expression, she adopted one for herself so as not to stand out.

"That is forbidden," Dack said. "Has he lost his mind?"

Maru nodded. "That is another rumor."

"Do you think any of this is connected to Arañalianza?"

Her answer would have to wait. A loud pounding on the store's front door startled them all.

"My curious clerk has returned." Maru stood. "Our conversation is over, and you should leave." She unlocked the eatery door. "Go back down the path that brought you here, and follow the signs for Aubrey's. That is who will take you to Edalés."

The four stood. Jandro, Amy, and Licha put on their knapsacks and cucabezas before thanking their hostess and going out the door. Dack swung his knapsack over a shoulder and then hugged the large quimera. His hands didn't meet at her back.

"*La Reina* be your guide." Maru shoved him out the door. "Go now."

She closed the screen door on them, as Dack donned his cucabero and led the others away. Amy followed Dack.

"How could she have learned about what happened at Winter Outpost? She said she'd heard it from a trotéjo."

"I sent a mensáneo—a coded message—to a comrade in Alvela. He was to spread the confirmation of your arrival to other comrades."

"And you left out the part about Tamezo being Arañalianza and you having to kill him."

Dack nodded. Amy didn't need to ask him why. If one arañalianzan could infiltrate the Trotéjo, who knew how many others had. They continued on in silence.

Halfway to their destination, they had to stop at a cross bridge to let several quimerté, loaded down with what looked like gigantic, legless, eyeless grasshoppers, as big as large trout, pass. Jandro whispered to Amy that the quimerté were carrying libélosa libillo.

"You mean that's where the nectar comes from?"

"I don't think so," Jandro said. "That's libillo ... um ..." He thought for a moment. "They're libélosas before they get wings. They live in the water so I don't think anyone could harvest nectar from them. Unless maybe they squash them or something."

Amy gagged a little. "Jandro, stop." She shoved him ahead when the quimerté passed. She didn't want to think about what libillo grew into.

When they reached the islet where the boat for hire was located, Dack didn't quibble over the price. He paid the quimero and boarded a flat boat that was poled across the water by two shaggy quimero on either side of the stern. Although the boat could have held as many as fifteen, they were the only passengers. The four sat at the front far enough away from the quimero guiding the boat through the increasingly shallow waters that Dack felt it was safe for Amy to ask questions, as long as she kept her voice down. Her first question was to ask what, now that they were in Primerabrigo, he planned to do next.

"When we reach Edalés we will take a train to Navercío and go to my family estate before seeking audience with the viceroy."

"Why before?"

"Because my mother has some sway with him and we can use all the help we can get."

"What are you going to tell your mother? How are you going to explain me?"

"I'm going to introduce you to her as my betrothed, who I met at Winter Outpost."

"Betrothed?"

Dack cocked an eyebrow, which was difficult to see through his cucabero. "Would that be so bad?"

"No." Amy laughed. "It's just not … never mind."

"It's just not what?"

"It's just not something I expected, that's all."

Dack looked away. "I have to come up with something other than claiming you to be a cousin. Any of my relatives would know that to be a lie."

Amy wondered if she'd inadvertently hurt his feelings by laughing over the notion of being his betrothed, but didn't worry about it. She had too many other questions. "Why were you so shocked when Maru said there were rumors that the viceroy wanted to be king? Why is that prohibited?"

"It was an agreement made thousands of years ago, the same agreement that allowed Primeróte descendants to rule the three nations. There would be no kings or queens in the post-*Morphósis* world, out of deference to *La Reina*."

"Even after her name and face were forbidden?"

Dack nodded. "Even after that."

The boat ride to Edalés was considerably longer and slower than the boat ride across the river. Their destination took several hours to reach and the last few were under the cover of darkness. Despite the constant full moon, Amy didn't know how the quimeros guiding the boat knew where they were going. The árbosgo trees had become scarce and, as they grew less abundant, they became less moss-covered. Without the hanging moss, they looked naked; or worse, they looked like skeletons. The cucabezas were no longer needed as the swamp opened up. Licha and

Jandro kept theirs on nonetheless. Amy was happy to take hers off. Dack merely flipped the mesh part of his cucabero up off his face.

The night was extremely quiet—apparently, there were no crickets in this world—and for the longest time, the only sound was the boat slowly gliding across the water. Then suddenly there came the unmistakable hum of a flying insect buzzing overhead. Amy, who had nearly been lulled to sleep by the gentle *swoosh* of the poles cutting through the water, sat up and looked around. Jandro and Licha, pressed against each other like bookends, were asleep. Dack was awake and was looking up at the sky. When Amy looked up, she saw the silhouette of something large cross the moon. For a moment she was reminded of the night before she'd left for Palm Springs, when she'd thought there had been someone very tall standing at the end of her bed. This silhouette was nothing like that, though.

She grabbed Dack's arm. "What was that?"

Dack looked up. "That was why we don't use a paluz in the Lagosla Region."

The creature overhead had to be two feet long with a wingspan twice that. "What is it? Is it dangerous?"

"Only in the sense that it can knock you over and take a chunk from your flesh. They're not poisonous, if that's what concerns you; otherwise, you wouldn't be able to drink its nectar."

Amy involuntarily flinched. "That's a libélosa."

"It is indeed."

"How does it make nectar?" Even without the mesh, it was too dark to see Dack's face clearly, but she had an idea that he was smiling.

"You probably don't want to know."

She was willing to leave it at that while she held onto his muscular arm and searched the sky. He didn't seem to mind.

Near midnight, the boat stopped because the water had become too shallow to go any farther. The dock where they disembarked was twice as long as the one that had led from the river into the swamp and Dack claimed that it needed to be lengthened yearly because the water was receding.

"Don't tell me," Amy said. "The water is receding because the world is shrinking."

"That could be the reason, I suppose. I think it has more to do with it seeping underground as Navercío uses more and more water these days." When Amy looked at him questioningly, he further explained. "There's an underground river that runs through the Taplanas Mountains. It's the main source of water for Navercío."

Jandro and Licha were groggy, and Jandro practically dragged his knapsack behind him as they lumbered down the dock. To perk them up, Amy told them about seeing a libélosa. The two seemed too tired for conversation so she focused her attention on what lay ahead. Soon she saw lights.

"That's Edalés," Dack said. "I haven't been there since I was a quimerito. My parents liked to vacation there when my sister and I were young. Of course, that was back when this region was less of a haven for venbados."

"You've never mentioned that you have a sister."

"Had. She died many years ago, the same year I left to join the Fensoré."

"Oh. I'm sorry to hear that." Amy wanted to ask him more about it, but she had the feeling he'd rather not speak of it.

Jandro had perked up some and walked between them. "What about you ... Amy? Do you have any brothers or sisters?"

She heard the hesitation in his voice when he said her name and tried to recall if this was the first time he had actually used it. "No. My mother passed away when I was very young. My father remarried but his new wife didn't have ... quimerito of her own and they never had any together. I guess I was handful enough."

Dack laughed. "I can imagine you were."

"His new what?" Jandro asked.

Amy was unsure what he meant.

"You said your father had a new something who didn't have quimerito."

"Wife. His new wife."

"What's a wife?" Licha asked.

Amy glanced over her shoulder where Licha lagged behind. "The female half of a married couple. The male half is called a husband."

"Interesting," Dack said. "You have different words for the sexes. Here, a spouse is a spouse."

Edalés wasn't walled in so there were no gates to have to pass through, which meant there would be no one to question them or otherwise impede their passage into the city. But no gate also meant that there were no guards, and that, of course, meant that the streets weren't particularly secure since anyone could make their way through them. Rather than risk their safety, Dack suggested they look for an inn to spend the night. It would be easier to find the train station in daylight and, most importantly, it would get them off the streets. The jetty crossed over dry ground the last hundred threestrides or so, ending at well-lit plaza. Several quimerté walked about, including one who pushed a cart and sold something on a stick that could have been fruit or a lump of libélosa flesh, for all Amy knew. Dack asked him for directions to the nearest, cleanest inn. The horned quimero happily supplied the directions once Dack pressed his palm with a silver coin and even offered to take them there. Dack declined but thanked him for his help.

"He would have wanted more silver," Dack explained. "We can find our way ourselves."

Unfortunately, either the quimero had given him the wrong directions or Dack had simply not followed what he had been told. Soon it became obvious that they were lost and deeper into the city than Dack had wanted to go and he kept his hand on the sword hilt ready to defend them if the need arose. Amy, however, was delighted to wander the cobblestone streets. So far what she had seen of the city evoked the French Quarter of New Orleans, although she was aware that she was probably giving it more credit than it was due in that regard simply because the swamp they had come from had reminded her of Louisiana. Still, there were striking similarities, particularly the architecture. The majority of buildings were multi-leveled with ironwork galleries on the upper levels where plants hung alongside open windows and doors. Unlike Winter Outpost, Edalés didn't seem to have electricity. All the streetlamps were gas operated, as were the lights along the buildings. She found it romantic and wanted to linger and take in the atmosphere, but Dack would have none of it. He took Amy's arm and guided her along to keep her from stopping to look at whatever caught her eye.

Eventually, they stumbled across an inn and Dack hustled the others inside. The building's interior was no less reminiscent of New Orleans than the outside had been. The lobby walls were covered with striped paper, peeling slightly at the corners and around a few flickering wall sconces. Dack stood at the reception desk and charmed the quimera—a not-too-distant relative of Maru's, if coloring and size counted—into assigning them two adjoining rooms. She had been hesitant to do so because he had introduced Amy as his betrothed and the quimera said it would be more appropriate if their rooms were on separate floors.

"That won't be necessary." Dack took Licha by the shoulders and held her in front of him. "Although my beloved's iado is small, she packs a mighty wallop. She'll keep me in my place."

The quimera laughed delightedly and handed him two sets of keys.

"One question before we go to our rooms," he said as he took the keys. "Actually two. Are we near the train station? And where is the nearest couturier? My betrothed wants something more appropriate for travel."

When the quimera didn't question this Amy guessed it was because they were near the Lagosla Region. If venbados abounded, as Maru indicated, it was probably best to mind one's own business.

The quimera told Dack that the train station was on the other side of town, but he could hire a cab to get them there in the morning, and just one street over was a lovely couturier. Dack thanked her again and the traveling party climbed the stairs.

Though she had to share it with Licha, Amy was thrilled to see a bed. Even more so than after the trek to Winter Outpost, the mere idea of sleeping on a real bed, underneath real sheets, her head atop real pillows, had her quaking with joy. The double doors between the rooms were unlocked and opened wide and Dack shoved a dresser in front of the door to the hall in Amy and Licha's room. He wanted to be sure that if anyone tried to get in, they would have to go through his room first. Amy turned up the gas lamps to better light the rooms, but doing so made the room more stifling than it had been when they walked in, so she opened the windows and the balcony doors. The street below was dark and deserted. While Amy didn't feel the need to unpack the knapsacks, as she would have done if they had been luggage, she did hang up all the cloaks in the hope that the humidity would soften the wrinkles.

"Unless, of course, you're planning to buy us new ones," she said to Dack.

He looked up from his knapsack in his lap as he sat on the bed in his room. "Those will do, even if they are wrinkled." He turned his knapsack over and opened a hidden pocket underneath from which he removed a drawstring bag filled with silver coin. Jandro searched the bottom of his knapsack for a similar hidden pocket but found none.

"I should have just enough to buy us passage on the train and a proper coat for you and me." Dack returned the coins to the drawstring bag, as he addressed Jandro and Licha. "You two will wear the garments given to you at the garrison."

They looked at each other.

"We don't have them," Jandro said. "We put them into the bag that these clothes came out of."

"What? I told you to keep them."

"No you didn't."

Dack stood, menacingly. "I distinctly recall telling you to keep those garments."

"Then your memory isn't as distinct as you believe." Licha also stood, albeit without any menace at all.

Because he looked as if he were going to bite their heads off, Amy also stood. Dack took notice of the scowl on her face and immediately backed down.

"Perhaps I meant to tell you but forgot in the heat of the moment." He looked at Amy for apparent approval. She smiled at him. "I suppose I'll have to stretch out what coin I have to buy new servant garments. We have to be convincing when we arrive in Navercío."

The inn proprietress sent up a basket of bread and fruit and a jug of the wine that tasted like butterscotch. The wine made Amy sleepy and she bid the others good night while they were still eating. She closed the door between the rooms so that she could undress and take full advantage of a water basin and pitcher atop the dresser that had been pushed in front of the door. She undressed and removed all of her bracelets, careful to put the Cocúlta on top of the stack. The bracelets they'd procured in Lagosla were very close in appearance, but the Cocúlta was slightly thicker. Licha had pointed that out.

Being out of her soiled clothing, including the red bustier she'd worn for what seemed like weeks, felt wonderful and Amy was loath to put anything back on. Once she had washed every part of her body, having made sure to leave some water for Licha's use, she crawled into bed and hoped that Licha wouldn't mind if she slept in the nude. The bed wasn't that wide.

With the exception of Dack, who was up at dawn, they slept late the next morning. Despite that the bed was lumpy, the pillows flat, and the sheets threadbare, Amy reveled in the luxury and lingered there even when Dack returned with boxes tied together with string.

With the top sheet modestly wrapped around her, Amy stood while Dack untied and opened the boxes he had brought back to the room. The first box contained what ocático wore in Primerabrigo similar to what Amy had seen the members of the Trading Guild wearing at Winter Outpost. Jandro was disappointed that he had to wear another cropped shirt, but Licha was surprisingly amiable about wearing another turban when Dack took it out of a box. Before giving it to her, he pulled the scarf from Licha's head. Her white hair was about half a knuckle long.

"Your hair has almost grown out enough that you would look fashionable. In the meanwhile, I'm afraid you'll have to wear one of these again." He gave her a dark blue turban, which matched Licha's eyes. This turban was more decorative than the one she had worn at Winter Outpost. At the front fabric folded around a ring, giving it just enough flair as not to be plain. Licha took the turban without question and, as she looked it over, a smile spread across her face.

"I like it. Thank you very much."

Completely pleased with himself, Dack bowed slightly. "You're welcome."

Amy looked at what Dack had bought. "I can't believe you had enough for all this."

"I didn't. Fortunately, there is a pawn shop nearby and I was given a fair price for Licha's and Jandro's swords."

"Hey!" Jandro acted upset, even though he had yet to use his sword for more than poking at a dead medorocas.

Dack explained that servants didn't carry swords in Navercío. The knapsacks were no longer appropriate either, so they were stuffed into the boxes the clothing had come from and tied so that Jandro and Licha could carry them. Licha left for a quick sponge bath and returned fully dressed, including the turban. Dack only had to replace the shirt he wore with the new one, and when he took it off, Amy wished she could get a closer look at the three moles under his left pectoral muscle. Surely, they couldn't be actual moles. The very idea that quimerté were marked from birth as belonging to a secret society was ridiculous even in a world were beings had horns growing from the bridge of their noses.

Dack pulled on his long-tailed jacket. "I'll ask the proprietress to hail us a cab. The rest of you finish dressing and meet me downstairs. Amy, it is appropriate for you to wear a sword, so please be sure to put yours on."

"I will," she said.

"Splendid. Don't be long."

When he left, Amy returned to her room to put on her new clothing and the bracelets she had taken off the night before. Only she continued to wear them. Now that they were out of the Lagosla Region, Dack no longer thought it necessary anyone else have bracelets. Licha helped her into her new maroon bustle-jacket, which had buckles to attach the scabbard. Once Jandro finally put on his cropped shirt, grumbling about it all the while, they went downstairs. Amy offered to carry some boxes, but Licha reminded her that she was ocático and they didn't carry anything. Dack was waiting next to the cab.

Unlike the previous night, no doubt due to their late arrival, the city was awash with quimerté. Amy had thought the plaza at Winter Outpost had been crowded but compared to the streets of Edalés it had been an empty square. Beings of all shapes, colors, and sizes dodged in and out of the carriage traffic. Carts pulled by avestrotés and avestrandés, quimerté riding radamias and pulling srudas that were piled high with everything from ears of corn to stacks of wood, clogged the streets. Amy certainly hadn't expected the hustle and bustle and, apparently, neither had Dack—who continually reminded the driver that they had a train to catch.

Amy had to be told again, by both Licha and Jandro, that she shouldn't ogle her surroundings with her mouth agape. She was supposed to be ocático and would be better suited by acting annoyed on the verge of anger, as Dack was doing. They were right, of course, but she found it difficult not to marvel at the activity. She did her best to at least keep her gaze forward and not look to the sides or behind her and was doing a rather good job of it until the carriage passed a group of tiny quimerito hand-in-hand following what she guessed was their teacher. She hadn't seen many youngsters at Winter Outpost or in the swamp and was taken by their inherent cuteness. They couldn't have been more than four or five years old and were as varied in coloring as the throng they passed through. Although she had never had any real maternal instincts, it didn't stop her from wanting to grab a quimerito and squeeze it tight like she would a ...

*Like I would a stuffed toy*, she thought.

Something about that resonated through her mind and she listened to the resonance for a bit, but was never quite able to hear it. All she was sure of was that the memory fragments had something to do with her childhood—something to do with her *early* childhood because she didn't keep stuffed toys after she and her father had moved up north to live with Alice. Or had she? Unfortunately, that was the part of her childhood she remembered the least.

When they reached the crowded train station, Dack hurried them into a long brick building. The station was filled with quimerté departing a train that had recently arrived and those headed for that same train, which was about to leave. They managed to find their way to the platform where quimerté were already boarding the train. As Dack argued with a conductor about something Amy couldn't quite hear, she stopped to look about. The quimerté were as diverse as those she had seen elsewhere, although there were quite a few more dressed in similar fashion as she and Dack. Several stood out, quimerté dressed entirely in blue. Their long-tailed jackets, high-collared shirts, and pleated trousers matched in color exactly. As one of them hefted a long-barreled rifle to his shoulder, she realized they were wearing some sort of uniform. When he turned toward her, she turned around to study the odd-looking engine car.

The train was a steam locomotive—that much was obvious—but the engine was at a curious angle. Its front end was close to the ground while its back end was up in the air like a stinkbug's. Twelve quimerté in bibbed overalls held onto a long pole, six to a side, and were apparently jacking up the front end. The pole extended underneath the cowcatcher and they used it like a lever to raise the front of the engine, while three other quimerté, including the engineer who remained on the train, stood by making sure it was leveling correctly. Amy had never seen anything akin to this. The quimerté were obviously experienced in doing what they were doing, so it couldn't be that the engine had collapsed to its figurative knees, but she couldn't imagine what would have caused it to be in that position in the first place.

Dack pulled her away and herded his group down the long row of passenger cars rapidly filling with quimerté. Burdened with the boxes and the cloaks, Licha and Jandro found it difficult to maneuver through the crowd, but when Amy stopped to assist them Dack tugged on her arm and reminded her that they were iado and would find a way to manage. Still, she continued to look over her shoulder making sure that they weren't entirely lost in the crowd, wondering if that was Dack's plan all along. Not being able to stand it any longer, she yanked her arm from his hand and returned to assist her friends. She knew that she had to keep up appearances so she berated Licha for dropping one of the cloaks and demanded that the quimera hand them over lest she ruin them for good. Licha seemed to understand the ploy and gladly gave over the cloaks. Marching angrily and muttering rather loudly about incompetence, Amy hurried back to Dack with the cloaks in her arms. With one hand free, Licha helped Jandro with his boxes and they were able to keep up. Amy noticed another of the uniformed quimeros and asked Dack who they were.

"Centación, the Primerabrigo military. Considering what Maru said about the black market, I'd rather they not take notice of us so get on board."

He stopped at the entrance of the last passenger car. The four cars at the back were considerably smaller than those at the front. He ushered everyone aboard but remained at the entryway peering out surreptitiously.

The reason for the passenger car's smaller size became apparent when Amy stepped inside. She had only seen a private car once before while vacationing somewhere with her father and Alice. They had to have been on some type of tour because they hadn't ridden in the car, only walked through it, but she distinctly remembered how ridiculously luxurious the private car had been. The same could be said for this one. Jandro dropped the boxes he carried to the floor and stared agog at the sumptuous traveling room. Licha was careful with her boxes. She set them neatly on a table at the back near two daybeds and took the cloaks from Amy to hang on hooks across from the powder room. She seemed to be less impressed with the car than was Jandro, who *ooo*-ed and *aah*-ed for the first few minutes. For Amy, it was like stepping into the past when oil barons ruled the railways in her world.

She removed her bustle-jacket and sword before perching on the red velvet bench so that she could look out the window. Dack remained at the entrance scanning the area while remaining in the shadows. He hadn't said anything about meeting anyone at the train, so she had no idea who or what he could be looking for. Then, darting from the crowd, a young quimerito ran up to the car with paper in his hand. Dack pulled him in, wrote something on the paper and returned it to the quimerito, who started to take off until Dack stopped him and said something more. When Dack gave him a silver coin, the youngster's his face split into a grin. As the quimerito disappeared into the crowd, Dack finally boarded the passenger car.

"What was all that about?" Amy asked.

Dack removed his jacket and draped it over a chair arm. "He's a porter. I'm having him send a message ahead and procure some food and drink for the car before the train departs." He unbuckled his scabbard and sat down on the chair across from Amy.

"A message? Who to?"

"My mother. I told her we would be arriving tomorrow and to be prepared."

"Tomorrow? It's going to take that long to get there?"

"Yes. Halfway to Navercío the elevation increases substantially and the train slows down considerably, giving my mum plenty of time to make arrangements for us. Oh, and I also told her to have coinage waiting for me at the station. That's what I was arguing with the conductor about. He wasn't going to allow us to board without prepayment. I had to pull rank to get him to agree to accept payment when we reach our destination."

"I thought you didn't want anyone to know you were a Fensoré colonel," Jandro said from the back. He had taken over a daybed.

"I didn't tell the conductor I was a colonel. I told him I was a Sangcertigre. Privilege does have its privileges." He wiggled his eyebrows, making Amy laugh.

Twenty-five minutes later the quimerito returned with a paper receipt indicting that Dack's message had been sent and a large basket filled with food and wine. The car supplied water and serving utensils. Dack paid the youngster with the last of his coins and sent him on his way.

Jandro watched him go. "Now that's a job I would like to have."

Licha swatted at him. "You would not. You would have to be on the move all day."

"Isn't that what I've been doing for the past few weeks?"

"I don't know if you would have to be on the move *all* day," Dack said, "but you'd have to hustle whenever the train was here. Porters are paid in tips."

"Seguidosts aren't paid at all."

Licha swatted at him again, this time making contact with his bald head. "Jandro, how can you say that? Seguidosts are paid in food and shelter and camaraderie. If it were a salary you were looking for you would have been better off becoming Fensoré. They're ..." She trailed off when she looked at Dack, who was shaking his head slowly.

"Licha, you—and Jandro—must stop thinking of yourselves as seguidosts. I've said it before and I'll say it again. There can be no discussion about it, not even among yourselves."

"I suppose we should just think of ourselves as your servants and not servants of *La Reina*." Licha rolled her eyes.

"Everyone serves *La Reina*." Dack looked through what the porter had brought. "As for you two being *my* servants, that's only for show and that's only for now. When we accomplish our goal in Navercío, things may change."

"How so?" Amy asked.

Dack stood briefly to step across the aisle where he stretched out on the velvet bench. He placed one of the many emerald green pillows scattered on it under his head. "When we are able to read the full prophecy we will know exactly what needs to be done. It's my guess that we'll be returning to Pliada."

"Why there?" Jandro didn't seem all that anxious to return.

Dack turned onto his side and tilted his head back so he could see the young quimero. "As I said, it's just my guess, but I think we'll be traveling to Nieblota."

"No one can go in there. Or, at least, no one can go in and come back out."

Licha removed her turban and scratched her head. "Nieblota is where *La Reina* resides. Of course we'll have to go there."

"Only the Carados believe that," Dack said. "Nevertheless, I believe Nieblota will have something to do with the prophecy."

Licha ambled down the aisle and sat in the chair across from Amy that Dack had just given up for the bench. "I don't understand. I thought that the fabled Trotéjo believed in *La Reina* the way that the Carados do. And we—they—believe she still dwells in Nieblota watching over us."

"Trotéjo believe in *Lacáruna*." Dack sat up and swung his long legs to the floor. "She's the only reason the Trotéjo exist." He reached for the food basket just as the train started to move.

"It's nice to know that a man believes in me and I'm the only reason he exists," Amy said with a grin. "Finally, someone gets it."

"Man?" Dack stood.

Amy groaned softly. "Quimero. Man means quimero in my world."

Dack began unloading the basket. "Anyone hungry?"

They settled back onto the benches and chairs while Amy and Dack sipped on the butterscotch wine. Despite its overwhelming sweetness, Amy was growing quite fond of it. She hoped it wouldn't make her sleepy, as it had the night before, because now that they had some real privacy she had many questions to ask.

"Speaking of worlds," she said, although no one had been, at least not for a while. "How many are there?"

"No one knows." Dack passed around the basket and everyone

took out something to eat. "Scholars and clergy have argued about it over for the past three thousand years. What *is* agreed upon is that, other than this one, there are at least three different worlds—one for each Primeróte couple. Most quimerté believe that there had to be many more, hundreds more, because the world was first populated by beings from somewhere else. But three is what's agreed upon."

"Wait." Amy set down her wineglass. "You mean more than just the first three couples were brought to *La Reina*'s world?"

"Of course. So were *La Reina* and *La Rata* and *El Hámster*, her iado."

*A queen, a rat, and a hamster,* Amy thought. *Must have made for one interesting castle.*

"Once the Primeróte settled in the flatlands, more and more quimerté appeared in the world to populate it."

"Maybe Amy comes from one of those worlds," Jandro suggested.

"Possibly." Dack clasped his hands and rested his chin on them. He looked at Amy. "I doubt it, though. She doesn't look like she came from any of those three worlds, but I'm not a scholar so I'm not the best judge."

Licha agreed. "She looks like she came from our world."

"Which works to our advantage."

Amy sipped her wine. "How do you know that the Primeróte came from three different worlds and not just one?"

"Because that is what is written in the Extiguo translations. The three couples claimed not to know anything about the others' worlds. They were dropped in this one along with *La Reina*."

"Then there were *four* worlds. If *La Reina* was dropped here too."

Dack sat back. "There have been great debates over that. Many scholars believe that she wasn't brought to this world, but that her world changed around her and became the one she shared with the Primeróte."

"Scholars believe that?" For some reason, Amy found that a bit disheartening.

"Not all. The Trotéjo share that belief because that is what happened at the time of the *Morphósis* when this world expanded. Others believe that *La Reina* did indeed come from a separate world from this and from the worlds of the Primeróte, which the Translations seem to support. Although, again, not everyone agrees with that interpretation."

Amy nodded her head slowly while taking all of it in. "So the prophecy may be about a third *Morphósis* and not a second."

"Exactly, which is why it's called the *New Morphósis*. It keeps the squabbling down."

She set her wineglass on the table across from where she sat. "All right, I think it's time you explained to me who the Primeróte were ... or are ... and what significance they have other than extending privilege down their bloodline."

Dack laughed as he leaned back and put his hands behind his head. "The Primeróte are the first six beings brought into this world to propagate and fill it with subjects for *La Reina*."

"Brought by who?"

"That's a question better suited for the clergy. Religions have splintered over it."

She recalled what the apósto had told her. "The angel. That's who you mean, right?"

"For the sake of simplicity, let's skip that for now."

When Amy agreed, he continued.

"The first two Primeróte are my ancestors: Thomas and Audrey Certigre. They appeared in *La Reina*'s castle at the same time as the second couple: Raul and Pen-Mai Peroso. The last two to appear were Hagos and Salama Tamus. Because the six were the only quimerté to appear in the castle, besides *La Reina* and her iado, she bestowed on them special privilege and gave each of them a town to govern."

"Towns? I thought *La Reina*'s world was empty before she

arrived."

Dack held up a finger. "Ah, you've discovered why some scholars believe she wasn't actually brought to a new world but that her old world changed around her. In the translation of the first Extiguo there is one line about how, after the Primeróte left the caste for the flatlands, they built the first town on pre-existing foundations.

"Over time, more beings began to arrive, but none arrived in *La Reina's* mountain castle, as had the Primeróte. The others appeared across the land, in and around the Primeróte cities. Now, there are hundreds of stories about those days but most are likely to have no relevance to the prophecy, so there is no need to go into them right now."

Jandro leaned over to Amy and whispered. "I know a bunch of those stories. I'll tell you later."

Dack continued. "For hundreds of years, the pre-*Morphósis* world remained as it was. The Primeróte's progeny continued to govern the cities that *La Reina* had bestowed upon them, but dissension among the quimerté grew and *La Reina* believed the strife below was *La Arañota's* doing. The Spider Queen—"

Amy groaned dramatically. "Why does it always have to be *spiders?*" She shuddered, making Dack laugh.

"I'm only relaying the—some say historical facts, some say legends—of how this world came into being. *La Reina's* mortal enemy was an enormous spider who claimed to be the true queen of the land and that *La Reina* was a usurper undeserving of the crown. But *La Reina* knew that *La Arañota* was the Queen of Lies, which was how she and her minion sowed discord across the land. There, in the mountaintop castle, a great battle was waged, witnessed only by the participants and *Dendos* before he became one."

"One what?" Amy asked.

"One being."

"Oh, right. The apósto said something about *Dendos* being two into one, or something like that. Who was he before he was two? Wait, don't tell me." She tried to recall what Apósto Baruti had told her.

Dack dropped his hands to his knees and pushed off them as he stood. "I've been meaning to do this for a while and I suppose now is as good a time as any." He walked to the back of the car where the boxes were stored and rummaged through them until he found his knapsack. From the same hidden pocket where he had removed the last of his silver coins, he pulled out a medallion on a chain. He returned to the front and sat back down, but nearer to Amy so that he could show her what he had.

"This belonged to the apósto. I removed it before ... before his burial."

Amy had seen the medallion when Apósto Baruti had shown it to her. In relief, it depicted a being with two heads, back to back. "The rat and the hamster."

Dack nodded. "*La Rata* and *El Hámster.*"

"See, now that's something I don't understand," Amy said. "You're telling me that before he became *Dendos*, he was a rat and a hamster. An actual *rat* and *hamster.*"

Dack didn't seem to understand her question.

"Rodents."

Now he seemed confused. "They are referred to as rodents in the Translations, and it is believed that is what all beings from their world were called."

"So, their entire world consisted of little furry creatures running around on all fours with tails—"

He cut her off. "All fours? Do you mean on hands and knees? How can anyone run around like that?"

"Because that's what rodents do, and not on their hands and knees but on their four feet. Rodents don't have hands. Well, not these kind of hands." She held hers up as an example.

"But those *are* the kind of hands *Dendos* always had," Jandro said. "Even when he was two."

Amy tried to envision a creature such as Jandro described. "So they were a rat and a hamster, but they were shaped like ..." She looked at the beings surrounding her. Although they were odd-looking in human terms, they had the same form as she. "They were shaped like us,"

He took back the medallion. "Yes. They didn't look like us, but they had arms and legs, a head and a torso, hands and feet. And—unless you've been hiding something—also like us, they had no tails."

Dangling the medallion by its chain he held it out for Licha to take. "I think you should have this. But keep it well hidden."

Licha nodded and with a trembling hand, she took the medallion from him. Tears fell from her eyes. "I will keep it safe."

Dack poured himself more wine. "In short, the war waging in the castle reflected across the land and the situation became dire. Eventually, *La Reina* bested *La Arañota* by chopping off her head."

When he paused, Amy wondered if he were thinking about what he'd had to do to Captain Tamezo. The pause was brief.

"But even with her head separated from her body, *La Arañota* promised that she would someday return and take back the crown. *La Reina* had seen what sort of destruction *La Arañota* could cause and knew the only way to keep *La Arañota* from returning was to take the world out of her reach."

"She changed the world." Amy began to understand the meaning of the *Morphósis*. "She changed the world around her by expanding it."

"Exactly. Cities became nations; mountains became mountain ranges; lakes became seas; ponds became lakes. The tracks that this train travels upon is said to have once stretched from city to city before the *Morphósis*, but after the expansion all that remained of it was this small section."

Amy scowled. "Oh, come on. You don't really believe that these train tracks could be three thousand years old."

"Of course not." He gulped some wine. "I'm sure that was something that a Primerabrigo viceroy made up a long, long time ago just to give our nation a bit more importance than the others."

"All right." Amy picked apart a hard roll she'd taken from the basket and ate it bit by bit. "I get that the world changed, but how does expanding it keep it out the Spider Queen's reach?"

"Apparently, she didn't—at least not far enough. The return of Arañalianza indicates that *La Arañota* has once again found us."

Although she wasn't sure she comprehended the shrinking/expanding part of the legend, Amy nodded. She wanted to move on. "Back to what you said earlier about the Primeróte descendants governing the land, that still stands to this day?"

"It does," Dack said. "The current viceroy is my third cousin, thrice removed, or perhaps only twice. You'll have to ask my mum if you want to know exactly how we are connected."

"Mum." Amy chuckled.

"Why do you find that amusing?"

"Because it's a word from my world. A word used pretty much only by quimerté who have the same accent as you. My stepmother has that accent."

Jandro's eyes grew comically wide. "Maybe your stepmother is a Primerabrigite."

"No, she's British."

"What does that mean?"

"It means she's from a place called Great Britain."

Dack raised his eyebrows, crinkling the stripes on his forehead. "Perhaps my ancestors were taken from your Great Britain and brought to *La Reina*'s world."

"Did those ancestors have stripes on their faces like you?"

"One did."

"Then probably not. No one in my world has stripes, unless

they've put them there themselves." Even so, Amy still thought there had to be some sort of connection. She just couldn't figure out what it was. Yet. "Back to what you were saying. Is the viceroy on your mother's side of the family or your father's side?"

"My mum's side. Family lines are followed through the mother. Isn't that how it's done in your world?"

Amy guffawed. "Hardly. Like surnames, the bloodline tends to run through the father's side."

"Really?" Dack seemed genuinely surprised. "Surnames also come from the mother. How else can you be sure that the bloodline remains true to any family?"

"You're preaching to the choir." She could see that went over his head and continued on. "So Sangcertigre comes from your mother. I take it the viceroy—"

Dack clapped his hands loudly, as if to wake everyone up. "Lessons are over for the day."

He stood and opened another bottle of wine. With the bottle, he gestured to Licha and Jandro, asking if they wanted any. Licha declined but Jandro accepted. It was his first taste of wine and he took an instant liking to it. Amy, however, wondered if the wine had any alcohol at all. She'd consumed two wineglasses full of it but could feel no effect. Maybe wine was just another word for beverage in this world. Licha returned to the back of the car, and Jandro joined her after swallowing his wine in two gulps. Dack filled both his and Amy's glasses. He drained his and stretched out on the velvet bench, closing his eyes. Amy wasn't tired and, with nothing else to do, she looked out the window while sipping her butterscotch-tasting wine.

The Primerabrigo landscape was far lusher than anything Pliada had to offer and reminded her of Southern California, especially when the train passed a humungous grove of very tall date palm trees. Seeing the dates reminded her that the shop owner at Winter Outpost had given her something that he said she couldn't get in Primerabrigo, but Dack made her save for later when she returned to the garrison. She couldn't remember what the date cake had been called. Nor could she remember what had happened to it. She knew she had brought it back to her quarters but that had been immediately before the funeral procession and that's the last she'd seen of it. She hoped that Licha and Jandro had eaten it; she hated to think it had gone to waste.

While seeing the date palms had made her mouth water it, surprisingly, hadn't made her homesick. Amy found it curious that, other than wanting to return to her world because her life was in danger in this one, she hadn't give her life there much thought at all. Did she really have so little to return to that it hardly ever crossed her mind? Granted, she'd wondered on occasion what was going on regarding her absence, but really it was more about what was happening with projects at work than it was wondering whether anyone was looking for her.

Amy shifted on the seat so she could look at her traveling companions, all of whom seemed to be asleep. Maybe it was caused by the excitement this adventure brought about but she felt closer to the three of them than anyone she'd left behind—even Henry, the man she'd been dating for the past few months. With these three she'd formed such an implicit bond of trust that she'd never had before with anyone including her ex-husband. She hadn't had what she would call a *close* friend in years. She had *good* friends but none were as intimate as they had been in the past. Maybe it was because she'd always been one to put her job first. For that very reason most of her socializing was over lunch. Catching up with old friends seemed to happen less and less after the topic of her divorce played out and soon most of her luncheons were with colleagues or clients.

Finding the train of thought a bit depressing, Amy looked back out the window. The date grove was long gone and with nothing to hold her attention she lay down on the bench, an emerald pillow under her head, and closed her eyes. When she opened them some time after, Dack was kneeling on the floor next to the bench. His face was so close to hers she could see the yellow flecks in his otherwise green eyes.

"We've stopped," he said, softly. "Would you like to disembark and stretch your legs?"

Although her legs really didn't need any stretching (they'd been stretched out along the bench while she dozed), Amy sat up and looked out the window. They were at another station, a much smaller one if the brick building beside the track was an indication.

"Where are we?"

"In Piedél." Dack stood. "It's a small town at the foot of the mountain where the train converts."

"Converts what?" Amy looked at the back of the car; the daybeds were empty. "Where are Jandro and Licha?"

"Out watching the train convert. I thought you may be interested in seeing it, since you were so fascinated with the engine this morning." He held out his hand for her to take. "Come."

She accepted his help and stood, but before they left the car, they donned their jackets at Dack's insistence. He wanted to keep up appearances, although for whom they were keeping them Amy didn't know. He let her leave the car first and then bumped into her when she stopped abruptly. With her head turned toward the front of the train, she was entirely unprepared to see that they were at the foot of a slowly sloping, but very high mountain and had stopped. Dack's bump propelled her forward once again.

"When you said that we would reach a higher elevation, you weren't joking," she said.

"I wasn't." He offered her his arm and when she didn't take it, he grabbed her hand and placed it on his arm anyhow, reminding her the importance of appearing to be a couple. "Navercío sits atop a large mesa. That is why it's necessary for the conversion and why the next portion of the trip will be so slow."

A crowd had gathered near the front of the station, and Dack pushed his way through it. Initially embarrassed by his rudeness, Amy soon realized that he wasn't pushing anyone; the quimerté were actually stepping out of his way. Licha and Jandro were among those standing at the front of the crowd and when Jandro saw Dack and Amy emerge, he pointed excitedly at what was happening with the engine.

Dack gave him a stern look. "Calm yourself, Jandro."

Jandro dropped his hand, but his enthusiasm was justified. Standing in the track were more overall-wearing quimerté holding the long lever/pole that reached underneath the cowcatcher. Only this time, rather than jacking up the front of the engine, they were jacking it down. She was confused as to why they would need to position the engine in such a manner until she noticed a third rail running down the center of the track. The middle rail was notched.

"Rack and pinion," Amy said.

Dack looked at her with surprise. "Splendid. When the quimerté reposition the engine wheels drop and will catch the middle rail, which is needed to keep traction and help pull the train up the mountainside."

Amy nodded. "And the engine will remain relatively horizontal. Which it needs to do because it is steam powered and water in the boiler would otherwise rush to one end." Accustomed to having to figure things out on her own, she hadn't been able to do much of that since arriving in this world and congratulated herself. "What do they do on the return trip?" She found it difficult to imagine raising the front end of the engine to such an extent to keep it horizontal as it went downhill.

"It doesn't come back this way," Dack said. "From Navercío it will travel north to Port Audrey, the official northern border town where anyone coming into or leaving Primerabrigo is supposed to proceed. The slope on the northern side isn't so steep. From there it returns to Piedél where it rejoins the track back to Edalés."

"Do the other nations also have trains?" The crowd around them was loud enough that Amy felt safe enough to ask questions without being overheard.

"No, only Primerabrigo, which is ironic, I suppose, considering that both the train and the tracks were constructed in Maseprada. They, however, have their own unique way of traveling."

When the front end of the engine was lowered into position, the engineer inched the train down the track a few threestrides until the engine began to raise as the track sloped upwards. When the train stopped, the engine was again level and the crowd burst into applause.

With Amy firmly attached to his left arm and Licha and Jandro in tow, Dack led them through the dispersing crowd into the small station. It was filled with some of the passengers who had boarded in Edalés along with new passengers who seemed to be causing quite a fuss, clamoring en masse at a quimero behind the ticket counter. Struggling through the middle of the crowd was a train conductor trying to make his way out of the station. When he finally made it out of the unhappy throng, Dack stopped him before he went outside. The conductor threw up his hands in frustration.

"I'll tell you what I've told everyone else. If you don't have a ticket for the first two or the last three cars, you're going to have to wait for the next train."

"I boarded in Edalés and have a ticket for passage to Navercío. I only wanted to know what the trouble is here."

Although the conductor seemed relieved Dack only had a question, he nevertheless remained perturbed. "The fool at the ticket counter sold tickets for the third car even though explicit instructions were sent ahead that the third car would be unavailable."

Amy looked out the window at the six-car train and noticed for the first time that the third car had no windows. When they'd boarded in Edalés the platform had been so crowded and she had been so concerned with Licha and Jandro that she hadn't paid much attention to the cars.

"Why is it unavailable?" Dack asked.

"Because its in use by the Centación. Now if you'll excuse me."

Dack thanked him and moved out of the quimero's way. He looked out the window.

"I hadn't realized the third car was a freight car. Most unusual."

"I hadn't either," Amy said. "Why is it unusual?"

"Freight trains don't carry passengers and passenger trains don't haul freight. It could, however, explain why there were centacións at Edalés." He took her arm and pulled her away. "Let's get back to our car as soon as possible."

The station had a café and Dack, after ordering, asked to have the bill sent to his estate and left Jandro and Licha to bring along the food once the order was filled. While Amy would have liked to sit amongst the quimerté eating at the café, Dack insisted they return to the private car. She understood that he feared for her safety, but it seemed something else had him concerned. Amy followed him out, as he quickly walked down the platform. He slowed when they passed the freight car, but there was nothing to see and no centacións, which was what he said he'd been on the lookout for when they reached the private car.

"They're probably inside it."

Amy followed him aboard. "Why would they be inside a freight car?"

"To protect whatever it is they're hiding in there."

"Hiding?"

"The only reason there would be a freight car on a passenger train is because the Centación don't want anyone from the Trading Guild to know about it."

"Won't a freight car pulling into the station be a little obvious?"

"Not if you bribe the right quimerté." He looked out the window at the station platform. "Stay here. I'll be back shortly."

When he left the private car, Amy sat on the bench so she could watch him as he quickly found one of the overall-wearing quimeros. Although Dack never looked in the direction of the freight car, she was certain that's what he was asking about. They didn't speak for long and Dack returned.

"He doesn't know exactly what the freight car contains, only that it has an acerbic stench and sits upon large wheels. It was brought in from Lagosla the night before we arrived in Edalés and loaded into the car the following day along with several barrels. He didn't know what the barrels contained, but they seemed meant for the contraption."

Amy could see the wheels in his mind turning. "You don't think this has anything to do with me, do you?"

"I'm not sure what it has to do with, but it's very curious and that concerns me because it *might* concern you. I'll feel better when I get you to my estate." He sat on a chair. "Not that it would matter. I can't cloister you away there, even if I'd like to."

Holding up one hand, Amy looked down and shook her head fervently like a televangelist calling out to her flock. "Hold on. No one is cloistering me anywhere." She looked up at Dack before dropping her hand. "While I appreciate wanting to keep me from harm, I'm no damsel in distress, and I don't want to be treated like one."

Dack crossed his legs. His green eyes sparkled with amusement. "I don't know what a damsel is, but I'm sure you're not one of them."

Although she didn't want to, she had to laugh. "All I'm saying is that I don't ever want to be so protected that I'm locked away somewhere." She stopped smiling. "In all seriousness, I want to make sure that you understand and respect that."

"I do." He picked up a wine bottle and when it proved it empty, he set it back down. "Before your arrival at the garrison, I can't say I had a clear vision of who *Lacáruna* would be. To my knowledge, there are no descriptions of her in the prophecy. All that was known was that she would be female. I imagine all trotéjos had their own ideas about it. Raiquen—Captain Tamezo—did."

"What was yours?"

"I suppose I expected her to resemble the quimerté as they allegedly looked before the *Morphósis*."

"Like *Dendos* before he became one."

"Precisely."

"Well, I don't look like a rodent. At least, I hope I don't. I look very much like all the people—the quimerté—of my world."

"You resemble us more than I'd expected, which is why I was so skeptical when I first met you. Until you read what was written in that table, I was certain you were an imposter." Despite having just done so, he checked the bottle to see if any wine remained. "What I'm trying to say is that I never had a image in my head of what *Lacáruna* would look like, but the one aspect I've always believed was that she would be strong."

He reached across the aisle and took Amy's hand, placing it between his. "I can make this promise without hesitation. I will never, to the best of my abilities, allow anyone else to lock you away. You were meant to be free so that you can set *us* free and I will lay down my life to make certain that happens."

Unexpected tears welled in Amy's eyes and she turned her head so that he wouldn't see them. Never in her life, not even when her ex-husband had proposed, had a man spoken to her with such tenderness and sincerity. If Licha and Jandro hadn't returned to the private car right then she might have pulled Dack into her arms and kissed him, despite his odd appearance. The moment was broken, however, by Jandro's loud announcement that the café didn't have wine.

"They only had this." He pulled out a bottle from the large basket Licha carried. "It's from Maseprada. I hope it's not libélosa nectar."

Dack sat back and groaned as he took the bottle from Jandro and looked at the label. "This is wine, terrible wine. Nothing like what we bought in Edalés."

Amy could have jumped for joy. Tired of the sweetness of the last wine, she snatched the bottle from Dack and looked for the corkscrew. She found it in a drawer where Licha had returned it after opening the other wine and quickly made use of it. If she hadn't known that wine needed to breathe, she would have taken a swig straight from the bottle the instant the cork popped out. She took a sniff, however; it smelled like a delightful cabernet. Because the car wasn't equipped with a sink she couldn't rinse out her wineglass, so she removed another from a cabinet below the red velvet bench, poured a bit of wine into the glass and swirled it. Although she was sure it needed more time to breathe, she just had to taste it. One sip and she was in heaven. The wine was dry and bold just the way she liked red wine to be. She licked her lips and closed her eyes. When she opened them she saw that the others were staring at her in fascination.

"What?"

"I don't believe I've ever seen anyone enjoy Maseprada wine as much as you," Dack said.

The train lurched.

"Time to sit down," Dack said. "Make sure everything is put away." He gestured at the basket of food that Licha held. "Don't unpack that. We'll just take from it what we need when the time comes. Amy, if I were you, I'd keep hold of that wine bottle."

When the car slowly began to tilt, as the train headed up the mountain slope, she understood why. She braced herself for the worst, but the tilt stopped somewhere around a fifteen degree angle, just enough to make keeping anything on the tables impossible. When the flower vases didn't move, she saw that they, along with all pieces of furniture, were bolted down. Even the emerald green velvet pillows remained in place, held there by the velvet covering the bench. Amy sat in a chair that faced forward, the wine bottle in one hand, the wineglass in the other.

"This is going to take some getting used to," she said.

Dack chuckled and took the bottle from her. He wedged it between the basket of food and the table it sat next to so that the bottle remained upright. "I'm glad you're enjoying this wine. It always takes me at least two glasses before it stops giving me indigestion."

"Then you should get started. There's another bottle in the basket."

An hour later, the sun had set and they had finished both bottles of the Maseprada version of a cabernet. Licha had declined an offer to imbibe, as she had done with the butterscotch-tasting wine, while Jandro had taken one sip, made a horrific face, and refused to finish the rest. Dack drank what he wouldn't. The wine wasn't as potent as Amy thought it would be, but it certainly had more of a punch than the other wine. She felt very relaxed as Dack and she took over the daybeds in the back of the car, lying on them backward due to the train's tilt. Jandro and Licha sat on the bench and looked out the window.

Dack lay on his side facing Amy, who was lying on her side as well. "The wine is giving you rosy cheeks."

"Maybe I should just keep drinking wine," she said. "Then I won't have to put on that cream again."

"Now that you're no longer my cousin, you won't need it. You must, however, imitate Licha's accent, as you did when speaking to Maru. We can't have anyone believing that you are from Maseprada."

"Why not? Couldn't we have met at the outpost? You said you didn't get many visitors, but I could have belonged to the Trading Guild."

Dack thought over her proposal and agreed that it was interesting; nevertheless, he didn't think it was a good idea to say she was from the Trading Guild. "Better to say you are a visiting scholar who is studying in Runakopolis. That will allow you to forgo a Pliadalé accent and continue to be considered ocático. Which reminds me … My mum thinks we're coming from Port Audrey; so, no mentioning the Lagosla

Region." He sat up slightly and shouted to the front of the car. "Did you hear that? When we get to Navercío, no talking about Lagosla. We never went there."

When Jandro and Licha agreed, he lay back down.

"What's she like?" Amy asked. "Your mother."

"She's an earnest individual. She was once quite a character, gregarious, even a little outrageous at times, but my sister's death struck her deeply. I don't mean that to sound as if she sits staring out windows with tears running down her cheeks. She's simply more subdued. Now that my father has also passed, she lives alone at the estate and seldom leaves it. These days she spends most of her time sculpting. She's quite good at it."

Amy adjusted the hand supporting her head. "You do realize she's going to be full of questions about me."

"What makes you say that?"

"She's a mother. Her son is bringing home his fian … his betrothed for her to meet. How could she not be full of questions?"

"Leave that to me. I know exactly how to staunch a flow of questions should she have them, which is doubtful."

"All right. But she's not going to like me, I already know that much."

He laughed. "How could you possibly know that?"

"I've been through this before. That's not the only reason, though. You said that surnames and bloodlines follow the mother, right? That, of course, means that by marrying me, your offspring won't be Sangcertigre. They'll lose whatever privilege the name brings with."

"Not exactly. Because I have direct lineage to the Primeróte, I may pass my name onto my son. He may marry back into the Sangcertigre line and restore our branch of it. He can't, however, pass the name onto his son should he marry outside of a *sang* line."

"What about daughters?"

"This is the only instance when the male's name overrules the female's, but it may only occur one generation down."

"Was your father a Sangcertigre?"

"Yes, he was."

"Talk about inbreeding." Amy grinned, wickedly, which made Dack laugh.

"Not at all," he said. "As you can imagine, our ancestor tree has grown many branches over the past three thousand years."

"That's what you said to the quimero who rowed us across the river." Amy sat up. "What did he mean that his nose should be enough to convince you that you two were related?"

"According to legend, all quimerté before the *Morphósis* looked different from those of us who came after. As I'd mentioned, I had expected the same of you. The quimera he spoke of, Charvi, was alleged to have had a *very* long nose. Of course, there's no actual proof that their appearances were so different from ours before the *Morphósis*. We have only the Translations and artwork created hundreds of years later to go by. There is a museum in Rescatazo with dioramas that depict the Primeróte and others according to the premise. It's quite amusing, actually."

Amy returned to her prone position. "I'd like to see that."

"What about your mum?" Dack asked. "What was she like?"

"Because she died when I was very young everything I know about her has been filtered through the rose-colored glasses my father had undoubtedly placed over his memories." She could see that he didn't understand the metaphor, but didn't explain it.

"You've said that you had no siblings. Was it lonely?"

Amy had to think about it. Although she never could really remember much about her early childhood, what she did recall had no sense of loneliness included. She'd had plenty of friends and her father had said she'd always been proficient in keeping herself entertained. "The only time I felt lonely is when my father remarried. By then, I was nearly a teenager and the loneliness stemmed from having to leave my friends behind and make new ones when we moved to a different area."

"I imagine it didn't take you long to make new friends."

"Actually, it did. Everyone was so different from what I was used to back home."

"How so?"

"They all had money and I …" She raised her head to look at the front of the car. "My moving would be analogous to, say, Jandro … Actually, I don't know what his background is, so let's make it Licha. If she had been taken from Pliada as a … what's the word for female youngster?"

"Quimerita."

"If she had been taken from Pliada as a quimerita and brought to Navercío to live with your family, I'm sure you can imagine the difficulty she would have had."

Dack nodded.

"I did the only thing I could do. I knuckled down, bit the bullet, and cowboy-ed up until I was eventually accepted."

"I haven't a clue as to what you just said, other than the part about being accepted."

Amy chuckled. "Suffice it to say, I had to work hard to become a part of a world I knew nothing about."

"So this isn't the first time you've been dropped into another realm."

Amy smiled. "I suppose it isn't." She rolled onto her back and looked up at the damask-covered ceiling. The chandeliers hanging at the same angle as the train threw strange shadows throughout the car. "You'd think I'd be used to it by now."

They remained silent for a while. Amy thought about all the times she'd been thrust into a foreign situation. Not all of them were as jarring as when her father had married Alice, but a few came close. Nothing, however, could compare to stumbling into a world filled with odd-looking beings that weren't quite human and seemed to have animal characteristics tossed into the mix. She had to wonder, then, why she found that easier to accept than the possibility that she was the female mentioned in a prophecy? Some things couldn't be taken on faith alone.

"Dack, why am I *Lacáruna*?"

The answer never came. Dack was asleep.

Amy closed her eyes.

◉   ◉   ◉

Upon waking the following morning, and hardly for the first time, Amy wondered why she never remembered her dreams. *Ever.* One of her college roommates used to joke that she'd be the worst candidate for psychoanalysis because no one would be able to study her subconscious. She would respond by saying that dreams were overrated and they were only tools to assist the brain in filing away memories. It was human nature to want to string them together as some sort of narrative that inevitably never made any sense.

Her legs were a bit stiff from having been curled for most of the night. The daybed's raised head had been at her feet, and while the tilt of the car had compensated for that at the beginning, when the train reached the mountain mesa the car returned to its original horizontal level. Rather than spinning around, as she had noticed Dack had done, she'd remained where she was and curled in a fetal position. Not such a good idea, now that it was morning. She stretched and sat up. The daybed across the aisle was empty. She looked at the front of the car and saw that Dack was sitting at the table with Licha and Jandro.

"Good morning," Licha called out when she saw Amy stand.

Amy waved. She had a bit of a red wine hangover, which left her with a slight headache and a considerably dry mouth. Stumbling up to the front of the car on stiff legs, she made her way to the bench across from where the others sat and plopped down on it. She groaned when she saw herself in the mirror over their heads. Her hair had come undone from the ponytail and she looked a mess.

Dack smiled at her. "Care to break the fast with us? We have a particularly delicious soft cheese from Rescatazo to spread on a piece of bread, if you'd like to try it."

"What I would really like is a cup of coffee."

"What's coffee?" Jandro asked. He had what looked like a plum in his hand, ready to take a bite out of it.

"It's a liquid made from a bean that is dried and then ground up and steeped in hot water." Amy tried in vain to do something about her hair.

"That sounds like marrón syrup," Dack said, "something we use when we have digestive issues. Are you having any?"

"No, what I'm having is a bad hair day." She gave up trying to corral stray hairs into the ponytail and pulled off the ribbon. "Please tell me I will be able to take a real bath and wash my hair before we go to your estate."

"I can arrange it if you'd like."

"I'd like."

Free from the confines of the ribbon that had pulled it back, Amy's usually limp hair was surprisingly fluffy and didn't look half-bad. If her scalp hadn't itched, she might have considered leaving it unwashed. Licha handed her a slice of brown bread with the soft bright green Rescatazo cheese smeared across it. Amy took a bite expecting something that tasted like cream cheese but instead the spread had a raspberry flavor. She ate the bread and drank two cups of water. The sunlight streamed through the window at an angle casting an orange glow and she guessed it couldn't have been much past dawn. As she began to feel more awake, she leaned back and looked out the window. The sun was indeed just coming up over the horizon.

For a moment (it felt like several minutes but couldn't have been more than a few seconds) Amy was confused not only by what she saw, but also by the time of day. One part of her mind insisted that it had to be dusk, not dawn, because there in the distance was the silhouette of the downtown Los Angeles skyline with the sun setting (*no, it was rising*, another part of her mind argued) behind it. Though she had no liquid in her mouth, she began to sputter and choke. Dack jumped to her side and pounded on her back, as if to dislodge whatever it was that was stuck in her throat. What he couldn't know was that the only obstruction was in her mind, and it was determined to keep her from accepting what she saw. She jabbed her finger in the direction of the silhouette.

"What? What do you see?" Jandro jumped to her side to look out the window. "What is that?"

As Amy's sputtering died down, Dack stopped pounding on her. "That's Navercío," he said. "You can just see the top of it from here."

Amy sucked in breath. "No, it's not. That's where *I* live. It's not called Navercío; it's called Los Angeles."

The others looked at her, and at one another, utterly confused.

"I don't understand what you're saying," Dack said. "I can assure you that skyline belongs to Navercío. Believe me, there is no other skyline like it."

"And I'm telling you there *is* another skyline like it. *Exactly* like it."

Looking out the window again, Amy could see the distinct outline of the crown belonging to the seventy-two-story Library Tower, which, in Los Angeles, stood head and shoulders above the flat-topped, dozen or so rectangular buildings around it. Amy had seen this very view dozens of times while returning to L.A. from Palm Springs, traveling west in the late afternoon driving down Interstate 10.

Dack placed his hands on her shoulders and turned her away from the window to face him. "Help me to understand what you are talking about. Right now, you sound a little hysterical."

If he had been any other male she would have accused him of gender bias simply for using the word *hysterical*. He wasn't any other male, however, and even if he was, she had to admit she was feeling a bit unnerved. She took a few deep breaths before speaking.

"In my world there exists a skyline that looks exactly like the one out there, belonging to the city where I live and work." She glanced over her shoulder. "I know that one is not my city, but I'm telling you, from this distance, it certainly looks like it is."

Keeping a tight grip on her shoulders, Dack looked over Amy's head and through the window. "I don't doubt you. This must mean that there is a connection between our world and yours."

Wiggling out of his grip, Amy stood. She began to pace. "There's more than one connection. There have been many. Until now, I just haven't put them together."

"What other connections have you found?" Licha's voice was concerned and her eyes full of worry.

"Lagosla, for example. Lagosla was very much like a place I lived when I was in my early twenties. And … And … Well, the landscape almost everywhere. From Esterenas to right here, it's been familiar, even if it isn't exactly the same."

As she passed him, Dack grabbed her right hand, pulling her to a stop. "It makes sense that you would find similarities here. The Extiguos say that the Primeróte came from worlds similar to the one they had been delivered to."

She pulled her hand from his. "I'm not a Primeróte, Dack."

He wouldn't let her escape, and took her hand again. "I'm aware of that. But you are *Lacáruna*. As far as I'm concerned, there should be a connection between your world and ours. But tell me why it upsets you to know that."

Amy wanted to yank her hand out of his again, but he covered it with his other hand and held her tightly. She forced herself to relax.

"I don't know. I suppose it was just the shock of seeing …" She sank onto the chair Dack had been sitting in when she stumbled up the aisle bleary-eyed. "The other things that seemed familiar were only reminiscent of my world. That—"she had to use her left hand to point out the window; he held onto her right—"skyline is exactly like my skyline. Not reminiscent of, but an exact copy. I was stunned."

Dack dropped her hand. "I don't know what to tell you. Perhaps it means something; perhaps it's coincidence. Either way, we must go to Navercío."

"I know," Amy said. "Don't get me wrong. I'm not afraid to go there. In fact, now I'm more anxious to go there than I have been before."

Dack looked into her eyes. He must have liked what he saw there, because he smiled. "Good. I didn't know what I would do if you had wanted to jump off the train."

"I may have been in a bit of a panic, but I didn't suddenly lose my mind altogether."

Licha was obviously relieved. "That's good to hear." She returned to the table. "Would you like another slice of bread with cheese?"

Amy could see in the young quimera's eyes the desire for everything to return to as it had been moments before and it served to remind her, yet again, that there were others who had been taken out of their element and tossed into the unknown. She thought back to the night when she had held a knife to Licha's neck and how Licha had shown no fear, only a desire to help her, to comfort her, and felt ashamed. She'd forgotten that they needed her help, as well. She smiled at Licha.

"That would be lovely. Thank you."

Determined to remain casual, Amy sat on the velvet bench and peered out the window for the remainder of the trip. Her belief that the skyline was precisely the same as the downtown Los Angeles skyline never abated, but as the sun moved higher in the sky and the train grew closer she came to realize that it was only the *silhouette* that had been the same. What she had taken for several buildings meshed together in shadow by the rising sun actually *were* only three buildings—three gigantic buildings. A half an hour from Navercío with the sun almost directly overhead, she could see the buildings clearly. Dack explained they'd been chiseled out of what had once been a mountain of red sandstone. What they traveled over hadn't always been a mesa.

"Legend has it," Dack said, "that, after the *Morphósis*, the city that was governed by my ancestors discovered that it had been moved to the foot of the largest of the Taplanas Mountains. They decided a city unlike any ever known would be created. For over a thousand years the mountaintop was carved away and used to build Navercío, block by block—the largest of those used to create the three governing buildings: the Trade Building dedicated to all things commerce, the Palace Building, which housed all Primerabrigo government offices and home to the viceroy, and the Centación Building. The Guardians of the Western Access were created from the last of the blocks mined from the mountain. You'll see them when the train passes into the city."

While she tried to see in her mind's eye what he described, Amy had a question. "You said that according to legend the original city was relocated to the foot of the mountain. If that was the case, why did they move it to the top?"

Grinning, Dack would only say, "You'll see."

She looked back out the window. For the last several wheels into Navercío, the tracks crossed austere red-tinged ground. The train turned slightly on approach, just enough that it headed straight for the city, and the skyline could no longer be seen as clearly unless she wanted to stick her head out the window.

"Ocático do not stick their heads out train windows." Dack was adamant about that.

"Then there is nothing to worry about," Amy countered. "In order for a ocático to see me sticking my head out the window, they would have to have theirs out as well. Since they don't do that, they won't see me doing it either."

She pulled down the top window and kneeled on the bench in order to look out. Licha and Jandro were curious as well and popped their heads out next to hers. Because the train was slowing the wind in their faces was at a minimum, just strong enough to dry out Amy's eyes but not so strong she couldn't keep them open. The skyline loomed large up ahead, slightly deeper red than the ground the train traversed. She could see that dotting each of the mammoth buildings were horizontal and vertical openings—windows and doors—and what had to be walkways and balconies. The train was close enough that the wall surrounding Navercío was visible. Not as tall as the wooden wall surrounding Winter Outpost, the Navercío fortification was only a half circle. Dack said the city had been built on the eastern edge of the mountain so a wall was only needed to protect one side. Seated on either side of the open gate directly in center of the wall were the two guardians he had spoken of. Awe couldn't fully describe what Amy felt when she saw them.

The colossal statues were posed like depictions of Egyptian royalty: stiff backed, knees together, arms tight against the sides, hands atop thighs. But while the statues' posture mimicked each other, it was all they had in common. The statue to the left of the gate was female and clothed in a high-collared, long-sleeved dress with a full skirt beneath which the tips of her shoes were visible. The statue on the right was male and dressed in an old fashioned suit with a high-collared shirt, bowtie, and vest. What made the statues extraordinary wasn't their carved attire, but what sat atop their shoulders. Despite that both statues were worn from age enough detail remained to see that female had the head of a pig and the male had the head of a tiger.

Amy pulled her head back inside. "Those are …"

Dack smiled as he nodded. "Two of the Primeróte, yes. Thomas and Audrey Certigre." He seemed to take delight in her surprise. "As you can see, like *Dendos* before he became one, they looked considerably different from the quimerté who came after."

"A pig and a tiger." She wasn't sure why their appearances surprised and, oddly, disappointed her. All she could think of was that somewhere in the back of her mind she'd held out the hope that other beings taken from their world and dropped into this one be more like her, more human. She looked at the guardians and thought them a curious pairing of predator and prey, like a lion and a lamb. Only these two not only lay down together, they procreated. She looked at Dack. His tawny skin coloring, black stripes on his cheeks, white muttonchops-like facial hair made sense. He was descended from a tiger … person. She didn't see any pig in him; though, when she looked at her own arm still slightly stained with the pink-tinged cream he had given her, she recalled him saying that it was the color of some family members.

"What's my last name going to be? I don't think Darlidale is going to cut it here in this world."

"Is that your surname?" Dack asked in turn. "Darlidale?"

Amy nodded.

"Does it mean anything? What I'm asking is, does it refer back to anything the way that Sangcertigre does."

"Maybe at one time. All that it means now is that it was my father's name and his father before him. And on and on back to whoever made it up in the first place."

"I find it extremely fascinating that the quimerté of your world take their father's name. It must make for some exceedingly embarrassing births."

"I'm sure it has. I can only tell you that I know I am my father's daughter because I look enough like him."

"Then he must have been a very beautiful quimero," Dack said.

If not for being startled by a loud whistle as the train entered Navercío, Amy very well may have blushed.

The train slowed to a crawl while it passed through the gates. A road beside the tracks was filled with carriages and carts arriving into and departing the city. As the train came to a stop just inside the wall, Dack stood and looked out the window.

"This isn't right," he said.

"What isn't right?"

Amy was about to stick her head out the open window again, but Dack stopped her. He told Jandro and Licha to pull their heads back into the car. He took Jandro's place and slowly leaned out just enough that he could look towards the front of the train.

"We're not at the station. I'm not sure what's going ..." Abruptly, he jerked back and shut all the windows. "Move away from the window. All of you."

As Amy moved off the cushioned bench, she asked him what was wrong.

"All that I'm certain of is that the Centación is responsible for stopping the train before it reached the platform. There has to be a dozen or more out there."

Amy reminded him of what he'd said about the freight car. "Could it be that they're unloading whatever is in it?"

He shook his head. "I don't believe so. They were boarding the two front passenger—"

The pounding on the car door stopped him. He looked around frantically and settled his gaze at the back of the car. "Go into the powder room. Now."

"All of us?"

He nodded. "Go."

Amy herded the younger two to the back of the car and squeezed into a space designed for one. She could barely get the door closed as she heard the pounding cease and the muffled voice of Dack talking to someone. A moment later, Dack opened the powder room door and the three practically fell out of the small room. He had cloaks in his hand and shoved them into Amy's.

"The centación I spoke with just now told me to wait because a commander wishes to speak with me."

"What about?"

"I don't know, but I told him I was alone. The three of you need to get off this car." He nodded at the rear door.

After a bit of struggle, Jandro opened the door Dack indicated and looked out. Amy could see the front end of the car behind.

"What do you want us to do?"

"You're going to have to find a way into the station and wait for me there."

Licha pointed to the boxes they'd brought aboard. "What about those."

Dack rushed to where they were stacked and picked them up. He tossed them to Jandro, who grabbed at the string that held the boxes together. Licha snatched Amy's bustle jacket and scabbard from the hook where it hung. She and Jandro quickly stepped outside. Amy hesitated.

"Dack, what if—"

"Get to Threeline. That's my family's estate. You can take a cab outside the station." He rummaged through his pocket and took out the piece of paper that was proof his message to his mother had been sent. "Here, take this. Show it to one of the iado at the estate and he'll know who you are."

They both heard the door at the front of the car open. Dack pushed Amy out and, as she turned to shut the door behind her, threw himself on one of the daybeds. In his hand was one of the empty bottles of wine. Amy closed the door.

Standing on the balcony, she held a finger to her lips and carefully looked to the left side of the train. The road paralleling the tracks was now behind a wall. The area between the wall and train was clear so she told Licha and Jandro to climb down. Although concerned that remaining where she stood she risked the chance of being discovered, Amy had to find out why a commander wanted to talk to Dack so badly that the train had been stopped before it reached the platform. She pressed her ear against the crack next to the door and strained to hear the voices within. A quimero inside introduced himself as Commander Ovejanode and Dack apologized for his disheveled appearance.

"I spent most of the night drinking this awful wine I procured in Piedél."

"We expected you at Port Audrey, Colonel Sangcertigre," the commander said. He too had the slight British accent.

"Oh, and why would you be expecting me at all?"

"Because the carriage you left Winter Outpost in was found along Trade Road with three dead fensorés inside."

Amy gasped and quickly covered her mouth, as the commander continued.

"If not for one of them having a letter from you in his pocket explaining that you had been dropped off earlier, you would have been taken for dead—or a deserter."

"As you can see I am neither."

"I can see that you appear untroubled regarding the dead fensorés."

"On the contrary. I am greatly disturbed by this news and as soon as I get off of this train I will make further inquires. But tell me, commander, why would the Centación concern itself with matters beyond its jurisdiction?"

There was a long pause. Amy held her breath ready to spring from the door should she see the doorknob move, but, the commander's next question indicated that the pause came as he'd looked about.

"You hired an entire car for yourself alone, Colonel?"

"Sangcertigres don't ride in passenger cars."

The commander harrumphed.

"What is this about, Commander?" Amy heard the irritation creeping into Dack's voice.

"The letter that was found on one of your dead guards said you'd been dropped at an undisclosed location because you were on some sort of covert mission. The commissioner would like to know more about that, since it's brought you to Primerabrigo."

"How did you know I was coming to Primerabrigo?"

"We weren't until you sent a message from Edalés." The commander paused again. "That's why I find it surprising that you're aboard alone. The message that was sent along to your family estate said you were bringing your betrothed to visit."

"I am."

"Where is she?"

"She's probably already at Threeline. There must have been some misunderstanding between what I said and what the messenger sent. My betrothed came in from Port Audrey and we're meeting at the estate."

"You can never trust how others interpret what you have to say, can you?"

One of the two chuckled. Amy guessed it was the commander.

"Commissioner Cabranode requests your presence immediately. I am to take you to headquarters."

Amy didn't hear Dack's response because the train began to move. Quickly, she jumped off the balcony and stood with Licha and Jandro while the train passed them. When the last car was near enough, they ran around behind it and off the tracks. The station platform was only a dozen or so threestrides away. They crept along until they could climb up to the platform as the passengers got off the train.

"What are we doing?" Licha asked.

"Dack wants us to wait inside the station for him."

Jandro shook his head. "I don't think that's where he's going."

Amy followed his gaze. Dack had stepped out of the small passenger car and was immediately surrounded by centaciòns in their solid blue uniforms.

"He's being taken to see the commissioner, whom I'm guessing is the head of the Centaciòn or at least someone near the top."

"Why?"

She told them what she'd overheard. Understandably, Licha and Jandro were both shocked to learn about the fensorés deaths. Without having to say so, she shared their belief that it had something to do with her.

"But how could anyone have known *Lacáruna* was in the carriage?" Licha whispered.

"I haven't any idea." And it was the truth. Both she and Dack had been suspicious of Siphiwe, but considering that she was one of the three dead guards they had to have been mistaken.

As more passengers began to fill the station platform, Amy told Licha and Jandro to put on their cloaks. After she did the same, they joined the crowd as it moved from the platform into the station itself. Amy glanced over her shoulder and saw that some of the centaciòn were standing by the freight car, as if guarding it. A few others seemed to be scanning the disembarking passengers. Telling herself that was probably normal and they weren't actually looking for anyone specific didn't help to quell her nerves.

Following their fellow passengers, they entered the first of the three humongous edifices Amy had seen from afar. According to the sign Jandro read aloud the station was located within the Trade Building.

Although only half the size of Manhattan's Grand Central Terminal, the Navercío station bore a striking resemblance to it down to the four-sided clock in the center. Strolling across granite floors as if they did this all the time, the three headed for the exit and squeezed through the doors along with everyone else. Amy pulled Jandro and Licha to the side to get out of the throng so she could get a better look at her surroundings.

The Trade Building they'd come out of was the shorter and smaller of the three enormous buildings. Seeing all the blue uniforms going toward and coming from the building farthest from where she stood, Amy concluded the widest structure was the Centación Building. That left only the center structure with the crown that had reminded her of the L.A. Library Tower which had to be the Palace Building. The facade of all three buildings was distinctly Romanesque. Each construction had at its uppermost level nine huge columns holding up a pitched roof. The Palace Building had another row of columns above that holding up yet another, albeit smaller, pitched roof. A long promenade stretched across and connected the three edifices. A broad boulevard paralleled the promenade and, opposite it, a low wall bordered a narrow park.

"Where should we wait?" Licha asked.

"We're not going to wait. Dack told the centación questioning him that he was alone and was expecting to meet his betrothed at his family estate. So that's where she'll be." Although Amy didn't want to look at her companions—she knew their eyes would be filled with fear and she was nervous enough—it had to be done.

"Now pay close attention. We have to do this and we have to act as if it's nothing we've not done before. Understood?"

They both nodded.

"First, Jandro find out where we hire a cab."

He pointed to a long line on the promenade. "It's right there, but how do we know where to go?"

Amy took the paper Dack had given her out of her pocket and gave it to him. "This is the receipt for the message Dack sent to his mother. Is the address to Threeline on there?"

Jandro looked the paper over. "I think so. It says Threeline right there above the word *valley* and has some numbers and another name. Do you think that's the address?"

Licha said she believed it was, but wanted to know how they were going to pay for a cab. "Didn't Dack say he was to get coin when we arrived?"

Amy hadn't thought of that. She looked at the line waiting for the cabs. "Let's hope someone will pay the fare when we get to Threeline."

After negotiating with Licha that she wouldn't leave their line of sight and before they asked more questions, she left them to stand in the long line for hired cabs. She dodged traffic on the wide boulevard and made her way to the park on the opposite side. A large fountain stood in the park's center, directly across from the Palace Building, and within the fountain were two more statues of Thomas and Audrey Certigre standing side by side, Audrey's arm through Thomas's, dressed in Victorian finery. In front of them were two small quimerito, who were no less bizarre looking than their parents. Both had the head of a pig, but the quimerita, the taller of the two, had the same stripes as her father, as well as his ears. One of them had to be Dack's ancestor, as difficult as that was to believe.

She crossed the narrow park and stood at its edge beside a low wall, looking out over all of Navercío. The city had been built against the mountain's flat eastern side in four descending and expanding tiers. Each tier grew in width and the bottom level was so wide that she couldn't really see the end of it, nor could she the valley beyond in any detail. As grand as the view before her was, Amy couldn't give it the attention it deserved. With her hands grasping the railing atop the low wall she closed her eyes and took several deep breaths. Slowly in, slowly out. The trembling in her hands abated somewhat but the tension in her shoulders would be there for quite sometime yet. It didn't matter. She'd use it to keep the proper posture of an ocático. Because that's who she had to be and she would have to continue to play the part until … She refused to think too far ahead. Right now, she had to get herself and the younger quimerté to Dack's family home. That was the task at hand and she would concentrate on that alone. She took another deep breath, opened her eyes, and turned around. Before returning to Licha and Jandro she removed her cloak so that her bustle jacket and the sword in the attached scabbard were visible. Shoulders squared and head held high, she walked to the promenade.

Both Jandro and Licha continued to look frightened as they neared the front of the line. Amy smiled broadly at the two hoping to put them at ease, or at least to convey that they needed to follow her lead. She handed Licha her cloak. "The park is lovely. On our way home I'll take you through it so that you can see the magnificent view."

Licha smiled weakly, but Jandro nodded encouragingly.

"Thank you, señora. We would like that very much."

When they reached the front of the line, a carriage pulled by two avestrandés stopped at the curb. Amy told Jandro to show the driver the receipt with the address and, along with Licha, climbed aboard. She could hear Jandro telling the driver that he'd get paid at the end of the ride, not before. He said it with more authority than she'd heard him ever express and it made her proud. When he climbed aboard with the boxes, she told him he'd done a good job. Although he smiled, he looked as if he were about to throw up. Licha didn't look much better.

"I need the two of you to calm down. We'll be at Dack's home very shortly, and I'm sure he'll join us not long after."

She wasn't sure at all, but nevertheless had to keep up the pretense for their sake. Although she'd told herself she wasn't going to think too far ahead, she decided that should it come to it, if Dack hadn't joined them by the following morning, she would find a way to return to Lagosla and seek out Maru. At this point, the female trotéjo was the only one Amy knew to trust. She didn't allow that thought to linger, however, and quickly filed it away. As the carriage pulled away onto the boulevard, she kept her eyes on the Centación Building because Dack was in there somewhere.

This wasn't what she'd had in mind when she'd longed to have more control over her destiny.

Amy turned forward and took a deep breath.

# END BOOK ONE

# GLOSSARY

**Arañalianza**     *Enemies of Trotéjo bent on stopping the prophecy from taking place*

**Árbaguas**     *Tall umbrella-like trees north of the Chorgo*

**Árbont**     *Mesquite-like tree primarily in Pliada & northwestern Primerabrigo*

**Árbosgo**     *Moss-covered tree in the Lagosla Region of Primerabrigo*

**Avestrandé**     *Large pájastia used for hauling*

**Avestroté**     *Avestrandé/radamia hybrid used for hauling and riding*

**Carados**     *Spreaders of the Truth religion in Pliada comprised of many factions*

**Cénarra**     *An animal that tastes like lobster*

**Centación**     *Primerabrigo military*

**Círcudito**     *Small group of university scholars studying the same topic*

**Cucabero**     *Pith helmet-like hat with mesh to keep out gnats*

**Cucabeza**     *Mesh head cover to keep out gnats*

**Dendos**     *Two-Within-One prophet said to have come out of Nieblota*

**Escalétre**     *Carados mediation/prayer done alone or in groups*

**Esacado**     *Musket-like firearm*

**Esacueño**     *Musket-like pistol*

**Evocasado**     *Mystical rituals otherwise known as Bygone Practices*

**Extiguos**     *Nine books about La Reina's world before the Morphósis*

**Feinnomado**     *Primary religion in Maseprada*

**Fensoré**     *Pliada military*

**Iado**     *Menial Servant*

**Isolationist Tribes**     *Clans in the Outer Belt & mountain areas not affiliated with any nation*

# GLOSSARY

| | |
|---|---|
| **Knuckle** | *Measurement equivalent to an inch* |
| **Istanté** | *Member of an Isolationist Tribe* |
| **La Arañota** | *Foe of La Reina* |
| **Lacáruna** | *She who will fulfill the prophecy* |
| **Libélalas** | *Huge dragonfly-like creature in the Límitotas Mountains* |
| **Libélosa** | *Large dragonfly-like creature in the Lagosla Region* |
| **Nectar** | *Honey-colored beverage made from smashed libillo* |
| **Libillo** | *Libélosa larvae* |
| **Lupita** | *Monocular* |
| **Medorocas** | *Huge centipede-like creature* |
| **Mensáneo** | *Type of coded message used by the Fensoré* |
| **New Morphósis** | *The prophesized return to the expanding world* |
| **Pájastia** | *All bird-like creatures* |
| **Pálas** | *Wingless pájastia in Pliada that blends in with the landscape* |
| **Paluz** | *Glow stick created with paluzite* |
| **Pióna** | *Scorpion-like creatures* |
| **Polloté** | *Smaller domesticated pájastia with long claws - used for eggs* |
| **Polluelo** | *Medium chicken-like domesticated pájastia - used for meat* |
| **Pomalvados** | *Large vicious pájastia hunted for their meat* |
| **Primeróte** | *The Six Founders of the pre-Morphósis world* |
| **Pulabaza** | *Gourd-like plant found in Pliada* |
| **Quimera** | *Female* |

# GLOSSARY

| | |
|---|---|
| **Quimero** | *Male* |
| **Quimerita** | *Female child* |
| **Quimerito** | *Male child/children* |
| **Quimerté** | *People/Person* |
| **Radamia** | *Pájastia that can be ridden* |
| **Sand Runner** | *Avestrandé with webbed feet* |
| **Seguidost** | *Lower members of Carados under an apósto* |
| **Servadoré** | *Rescatazo military* |
| **Srudas** | *Two-wheeled cart* |
| **Threeline** | *Sangcertigre estate* |
| **Threestride** | *Measurement equivalent to a yard* |
| **Trinéot** | *Wagon-sled used in Esterenas* |
| **Trotéjo** | *Secret society who have vowed to protect Lacáruna* |
| **Tuercacha** | *Date cake* |
| **Venbada/o** | *Smuggler working in the black market* |
| **Ventégra** | *Rock similar to obsidian* |
| **Wheel** | *Measurement equivalent to a mile* |

# ACKNOWLEDGMENTS

I want to thank all of those friends who listened to me talk about this project for years, especially Mark Weaver, who actually read the whole series before it was whole (and sometimes twice). Thank you to Lauri Veverka for help with the Lizard Queen insignia; Kayrn Doran for her expert eye; editor Betsy Mitchell for her invaluable advice and direction and Helen Breitwieser for introducing me to her; and Renu Sharma, a wonderful artist who put up with my ever changing ideas.

Also special thanks for help with the map:
http://starraven.deviantart.com/art/Sketchy-
Cartography-Brushes-198264358

## ABOUT THE AUTHOR

H.L. Cherryholmes, author of *A Slight Touch* and *Come Back for Me*, was born and raised in Albuquerque, New Mexico but has spent most of his life in Southern California. Clearly, he really loves the desert. He has a BFA from University of New Mexico and a Master's degree in Playwriting from the University of California, Los Angeles. Currently, he lives in L.A. and Palm Springs with his husband, Ron Cogan.

Manufactured by Amazon.ca
Bolton, ON